DEAD TIRED

DEAD TIRED

Derek J. Pack

Cover illustration by Ryan Hall
actionhall.wordpress.com

This book is a work of fiction. Names, characters, places, and incidents either are products of the author's imagination or are used fictitiously. Any resemblance to actual persons, living or dead, events, or locales is entirely coincidental.

Derek J. Pack
Discover more at
derekjpack.com
facebook.com/derekjpack
instagram.com/derekjpack

First Printing: December 2018

ISBN: 978-0-578-43921-1

If you don't know what it is, don't mess with it.

—FATS WALLER

CHAPTER ONE

Happiness is a warning that sadness lurks around the corner. There's a concrete rule of life, right there. No matter how joyous, how free, how transcendentally ecstatic you feel, no matter how much your heart wants to burst from your chest, sprout wings and fly up into the sky, shock, panic and misery are little more than a few seconds away at any given moment.

A prime example: tall people at rock concerts.

One minute he was courting elation; an unobstructed view of the stage, unmuffled sound, a smile on his face – the envy of everyone. In fact, he could almost read the thoughts of the girl next to him standing on her tiptoes.

'I paid seventy-five bucks to see Weezer for this?! I can't even see over the sweaty, hairy back in front of me!'

But the next minute – BAM! A frantic ringing in his ears quite unrelated to being within spitting distance of the stage. The Doc Marten's attached to the flailing legs of a crowd surfer landing squarely on the back of his head. Again. Euphoria turned to nausea.

He could've seen perfectly fine fifty feet back – *but that's not satisfying enough, is it?* He'd always know that the sound could be louder, the pressure more fierce, the people next to him more frenzied. And perhaps an unimpeded view of Weezer, in such company, was worth the occasional concussion.

There you go. There's the thought process that'll re-attach your jaw.

His tendency to be a glutton for punishment was proven minutes later, before the ringing in his ears even stopped, when the very same crowd surfer, having been thrown bodily from the stage by a fearsome-looking security guard, grabbed him on the shoulder and screamed for a boost. He took one look at the two-hundred-pound bearded thirty-something gentleman, and instinct took over. Who could resist crowd-surfing? And so, well aware that his face would likely meet this man's boots again, he locked his fingers together around knee-height and braced.

3

He was, in truth, the author of his own pain.

"Are you still with me Seattle?!" Rivers Cuomo raised both hands above his guitar, bathing in the adulation of the crowd as the audience erupted in rapturous applause.

They'd been playing for an hour already and had whipped every man and woman in the arena into a state of near-hysteria. In perfect sync, the band launched into "Dreamin,'" one of his favorite Weezer songs. He screamed, his throat raw, his capillaries bursting in his forehead. Carried along on a wave of sound with ten thousand others, barely even aware of touching the ground, the words coming from somewhere below his conscious thought, he smiled.

Does it get any better than this?

One hundred and twenty decibels of musical honey. The blinding lights from the stage. The wave energy pulsating through the crowd of packed sardines moving as one mass.

At that moment, a thought occurred to him. He stopped jumping and looked around.

Why am I always the one lifting people up to crowd surf? How come it's never me crowding surfing? Just because I'm tall? How is that fair?

He turned to the guy next to him and motioned upwards. The man looked him up and down, blew out through his cheeks, and locked his fingers.

Seconds later, a flurry of hands carried him across a sea of hysterical fans. Limbs spread like a snow angel, he floated peacefully over the crowd, a smile growing from ear to ear.

Then the impossible happened.

Instead of being dragged to the floor by a security guard, a final boost from the crowd sent him sailing over the railing, rolling clumsily on to the stage with the rock legends themselves. As he found his feet, Rivers Cuomo threw a sweaty arm around his neck like they'd been friends from school and smiled. "You made it!"

While desperately trying to commit every moment of this experience to his long-term memory, conscious that this was the single greatest moment of his life and it would all be downhill from here, he managed to choke out the lyrics of the song into the microphone together with the frontman of Weezer.

Eventually, the song decelerated into a soothing breakdown, and Rivers Cuomo turned to his new backup vocalist. "What's your name, man?"

"It's Camden. Camden Walker."

Rivers shouted out to the crowd. "Camden!"

The crowd exploded with thunderous applause.

"CAMDEN!" he cried again.

Camden stood, blinded by the stage lights, heart threatening to give out completely. Every conceivable emotion seemed to be competing for attention. Half of him wanted to freeze and the other half wanted to run around the stage high-fiving the front row.

He wiped the sweat from his forehead and attempted to catch his breath. "Just breathe, man," said Rivers. "Stay with me." The rock star smiled and reached down for a bottle of water. "Let me help you."

He opened the bottle and dumped the contents over Camden's sweaty head—

"Camden! CAMDEN! Wake up man! You're gonna be late for class again!"

His eyes shot open. Jeremy, his roommate, was standing over him with an empty glass. The next second, feeling returned to his limbs with a vengeance, and all four of them jerked at once. His comforter flew over his head, and in attempting to kick it off, he tangled himself further. He must have looked ridiculous, lying there, feet kicking like flags in the wind, his entire upper body smothered by a great gray lump. *Enough!* He rolled to his side and hit the floor with a thud.

Jeremy was trying to contain his laughter. "Dude, you slept through your alarm. The radio's been on for half an hour. Didn't you hear it? You're gonna fail your class if you're late again."

Camden wiped away the water from his face. "What time is it?"

5

"Ten to eight. You've got ten minutes to get to class or Williams is gonna kill you!"

He propelled himself off the floor and killed the final notes of the Weezer song playing on his radio.

Why do all the best things happen in dreams? I guess that would explain why Weezer decided to cover "Quiet" from The Smashing Pumpkins...

His jeans on the floor were dirty and wrinkled, much like the Screaming Trees t-shirt he'd slept in, but they would have to do for today.

As Camden struggled into his hoodie, Jeremy smiled and shook his head. Jeremy Evans was many things Camden wasn't: smart, from a well-off family, an early riser, and usually in control of the situation. In spite of – heck, perhaps because of this – the two of them were excellent friends, though usually more so in the evenings than the mornings. Jeremy was also the only African-American studying computer science at the university, something that had been the cause of much hand-wringing amongst faculty staff for the first year. The college already had a reputation for lacking in diversity, and the presence of a solitary non-white individual managed to draw this to everyone's attention far more effectively than a blanket sea of beige.

At first, this had fired Jeremy's political frustrations, and he'd sent several strongly-worded emails to the university demanding that 'Something be done about this modern-day segregation!' But politics had never been in Jeremy's blood - both his parents had had upbringings of reasonable comfort and hadn't engaged particularly in issues of systemic injustice, and their only child hadn't been given much reason to break the mold. After immersing himself in his course and finding it far more engaging than the righteous fury of politics, he simply ignored his racial solitariness and focused on making his grades the envy of his peers.

"Look on the bright side," said Jeremy, holding up his empty glass. "At least you don't have to take a shower now."

Camden rolled his eyes as he laced up his Vans. "Yeah, thanks. You're *such* a good friend."

A saliva spot on the open neurology textbook on his desk was still visible from last night. The book had doubled as a pillow before Camden migrated to his bed around 2:30 a.m. He closed the book, threw it into his backpack and headed for the door.

"Coffee's ready," said Jeremy.

"I gotta *go*!"

"Aren't you gonna eat something?"

Camden groaned, a long, low exhalation born of the belated realization that this day would be just like all the others. "No time."

Jeremy threw him a granola bar.

"Thanks."

Camden looked at himself in the mirror, ran his hand through his dark hair, and wiped the sleep from his eyes. The bags under his eyes were conspicuous in all their glory.

Yeah, there's no fixing that. Or any of it.

He'd just have to hope nobody looked at him all day.

He hurried down the stairs with his bike rattling at his side and out the front door of their apartment. The converted stately brick hotel from the 1920's stood in the heart of the University District. A fair few of the classic touches had survived the interior's modernization – broad banisters, shell-shaped lights in the stairwells. The rent wasn't cheap, but its proximity to both the university and to his work made it worth the price.

The bike ride to his class would take him ten minutes. He had five. Time to do for his med school run what Han Solo did for the Kessel: cut corners and try not to die.

He peddled faster, weaving between cars on University Way, the autumnal breeze cool on his unshaven face. Being late to class was the last thing he needed. There had been rain during the night and his tires were struggling to catch their grip on the asphalt. They needed replacing, but the coffers were empty.

No matter how fast he pedaled, and how close he came to being swiped out of existence by passing cars, he still couldn't wrench his mind away from the anxieties that bore down every morning on his way to class. The University of Seattle had a world-class medical school. Its lecturers were some of the best around, its alumni were busy wiping out tropical diseases and saving lives anyone else would consider hopeless. Its students would join the same path. Curing cancer, ending AIDS, reversing the effects of Alzheimer's and Parkinson's: all of these were likely to be Nobel Prizes won by graduates from this university. The kind of minds this campus held were ready and willing to bend the world to their will.

What I'd give to be among them.

He had no shortage of ideas – regrowing lost limbs from stem cells; heat-sealing broken bones for an immediate return to full strength – but med school wasn't a place for dreamers. There was no shortage of imagination rippling through the Class of 2023, but the difference between Camden and seemingly everyone else stared him in the face each day: others could back up their ideas with a cold, hard understanding of the science. They could fill their minds with new information, process and store it as easily as copying something to a hard drive.

For Camden, however, information seemed to drain through his mind like a sieve. As much as he hated to admit it, he simply wasn't clever enough. That was a depressing thought at the best of times, and even more so when cycling through the tree-lined entrance of the university he'd worked himself sick to get into ever since he was thirteen.

He loved the *idea* of being smart – who didn't, exactly? – but the reality was far different. Reading, writing, comprehension, understanding, application – everything took him twice as long as everyone else. Beyond that, it was simple math: he'd be using his evenings to frantically catch up with everything that had been considered in classes that day; everyone else would be pushing ahead, gaining extra credits and expanding their horizons.

Camden had become sick of bluffing his way through school – and through life. Making it through the first year of med school – never mind being accepted at all – had been the achievement of his life. But despite all his effort, each day he arrived to a marathon already exhausted, desperately trying to catch his breath as the gun fired and everyone else disappeared in the distance.

Sailing past Hendon Library, his bike cut through a flock of pigeons settled in the center of Red Square, scattering them in all directions.

His daily existential crisis overwhelmed him.

I'm in my second year of med school, and what do I have to show for it? Debt up to my eyeballs, grades that won't get me a job anywhere in the U.S. at the current rate – not anything legal, anyway – and I haven't had a good night's sleep in two years. Has it all just been a... a poor investment? A waste of time? Maybe I should just quit while I'm behind. Work my way up to manager at WestCo Medical supplies. It's not glamorous, but at least it's in the medical profession... sort of.

His bike bounced down the steps overlooking Mt Rainier in the distance. There was no time to soak in the view today. He rounded Siegfried Fountain and passed the rose garden, his bike screeching to a halt in front of the majestic Tudor-Gothic stylings of Peverels Lecture Hall.

No time to lock the bike.

He shouldered through the double doors, sprinting as quietly as possible up the stairs and down the empty hallways as he stuffed the granola bar into his mouth.

Gingerly, he approached the lecture hall entrance, took a brief breath and stealthily cracked open the door. If he waited until the professor turned his back, maybe he could slink into the room unnoticed.

Now's my chance!

He slithered in with, he felt, the deft skill of a green beret.

"Camden Walker!" said Professor Williams, still writing on the whiteboard. "How nice of you to join us today." His raspy voice was perfectly capable of peeling paint off the walls.

A hundred pairs of eyes turned on Camden, the proverbial deer in the headlights. The professor spun around to address his tardy student. "We were just discussing the effects of sleep deprivation on the prefrontal cortex and thalamus." He paused, a dry smile

9

spreading across his face. "But perhaps you don't have to worry about sleep deprivation, hmm?"

The snickering class produced a surge of heat in Camden's body which he was sure showed in his face. He would have quite happily had a meteorite hit the building right then, killing everyone for twenty kilometers in every direction. Or a nuke. Where was a maniacal dictator when you needed one? His head hung low, he sank into his chair next to Johnny and Sam.

Johnny leaned over and whispered. "Page two-forty."

Professor Williams, who was in his early sixties, went to great lengths to epitomize the college professor stereotype. Tweed jacket, sweater vest, full beard, glasses, and a slight paunch. Camden respected the professor, who had become a grandfather figure to him, but his respect was twinned with a healthy fear. He knew that this man, like all of his professors, could make or break his future. Camden opened his textbook and notepad while the learned doctor resumed his lecture.

"Over the years, the prefrontal cortex vulnerability hypothesis has received support in the field of sleep deprivation research. It wouldn't have taken them quite this long if they'd listened to me back in ninety-nine, but I'm not bitter, no, not at all. But! Other brain areas are also involved. For example, the exact role of the thalamus is debated. Some studies have demonstrated an increase in thalamic activation during sleep deprivation. Some speculate that this is due to an increase in phasic arousal."

Camden was drowning in a quagmire of words he only just about understood. Last night he'd fallen asleep exhausted before getting this far in the book.

Just another day playing catch-up...

"Now, please turn to page two forty-one. We'll discuss the study carried out at the Chicago Medical Institute in two thousand one. Can anyone tell me what the results of the study were?"

To Camden, it felt like everyone raised their hand except him.

"Yes, Jenny, please," said the professor.

"The results suggested that sleep deprivation might be linked to mental illnesses including psychosis and bipolar disorder."

"Fun! Yeah, exactly. Very good Jenny. What about the two thousand seven Harvard study on page two forty-three? Let's take Sara."

"It demonstrated that sleep deprivation causes the brain to become incapable of putting emotional events into proper perspective and incapable of making controlled, suitable responses to the events."

"Exactly. Well done. Not that I think any of us needed to have this proven by a medical study. I've been up for seventy-two hours straight before and basically forgot that control and suitability were even concepts that existed. So, make sure to get enough sleep tonight everyone. I don't want any of my students going psychotic! Definitely not good for my health."

The room giggled.

The rest of the lesson followed much the same pattern. Camden found it all fascinating, in theory. He could read *Clinical Neurology* like normal people could read John Grisham or Stephen King, and likely get a greater deal of pleasure out of it. But in practice, he could barely keep his eyes and ears open, fighting the feeling of swimming against the tide. Words simply flowed into his brain and out again: *posterior cingulate, presumes, fusiform gyrus, hippocampus...*

He knew what most things were, just about. He just wished it could all be on half-speed, or his mind on double-time, so he could process it properly.

As the clock neared nine, Professor Williams looked at his watch, then shrugged his shoulders. "Okay, all, I think I've taught you enough today. We'll call it here before I break someone. Pages two-fifty-five to two-seventy-one for tomorrow, thank you."

Camden, white noise in his ears, stuffed his textbook and notepad back into his bag, ready to join the massed ranks heading for the exit. Other ideas were had, however.

"Camden!" The dry voice once again cut through the room.

Oh no...

He raised his eyes to see the professor motioning him down.

Sam patted Camden on the shoulder sympathetically. "We'll see you at Allegro."

Camden nodded and sighed.

He plodded down the stairs towards the professor, who was slumped onto a folding chair, his fingers twitching the rhythm of a chain-smoker who'd been without tobacco for almost a full hour.

"Hi, professor."

The older man removed his glasses and focused his gaze on the weary pupil. "Is it too much to ask you to comb your hair before coming to class?"

Camden ran his hand through his head. "Sorry, professor. I slept through my alarm."

"Again?"

Camden nodded shamefully, trying his best to keep his frustration inside. A small amount managed to spill out. "Look, I'm really sorry I missed the start of the lecture. I'll do my best to not be late again. I think you made your point in front of the entire class."

Williams gave him a wry look. Camden grimaced internally. It wasn't smart, being so direct with the professor. But then, the professor stuck out his lower lip for a second, the universal language for *Yeah, well, life goes on.* He reached down for his small briefcase, stood and motioned Camden to follow him up the stairs and out the main exit.

"I know you're not late because you're lazy," said the professor, striding down the corridor. It wasn't packed – most students at this point would be heading to Public Grounds or the Ugly Mug, the campus coffee shops, or else the library. "Nobody who's made it *here* is blasé enough to be habitually late. Let alone getting the grades at college to even apply in the first place."

The professor hadn't looked once at Camden the whole length of the corridor. They reached a fire exit, which the professor pushed open and motioned Camden to go ahead.

"...Thanks," said Camden, feeling thoroughly uneasy. If this was the tipping point and he was about to be cut loose from the course, he'd rather just be told straight. This whole excursion had the feeling of a cigarette, a blindfold, and a wall. Nevertheless, he stepped out into the overcast passage.

Williams lit a cigarette and leaned against the wall. He sucked on the Marlboro for a good five seconds, incinerating half of it. Then he bent his head back and blew a foul-smelling cloud into the air.

Camden could never understand how an educated medical man like the professor could maintain such a filthy habit. Then again, Camden also knew perfectly well that logic and addiction were never on speaking terms. He'd never forget the chain-smoker he was roped to on Mount Rainier that lit up when they reached the top, ice pick in one hand, cigarette in the other.

Williams must have noticed the disgust twisting in Camden's face. "Yes, I know, I need to quit. It's on my to-do list."

"I didn't say anything."

"You didn't have to."

"Sorry."

"*So*, Camden."

"Yes, sir."

The professor rolled his eyes. "Don't look like you're about to be shot. I haven't brought you out here to beat you. You're not yourself, and I want to know why, because it troubles me."

"That's kind of you, sir. Not really sure what to say. Nothing's coming to mind."

"Camden. There's a time to speak, and a time to keep silent." Williams lit a second cigarette with the end of his first.

Camden hadn't expected to be going over this today and didn't want to let the professor into his business. But the tiniest leak had sprung, and he could feel that the rest would inevitably follow. So he took a breath and plunged.

"I'm behind, I'm *always* behind. Just chasing and chasing, and every time I think I can see everyone else in the distance, they just accelerate off again. It was like this last year and it's the same again this year. I probably work harder and get less sleep than anyone else in that lecture hall, and what do I have to show for it? Genuinely, what?"

The professor listened with one eyebrow raised. His forehead creased sympathetically. "Yeah, I can tell," he said, after a moment. "No one's ever going to question your work ethic, that's for sure."

"I'm working twenty hours a week to pay for tuition," Camden continued. "Plus my mom has cancer and I've been spending a *lot* of time taking care of her. Dad died when I was young so she doesn't have anyone close by to help her."

"Hmm... I'm sorry about your mom, Camden. I didn't know."

"Thanks."

The professor paused, then plowed on. "Look, Camden, it's the twenty-sixth of October today. There are more than seven months left until the end of the school year. These first two years of med school are extremely important to set you up for the rest of the curriculum." He paused again, stroking the grey hairs of his beard. "If you don't do well now... I don't want to pressure you, but I need to see some serious commitment between now and June eleventh. You need to figure something out – even with all your other responsibilities. If you can't turn things around..."

"I *will* turn it around. I have to..."

The professor sighed. "Look," he gestured briefly around him, "do you actually want all of this? Qualifying as a doctor, the pressures are ridiculous. You're living that, right now."

"I've wanted to be a doctor since I was five years old," replied Camden, with a hint of stubbornness. "That's the age where you're supposed to want to be a dinosaur or whatever."

The professor chuckled dryly. "Again, I can't fault your commitment, either. Those aren't the things on the table." He tossed his second butt to the floor and ground it under his heel, before turning back to look Camden squarely in the eyes.

"Look, Camden. You're a smart guy, and you're going to get smarter. You'll do fine for yourself. Probably find a nice girl and make an honest woman of her – and if you do, let me know how you did it. But it doesn't have to be *this* path. I know I normally say the opposite of this" – he rapped his temple with the knuckles of his right hand as if to psych himself up – "but genuinely, there's no shame in calling it a day. Horses for courses. This might just not be for you, and if so, that's *fine*. I'll shake your hand and wish you the best from the bottom of my heart."

Camden stayed silent. This was, if possible, even worse than being kicked off the course. At least then the decision was made for him. This just added another layer of anxiety to an already overwhelmed mind.

"But... okay, I'm not going to pretend it hasn't crossed my mind," said Camden, trying to think fast, in case this was his one chance to save his medical career, "but I've managed this far, haven't I? And I'm invested. I've got debts that could sink companies, I've got a whole load of specialized knowledge that will never come to anything unless I'm trained to make practical use of it. I..." he ran his fingers through his hair, gripping the roots hard, "I'm in too deep to leave now!"

"Huh," said the professor. A moment of silence ensued. "Well, if you want to know what I think, and this is free of charge, unlike everything else here: the longer you're here, the more in debt you'll be, while if you call it a day you can move to paying off your debts by next week. It won't help you to cough up for another year and then fail..."

Camden gritted his teeth. This wasn't what he'd wanted to hear. What exactly he had wanted to hear, he wasn't sure. But it wasn't this.

"Think of this conversation like... like an early warning system," said the professor. "Last year you just about scraped by. But let me tell you, boy, it's only going to get harder."

Camden dropped his head. "I know that."

"The university's not as up-front as I'll be, which is to say that you're not paying for a qualification, you're paying for four years of exam prep and the opportunity to take the paper at the end of it. Beyond that, they've washed their hands. I hate it, but, they pay me! So, I'm part of the beast. But look, Camden. I don't know how your other professors feel, but unless something dramatic happens, you should think about calling it a day... Come on, I have another class at ten."

With that, the professor headed back down the hallway. Camden joined him. If he quickly left behind that exact spot, perhaps the crushing negativity would remain there also. He didn't have another lecture until 11 a.m. and had hoped to spend the afternoon in the library, working on his neurological diseases paper before work began at four.

He decided, in the last few seconds before he was on his own, to try one final shot. "Something dramatic, professor. Any ideas? I'm open to anything at this point."

The professor gave a small, mirthless laugh. "Try giving up eating, sleeping and crapping. That'll give you six hours on everyone else every day. You'll catch up in no time." With a small wave of his hand, the professor left him.

Coffee? he thought. *Coffee.*

Moments later, he stood at the bike rack, his head buried in his hands. His shoulders dropped. Maybe if he wished hard enough, by the time he raised his head and opened his eyes again, the bike rack wouldn't be empty.

Nope.

He set off on foot.

The university campus, now buzzing with life, fanned out from Red Square, its avenues extending like spokes in a giant wheel. The red brick pathways and concrete concourses had burned themselves into his mind over the past five years, and now Camden could negotiate his way anywhere relying solely on a combination of peripheral vision and muscle memory.

Several coffee shops were scattered throughout the campus, ensuring that no shaking student was more than ten minutes from a caffeine fix. There couldn't have been more than three people in the entire university who were getting the recommended amount of sleep each night. Both faculty and students simply grabbed what they could; sacrificing calm, moderation and long-term health on the altar of keeping the pace. For all of Camden's self-pity, he knew that he was hardly the only one who regularly woke up with his forehead on a copy of *Brain&Life*. No one expected medical school to be a walk in the park, but the American public seemed alarmingly complacent about their next generation of surgeons, consultants and general practitioners amassing sleep debt to rival their financial debt.

Camden steered himself towards Café Allegro where Johnny and Sam were waiting for him. They met at the small café most days. Tucked down an alley, the small brick-faced establishment was the oldest espresso bar in the city and was iconically Seattle. He found the boys sitting next to the large poster wall which advertised everything from jazz festivals to local standup comedians and poetry readings.

"You okay, man?" Johnny asked Camden.

"That was harsh of the professor," said Sam.

Johnny and Sam Pappas were the kind of brothers every parent hopes they'll raise: inseparable, energetic, jovial and kind. An eclectic mix of a Mexican mother and Greek father, both of them could pass as Jewish. Outwardly, they resembled Mumford and Sons going through a Sex Pistols phase; a harsh, intriguing blend of leather and corduroy, piercings and mustaches. Although the first adjective that came to everyone's mind was inevitably *scruffy*, they had near 4.0 grade point averages and were Camden's loyal, longtime friends. He couldn't recall a single occasion when they'd ever let him down. Intentionally.

Sam prided himself on being the more outgoing of the two. The taller and better-built brother, with dark wavy hair and artfully-trimmed stubble, the general joke within their social circle was that he had to beat women off with a stick. This was always stringently denied by the man himself, to much eye rolling and ostentatious nods amongst his friends.

Johnny, by contrast, had a reputation for being thoughtful, contemplative, occasionally pensive. The smaller and slighter of the two, Camden would often find him staring into the distance mulling the mysteries of life. His most regular topic of conversation, in Camden's experience, was the beauty of knowing next to nothing about the universe.

Sam slid an espresso his way.

"Thanks."

Camden spent a moment meditating on the glory that was coffee. This would hopefully keep him alert at least long enough to get through his Health Care Ethics lecture. Another carefully-timed cup would give him the energy to get through work in the afternoon. It was like stopping at a gas station, if your car had a miniature gas tank and only cost four dollars to fill up.

"What did Williams want with you after class?" asked Johnny.

He loved these two men like family, but he'd never been comfortable talking about his insecurities with them. They seemed too confident, too at ease with the world. He had no doubt that they would listen attentively and offer good advice, but that wasn't the problem. He hated the idea that they would easily be able to come up with answers he himself would agonize over for days. All three of them were about the same age, but Camden didn't feel an ounce of their evident assurance. What did that say about him?

"He's concerned about my grades."

"That's pretty rough," said Sam. "This is a hard place to get ahead. We're all swimming against the current."

"Yeah, but some people have lifejackets."

Sam put his arm around Camden. "You know what you need?"

"I need a better brain!"

"No dude, you need a pint!"

Camden nodded. "That *does* always help."

"We'll meet you at Murphy's at eight, okay? Let's chat about it and see if we can help."

"Sounds awesome."

"And we're buying!"

A small smile crept onto Camden's face. "Even better."

CHAPTER TWO

Am I destined to stock shelves for the rest of my life?

Camden stood on the street corner across from WestCo Medical Supplies waiting for the light to change, ready for his 3:30-7:30 p.m. shift. He'd stocked shelves and filled orders here for nearly five years, and it was without a doubt the most boring job in the city. An interest black hole. A vigor inhibitor. It was unlikely that a single interesting thing had happened inside the building since its doors opened. However, it paid better than Whole Foods and more consistently than bar work. Of course, based on the events of the day, he'd probably be managing the business, as opposed to utilizing its products, by the time he hit forty.

Man, do they need a new sign.

He'd never really noticed before, but the giant antiquated plastic logo from the 1980s revealed a management stuck in the past. Seattle had underemployed graphic designers coming out of its ears! And yet whoever had the responsibility of making WestCo seem bright, relevant or in any way above mere utilitarian clearly needed to buck up their ideas. The façade was equally tired, hailing from a decade whose children were now pensionable.

The inside wasn't much different.

"Hey, Camden!"

That said, the people weren't all bad.

The young employee, bubbly as ever, greeted him with a broad wave as he tried to fake a smile.

"Hey, Krista."

Even in a white lab coat – their staff uniform, on the off chance any actual medical professionals came in who needed impressing – Krista Peterson reminded Camden of a benign version of Harley Quinn, Batman's famous punk-chic adversary. Red streaks pulsating through her dark hair, tattoos crawling up her arms, heavy blue eyeliner and lipstick, mid-calf buckled-up stomper boots, and a spike choke collar adorning her neck. She possessed an inner happiness bordering on insanity.

"You look sad," she said, putting her fingers to the sides of her mouth, creating the look of a depressed clown. "What's wrong?"

For some reason, her unironic concern for his well-being made him still more miserable. He'd have to snap out of this at some point – *or start a Cure tribute band. Hey! Another possible career for when I flunk out of med school.*

He shrugged and forced a smile. "It's just not my day, that's all."

Krista nearly smothered him with a bear hug while he looked wildly over the top of her head to ensure no supervisors were present. "Things will turn around, you'll see."

"I hope so."

She pulled away but then pushed her face up to his, with great big white eyes standing out from two dark clouds of makeup. "You wanna talk about it?"

He smiled and shook his head. She frowned and punched him gamely on the shoulder. Smirking, he attempted to return but she skipped back, giggling at him.

"You're in unusually good spirits, today," said Camden, shrugging on his white coat and clipping his name badge to the breast pocket.

"My boyfriend's visiting!" She did a little shuffling dance in the middle of the floor. "Been two weeks."

"Is this the one from the Czech Republic?"

"That's him! He's a bass guitarist in a metal band. He's got some amazing cheek tattoos."

Camden didn't know how to respond to that, so he just nodded.

She pouted. "I tried to get today off, but no one wanted to switch with me."

"Well, for the sake of my sanity – 'cause I've not had such a nice day as you," said Camden, pointing his finger vaguely in her direction, "I'm glad you're here. Work is a lot more fun with you on my shift."

She cocked her head, giving him a wry look. "You know what would be fun? I tell Ludek you said that. I wonder what he'd do. 'Hey Ludek, there's this guy I work with who said how much he likes working with me. He's also taller and better looking than you. But don't feel threatened, I only work with him every day or so.'"

Camden grinned, keeping concealed his vague feelings of alarm and terror. Krista's boyfriends were the kinds of men who could throw a car at him. "I don't think that'll be necessary."

"But it would be funny, right?" said Krista, following him to the warehouse door.

"For you, yes."

Krista laughed, unhooked a clipboard from the wall and strode off.

He collected his own clipboard, which listed dozens of orders to various medical facilities; hospitals, care homes, halfway houses, paramedics, the lot. His very first order was addressed to the University of Seattle Hospital.

He sighed and pressed on with his job, packing catheters, scalpels, incontinence pads, electrodes, and blood pressure monitors.

Maybe one day I'll be unpacking these boxes instead of packing them...

"Will you sit down, weirdo! You're always embarrassing us."

A regular watering hole for Camden and his friends, Murphy's Pub in Wallingford never let them down. And although he'd never been to Ireland, Camden imagined this was close to the real thing, a belief bolstered by the regulars who actually did hail from Limerick and Donegal. The pub was nice – but not too nice – and they did a killer fish and chips. He came here to unwind, to play darts, to hear stories, or to just take his mind off life. They all did. Tonight was no exception.

"Who am I embarrassing?" protested Sam, cut off by Johnny halfway through his rendition of *Spancil Hill*.

Jeremy and Camden quickly raised their hands.

Sam shook his head, slumping heavily back into his chair. "You guys are no fun."

Jeremy let out a sudden loud laugh, leaned back in his chair and pointed at Camden. "You should've seen the look on your face this morning."

Nice... I was brought here under the pretense of having my mind taken off the things that went wrong today. If you're gonna go through them all chronologically you're welcome to do it behind my back. "It was an awesome dream!" said Camden. "On stage with Weezer. I'd *die* to be on stage with a band like that."

"Don't worry," said Johnny, turning to Camden. "You're not the first person to sleep through their alarm."

Camden sank in his chair. "That'll be a comfort when Professor Williams fails me."

Sam shook his finger in the air. "We won't let that happen."

But Sam's usual method of alpha male-ing the problem away wasn't having its usual effect. Camden felt like he was slipping past morose to full-on despondent.

"I think I just underestimated how hard it would be. I mean, I knew med school would be difficult – everyone knows that – but I just don't have a *life* anymore! The deadlines, the studying, the stress! I'm giving all I've got, and failing at it." He groaned. "If I just had a few more hours in the day, I could cope."

Sam reached into his backpack, pulled out a white bottle, and shook it in the air. It rattled. "More hours in the day come from a bottle, my friend."

Jeremy read the label, rolled his eyes and shook his head. "Oh yes, the Modafinil route. A noxious culture. Are you stupid or what?"

Sam returned Jeremy's eye roll and stuffed the bottle back in his bag. "You can say what you want, but those babies have helped me through many a jam. Snaps your mind straight to whatever you need to do. Helps me focus, helps me remember."

"Where do you get the money for that?" asked Jeremy.

Sam just smiled.

"Plus, they're addictive! And what about the side effects? Have you had any internal bleeding yet, Sam? Hmm?"

Sam gave him a look. "I've been taking them off and on for... for a good six months so far. And you know what? Nothing. Well, maybe the occasional headache. But I can live with that." He pointed his finger firmly at Jeremy's chest. "*You've* had more wrong with you in that time than I have. I go to sleep at midnight, wake up at five, take just one of these, work out, I'm on fire. Rest of the day goes like a dream."

Jeremy shook his head. "You're a moron. You've gotta have a healthy relationship with sleep. There's no shortcut."

"Whatever..."

Johnny stared deep into his pint of Murphy's. "You know what?" he said, quietly.

Everyone turned politely to him. They had all long known two truths: Johnny often had very interesting things to say, and would get quite upset if nobody wanted to hear them.

"Sleep does get in the way, doesn't it?" said Johnny, lifting his head from his pint to look at nothing in particular. "It literally takes up a third of your entire life! We're *chained* to sleep – there's no way around it. You can't just say, 'Today, I'm deciding not to sleep.' *But*, what if you didn't need to sleep?"

Johnny smiled broadly. "Imagine having thirty years added to your life! Think of all the things you could to with the extra time. The places you could go, the things you could learn, the money you could make... You'd get more done, you'd have a competitive edge over everyone. Seriously – I mean, why can't we be more like machines? Why do we have to be slaves to sleep?"

Jeremy tutted loudly, as though highly irritated at the proposition that someone might question his carefully constructed normality. "That's like asking why we eat or drink. Or crap."

Johnny ignored him. "Take a fridge, for example. As long as it's plugged in, it runs twenty-four seven, right? It doesn't need to stop and rest. Why can't *we* be like that? We give our body fuel. Why do we have to shut down, and for *so long* every day?"

Jeremy gave him the same look a politician might give a voter who'd just demanded to know why people needed to pay taxes or have an independent judiciary. "Right. And what happens when the fridge needs to be repaired? Or it breaks? It shuts down! That's why we sleep. So the body can repair itself. So the brain can go offline." He held up his hands. "Look, I know I'm not in med school like you guys, but I think it's an unfair compari-"

"Oh c'mon Jeremy. You think I don't know that? I'm just philosophizing."

"Well look at you, a regular Plato. Don't you think I-"

"Hey, guys!" said Sam, bulldozing the conversation, clearly bored. "Check it out. That hot new barmaid's coming back!"

Johnny pointed sternly at Sam. "Don't you try that 'We're in med school' line again, okay? It never works."

"Whatever."

The barmaid appeared by the table. Tall, with long brown hair and a vibrantly curved figure, she successfully carried the gaze of every man in the room. Camden gave another groan, his mind now determinedly focusing on the cloud in front of every silver lining. *Look at her. She's got it made. Probably makes enough in tips every night to pay off all my debt and still stay smiling.*

"Can I get you boys another round?" she said sweetly.

"Oh, yes please," said Sam. "Medical school can be so stressful. We really need to unwind."

Johnny buried his head in his hands.

"Oh, wow," she said. "Are you all in medical school?"

Johnny snuck a hopeful peak through his fingers.

"Ah, yes. Yes we are," said Sam. "All but our friend over there. He's a techie."

Jeremy narrowed his eyes at Sam.

"That's really cool," said the barmaid. "I'm training to be a nurse."

Sam fired Johnny a look as if to say, *I told you so.*

"Really?" said Sam, his eyes widening with astonishment. "You know, you're going to make an amazing nurse. If I was suffering, I'd want you, and only you to look after me."

She giggled. The other three died a little inside.

"Can I ask...?" said Sam, conspiratorially. She leaned in. "I hope you don't mind me asking, but I've always wanted to pour my own pint. Do you think I could try?"

"Oh, sure thing!" She stood up straight. "Let me show you."

As Sam, who of course had poured many pints in his life, left to fraternize with the staff, Camden slammed his empty glass on the table. "This is all very entertaining guys, but I thought we were here to help me deal with Williams."

"Oh right," said Johnny. "So what exactly did happen today? I mean, you seem seriously down. Like, 'the Seahawks lost' down."

Camden blew out through his lips. He may as well catch them up on the day's events while the creamy pint of stout in his hand suppressed his insecurities.

"I wasn't expecting it – I mean, I was expecting to get ripped to pieces, 'cause I was late to his lecture, again." He paused.

"But..." said Johnny.

"Williams wanted to know what was up with me. He said I haven't been myself for a while, and my grades are down, and I explained... you know, I was honest. The truth is simple, and pathetic, and laughable: it takes me, ugh, three times as long to understand something than everyone else. Trying and trying and trying and trying. Plus my mom and all that..." His voice went up a pitch: "And I told him, I probably work harder than anyone else in that classroom, I get less sleep than anyone, and I'm still behind!"

"And?"

"He didn't say he's kicking me off the course or anything. I mean, it might have been better if he did – instead, he just said that... it might be better if I called it a day and took *myself* off the course, before I have to pay for a third year and fall even further behind."

"Serious?" said Johnny.

There was a moment of silence as Jeremy and Johnny digested this, accompanied by much shuffling in seats.

"That's rough," said Jeremy. "It's like he doesn't want to shoot you so he's offering you the gun and telling you that it's cleaner this way."

Camden blanched. This was a deeply unpleasant conversation topped by a deeply unpleasant image.

Johnny took a sip of his pint. "I see where Williams is coming from, but personally... You're a month into your second year of med school already. That's a lot of progress to leave behind."

"Yeah," said Camden, keeping a calmness in his voice that he certainly didn't feel. "Yeah, that's what I said to him. I'm kind of... just, in too deep. I just feel like I need to see it through to the end. Otherwise, why did I even start?"

The three sat in silence for a moment.

"What'd I miss, guys?!"

Sam thumped another round onto the table, breaking the silence.

"Check this out, guys," said Sam. "She made a shamrock on the top of your pints, but she did a heart in mine!"

Jeremy snickered. "It's meant to be, Sam." Sam stuck out his tongue in response.

"Listen," said Johnny, attention back on Camden, "how about this: you come over on Monday evenings for a while and we'll help until you catch up, okay? Just the three of us, no distractions, no drinking. We'll get some teriyaki and work hard."

"Thanks."

A couple of hours help once a week? Maybe I'd be better off on Modafinil. I'm sure I could cope with some internal bleeding...

CHAPTER THREE

"Good morning class."

Professor Williams raised his eyes over his reading glasses and smiled at Camden. "I hope you all had sufficient rest last night. Can't study sleep deprivation if you're sleep deprived. That would be *absurd.*"

A muffled chuckle rippled through the class.

"Yesterday we discussed the role of the thalamus in sleep deprivation. The thalamus is a key player in regulating awareness and activity in the brain. It's thought to play an important role in regulating our sleep, because something in there needs to shut down all the receptors and allow the mind to function with a lower level of sensory stimulation. Thalamic nuclei have reciprocal connections with the cerebral cortex. This forms what we call thalamo-cortico-thalamic circuits. These are believed to be involved with consciousness..."

Thalamo what? Agh, I'm hopeless.

Of course, staying at the pub till eleven didn't help...

Camden's internal monologue continued, waxing and waning alongside the professor's eloquent diction. He'd scramble to pages in the book, scribble notes as fast as he could, but still it seemed that everyone else in the class had the answers to each question on the tips of their tongues while he remained lost in a fog of his own misery.

After another torturous hour, Camden packed his bag to leave. He looked up to see the professor standing politely in front of him.

"Camden, do you have a minute?"

But I was on tiiiiiiiiiiiime! You've made your point, so at least give me the chance to choose the moment I throw myself out.

Johnny and Sam quickly slid by him, the latter giving him a sympathetic punch on the shoulder before heading for the exit. "See you at Allegro."

The professor smiled, which for some reason drove his discomfort straight on to nausea. "How are you, Camden?"

"Been better, thanks."

"Yeah, a day isn't very long, is it. Listen, I'll get straight to the point." The professor seemed jittery, clenching and unclenching his fist, clearly desperate to get outside and light up. "I was thinking about what you said yesterday – about how busy your schedule is, about how overwhelmed you feel. It's sad. I don't want any student I like to feel that way. So, I'd like to help, if possible."

He's gonna cut me some slack! The story about my mom paid off. Oh, thank you, mom! Something good will come of your crippling illness.

"Oh yeah?"

"There's a buzz at the moment in the medical community – *I'll catch you this afternoon, Jenny!*" called the professor to a young lady lingering by the door. Once she left, they were alone.

"Where was I? Right. There's a Seattle company called Drax Pharmaceuticals. Have you heard of them?"

Camden had. In addition to participating in a drug trial for them earlier in the year, Drax regularly bought equipment from WestCo. Increasing amounts in the last few months, now that he considered it.

The professor paused, almost unsure if he should continue. After a second of interlocking his fingers and blinking furiously, he said, "Have you heard of cognitive enhancing drugs, Camden?"

Seriously? First Sam, now the professor. Is this his idea of help?

"Of course. Some of my friends are on Modafinil to improve their concentration, or to keep awake."

"Right. There you go. Blunt instruments, right? Nosebleeds and migraines all over the shop. Well, over the last few years, Drax has been developing something a little more elegant. It's a new drug that's not so much about improving concentration as, well, something more fundamental."

"What do you mean fundamental?"

"It reduces the body's *need* for sleep. That was the goal when designing the drug. It sounds unlikely, I know. I study sleep, I know the extent to which mammals need it. But the test phases have been very, very interesting, and I'd be a poor academic if I ignored it.   Unlike drugs like Modafinil, there've been no significant side effects – addiction, cellular breakdown, they just don't seem to be an issue. It's amazing, actually. They seem to have made a major genetic breakthrough."

"Um." Camden wasn't quite sure what to make of this. He'd been in medical school long enough to have a healthy suspicion of anything that promised a grand breakthrough in an area that had remained static for millennia. "I've honestly never heard of it. Do you think it's something I should try?"

"You've never heard of it because it's not on the market yet."

"Oh."

"But, Drax is almost ready to conduct phase three trials. Mass trials. And, as I'm sure you know, that means that the drug has been successfully tested on animals and people. So it's nearly ready for submission to the FDA for approval."

"So it's safe."

"Exactly. The phase three trials will involve a thousand people. Anyway, long story short, I checked with Drax and there are still a few openings for the trials."

The professor ran a hand through his hair. "It's not in my nature to do this, but I feel socially obliged to mention it to you."

Hmm. Taking unproven medication in the hope of improving my grades is not exactly what I had in mind. "When do the trials start?"

"On Monday.   There's an orientation and screening this weekend."

"*Professor?*" One of the students from the last class stood in the doorway. The professor's tension ratcheted up another notch and he began rocking back and forth on the balls of his feet.

"Claudia, what can I do for you?"

"Sorry to interrupt, but when did you say the essay was due?"

"Next week on Tuesday.   There's a study group on Friday evening opposite my office. I'll see you there."

"Okay, thanks."

The professor walked up the stairs to the door and poked his head through into the corridor, ensuring they were unlikely to be interrupted again. He gently pulled the door closed.

29

"Look, Camden, this has to be between us. It's against university policy for me to recommend anything like this to you. However, this could be a good opportunity. It could be something that helps you in the short-term, and I know for a fact there are a few other students from the university that'll be involved. Plus you'd get paid a thousand dollars as a sweetener."

"Wow. It does sound interesting. Actually, I took part in a drug trial for Drax last January."

"Did you?"

"Yeah, some cure for the common cold they were working on. I don't know what ever came of it. Loads of us have done drug trials – except my roommate. Easy money. I don't think any of us have ever suffered anything worse than a headache."

"Well, in that case, you wouldn't have to take the medical exam again. It's good for a year."

"Cool."

"They've also moved to a new facility since January."

"They're not in that warehouse in Queen Anne anymore?"

Williams chuckled. "No. They've moved up in the world. City center."

"Well, um, thanks for thinking of me professor. I appreciate it. It would be great to make some quick cash."

"It may be some quick cash, Camden, but this drug might end up being far more than that."

The professor pulled out a leaflet from his jacket pocket. "Drax has been handing these out to several universities in Washington. If you go on their website, there's more information about the drug and what's involved in the trial. If you're interested, you can sign up on the website. Anyway, read it through, give it some thought."

Camden took the shiny leaflet from the professor and read the title out loud. "*Consurge*."

"That's what they're calling the drug."

"Does it mean anything?"

"Honestly? I haven't asked." The professor placed his hand on Camden's shoulder. The grip was tight. "Now, I want you to know that I wouldn't mention this to just anyone. But, well, I like you, and perhaps this can help. At least a little." A smile spread across his face. "I'm tempted to sign up myself actually! Imagine what you could do with more time?"

"Yeah, it's funny," said Camden, "we were just talking about that last night."

"I think it's a conversation that happens every night of the year on every campus around the world."

Camden weighed the leaflet in his hand. "Thanks, professor."

"See you in the week, Camden."

As he walked across Red Square towards Café Allegro, Camden examined the bright declarations of the leaflet.

'Consurge. Awaken to a full life.'

Hmm. Cheesy. Clearly a slogan agonized over and focus-tested to within an inch of its life. But... also intriguing. Even an extra hour in the day could give me the edge I need to bring up my game.

Camden grinned. He could almost feel himself being talked into it, and from where he was, things could only go in one direction. Of course, if he didn't like it, he could pull out of the trial at any time.

I wonder what Johnny and Sam will say? The opportunity to get in on the ground floor of something like this... Plus, I could use a new bike. And a lock...

Krista was right, Ludek has some amazing cheek tattoos.

After his shift at WestCo that evening, Camden unlocked the door to his apartment, threw his backpack on the couch and cracked open a beer.

The apartment epitomized the college bachelor pad. A ping-pong table wedged into one corner, an electronic drum set in the other, a dartboard on the back of the front door and a giant Guinness sign in the living room, the deep black glaring down at them ominously like the monolith from *2001*. Mini basketball hoops had been installed above the recycling and trash cans, both roommates attempting to save the planet while emulating Gary Payton on a good day.

Camden's room was much the same: a gigantic map of the world filled an entire wall; the other three were dotted with posters of Nirvana, Pearl Jam, Foo Fighters, and the Presidents of the United States of America. He never entered his room without a small feeling of melancholy, a knowledge that he'd been born in the wrong era for music, and a longing to have been 23 in 1990 rather than 2020.

That was the moment. That was the zeitgeist. Seattle in the first half of the nineties.

In fact, Camden made a point of watching Cameron Crowe's *Singles* at least once a year just to remind himself of what things used to be like in Seattle. This no doubt contributed to his undying belief that everything seemed better in the nineties, although he was only three when he exited the decade. Maybe it was also why he still used a ruled notepad in class. He owned a tablet, of course, but there was something irreplaceable about old fashioned pen and paper.

He jumped on the internet and sipped his IPA. He remembered the Drax Pharmaceuticals website from January – slick graphics and a winning design. They obviously budgeted far more for presentation than WestCo had ever thought to do. The link to the Consurge drug trial dominated their home page, and a click immediately started the playing of a promotional video.

"Would you like the opportunity to meet other like-minded volunteers and get paid for your time?"

Camden grinned, in spite of himself. *You want me to hang out with people like me? I should be paying you! And hopefully they'll all be as good-looking as everyone in this video.*

Next, he clicked his way to the trial protocol.

- Baseline MRI through external lab prior to trial arranged and paid for by Drax Pharmaceuticals
- 30-day drug trial

- 10-day monitoring period
- Must wear an in-home EEG sleep monitor each night
- Medical checkup every weekend during the trial
- Must not be 'needle-phobic'
- Must keep a daily online record of drug effects and side-effects for entire 40-day period
- Final examination required at the end of trial
- Drug may have mild side effects such as nausea, fainting and headaches
- All clinical tests correspond to regulations set up by the FDA
- Final MRI through external lab after trial arranged and paid for by Drax Pharmaceuticals

So far so good – nothing immediately stood out, except for the part about needles. One of the great failings of medicine is that we haven't yet replaced needles with patches. Or maybe developed a pill to stop people being scared of thin steel rods slipping under their skin, so that we don't focus on the possibility of them touching a nerve, where the muscle spasms and locks, breaking off the needle tip inside and causing excruciating, endless pain...

Camden took a deep breath.

Otherwise satisfied, he began working his way through the online application form. Name? Camden David Walker. Date of birth? June 20, 1997. Gender? When last I checked; but these days, who knows? Sexually active? Hahaha. Smoker?-

"What's this?"

Jeremy was standing in the doorway to Camden's room holding the Consurge leaflet.

"Man, you startled me! I didn't even hear you get home."

"Well, you seem pretty absorbed in whatever you're doing." The curious-aggressive tone was unmistakable. Camden considered the best way to respond.

"I suppose I am."

"So, what's this leaflet all about? It was on the kitchen counter."

"A drug trial. As I believe it mentions in the leaflet. I've done them before, as you know."

"Consurge?"

"It's a new drug," said Camden, brightly. "It's supposed to reduce the body's need for sleep."

Jeremy's eyes lifted from the leaflet and met Camden's. "You're serious?"

"Yeah. Completely. Sounds great, don't you think?"

Jeremy turned the leaflet over. "Awaken to a full life? How cheesy is that."

"I know, right?" said Camden, trying to keep the conversation light-hearted.

"And you're thinking of taking it?" Jeremy shot the question straight at Camden, who was taken aback.

It's okay. He's looking out for me. I'd do the same. You just need to explain the situation to him.

"Why wouldn't I? It's fine. Nothing makes this trial any different to the others. And any chance to get a bit more time in the day would be awesome. Or don't you remember our conversation last night?"

Jeremy shook his head in disbelief. "I can't believe you. And you think this is actually a good idea?"

"Yeah, why not?" As soon as he said it, Camden knew he should've never have asked. Jeremy always had a wealth of examples ready to go at any moment should an argument arise. It was far and away his most irritating trait.

"Don't you remember what happened during that drug trial in France a few years ago? People were left brain dead – or actually dead – from a drug trial."

Camden took a breath. "Yes, of course, I remember. I showed you that article because I was worried about the drug trial I'd just signed up for. But everything turned out fine. Besides, the thing in France was a stage one trial. This is a stage three trial. It's already tested safe. The final test is just a formality."

"Buddy, come on! You know I love you, but people like you can be so naive. These companies don't care about you. You're gonna pump yourself full of who knows what, and – well, who knows what it'll do to you. How much are they paying you? How much is it worth you poisoning yourself?"

Camden bristled. "Jeremy. Let's get serious. If nobody ever volunteered for drug trials, there'd never be medication available to treat diseases! You'd put back medical science two hundred years. Is that what you want?"

Jeremy held up the Consurge leaflet. "But this drug isn't treating any disease. It's totally unnecessary!"

"Maybe for you. You're smart."

"If I'm smart," said Jeremy, calmer now, his voice softer, "then listen to me. There's never justification in messing with natural processes like this. Not your grades. Not even your own future. Sleep isn't an enemy; something to be conquered. It's what nature intended."

"Jeremy - you know, just like me, that living as nature intended means a woman dying every two minutes in childbirth. We move beyond that, pushing if we need to." He waved at the screen. "This could be one small step."

Jeremy shook his head disapprovingly.

Camden clenched his teeth. "I don't know why you have to be like this. Johnny and Sam are in medical school and they think it sounds amazing!"

"Oh, big surprise! What did you think they'd say? Sam's already hopped up on Modafinil."

Camden rolled his eyes. "I knew you'd be like this. Look, I appreciate you caring, okay – I do. Just don't worry about it. It's not the first drug trial, it won't be the last, it'll be fine."

"It's a bad idea man."

Jeremy had finally pushed Camden to his breaking point. "You can be so limited in your perspective sometimes! Why do you limit yourself?"

"Ha. You call it limited. I call it shrewd. I don't need to take heroin to know what it'll do to me."

"Man, give me a break. You sound like you're in elementary school."

"Listen to me. Companies like this are just using you."

"How about this: I won't give you a hard time about the EMFs in your electronics if you don't give me a hard time about this. Deal?"

"There's no proof that EMFs cause-"

"Deal. Fantastic." With a final click of the mouse, Camden submitted the application and smiled. "There it is, my appointment with destiny. Ten o'clock, Saturday morning."

Jeremy shook his head, threw the Consurge leaflet on Camden's desk and walked away.

CHAPTER FOUR

I wonder how much their rent is!

Camden stood near the fountain in Westlake Plaza craning his neck towards the heights of the gleaming Seattle Investments Tower. Drax Pharmaceuticals dominated the top six floors, including the resplendent two-tiered arched glass roofs running the length of the building. However much they were paying, it was having the desired effect on him at least. This level of expenditure screamed power, ambition, and influence.

Professor Williams was right. They've certainly moved up in the world.

Trying to avoid any premature reputation for tardiness, he'd arrived half an hour early for his appointment. He crossed the street and made his way into the atrium of the building, looking straight ahead as he passed by a security guard. He didn't want to give anyone a reason to kick him out – he'd even worn his suit, though the suit was possibly one more matched to a Strokes concert than any sort of formal occasion.

Ascending an escalator, he managed to find the elevators and squeezed in with a group of mainly business people. One girl in a flannel shirt and jeans, crammed in between two men in suits, held a Consurge leaflet in her hands. At least he was in the right place.

By the time the elevator reached the top floor, he was alone with flannel girl. The door opened and he slowly poked his head through, a wave of nerves threatening to suddenly overwhelm him. He doubted he'd ever been anywhere so rarefied in his entire life.

Is this the Starship Enterprise?

Camden could tell by the girl's bulging eyes that she was taken aback as well. The lobby glowed with soft shades of white, blue and beige. An automatic door opened before them into a reception area. The feeling was that of the nicest hospital money could buy: subtly-frosted glass walls screening offices and conference rooms, mood lighting strips along the top of the walls, and a tiled floor so clean he could see his reflection. A giant Drax Pharmaceuticals logo dominated an entire wall.

"Welcome to Drax Pharmaceuticals. Are you here for the Consurge trial?"

A striking young Indian woman with flawless olive skin, a long black braid, and a delicious accent greeted him from behind a spotless glass desk.

"Yes, I am," said Camden.

"Please sign in here."

She looked at his name and handed him an information packet. "The auditorium is down the hallway to the right and up the stairs."

"Thank you."

"Enjoy the program." She smiled sweetly at him, then turned her attention to the girl. Camden waited for a moment, before realizing that he'd been dismissed.

Program? Is this a drug trial or the theater?

Camden's eyes widened as he entered the auditorium.

This must be the bridge of the Starship Enterprise!

The tiered seating descended before him, commanding a sweeping view of the city and Elliot Bay below, all framed by a thirty-foot-high arched window the width of the building. Light flooded in from the glass ceiling above, illuminating the room despite the cloudy Seattle day. Hanging from the ceiling, a home theater-sized screen displayed the Drax Pharmaceuticals corporate logo and a bright green countdown timer.

Walking slowly forward, he noticed a number of other people had also arrived early. Most of them had taken up residence near the front, but two guys had taken seats in the back row. Camden placed them in their mid-thirties. One of them looked up, saw him, and raised his eyebrows in greeting.

"Welcome to the party."

Camden smiled. "Gentlemen. How are you?"

He kept his voice pleasant, so as to not make it obvious that he'd used the word 'gentlemen' loosely. His first impression was of two hitchhikers who'd come straight from a week-long backpacking trip in the Cascades and bypassed the showers. Possibly with a hint of meth lab mixed in.

"Yeah, bro," one of them said. "All's good. Can't wait to see what this is all about. Seems too good to be true."

Both sets of eyes fixed firmly on him. Camden felt a mild tinge of apprehension. Was he supposed to know something they didn't? "I... assume we'll find out. That's why we're here. It sounds pretty exciting, though."

They shifted over. "Care to join us?"

"I'd love to."

It's a good thing I'm not Catholic or I'd have to go to confession for lying.

One of the men had a fire burning in his eyes. "I can't stop thinking about what I'd do with extra time." He chuckled gruffly. "You get more time to work, more time to make some moolah, and then where you gonna spend it?"

The other guy had clearly boarded the same train of thought. "You've got options. Strip clubs, bars, casinos!"

The two 'gentlemen' bumped fists.

"Hmm," said Camden, turning his head to roll his eyes.

Look, it's fine. They're no different from the idiots who crush up Modafinil and snort it. They'll be anywhere with easy money and free drugs. Just ignore them. You're here for something better than that.

By now, about 50 people had arrived. The countdown clock on screen ticked ever closer to zero and a palpable anticipation rippled through the audience.

The increasing din of the crowd was sharply silenced when, at precisely 10 o'clock, a lone man strode into the room. Camden couldn't place his age, but he looked to be in his sixties, though well-kept. He wore an immaculate navy suit and sported a neat goatee and slicked-back wavy hair. To an extent, he reminded Camden of another version of Professor Williams – but from an alternate dimension where Carl Williams hadn't become a professor, living inside a tweed jacket and smoking eighty cigarettes a day, joking with students and editing the occasional academic journal. This was something quite different: the figure below had the same skin tone, was roughly the same height and the build was not dissimilar, but a self-confidence and an aura of tight authority emanated from him in waves. The man walked briskly to the center with one hand in his jacket, scanning a calm eye over the audience. A dropped pin would have echoed.

After he had claimed sole ownership of the audience's attention for a moment, a much younger woman followed behind him. Camden's brain acknowledged her. Then he looked at her again. Then, as though struggling to believe his eyes, he looked at her a third time.

At that moment, Camden's entire world abruptly slowed down.

Graceful and tall, with red hair cascading past her shoulders, the woman had been extracted from his dreams. Under a plain white lab coat, she wore a purple shirt and simple blue skirt, the color adorning her beauty.

My lord, she's a vision. Look at those lips. Look at that hair.
Why did I sit in the back row!

A powerful voice soon broke through his reverie.

"Good morning. My name is Dr. Walter Johnson and I'm the owner of Drax Pharmaceuticals. I'd like to welcome you here today and thank you for making yourselves available for the phase three clinical trial of Consurge. We're confident that this will be a historic trial that will revolutionize the way society operates. And believe me, ladies and gentlemen, that's not a statement I make lightly."

Camden looked around to see people already leaning forward in their seats. Johnson clearly was a professional. Everyone – well, most people – had come here because they wanted to be part of something special, and that was precisely what he was providing.

He took a step back and gestured to the vision in the lab coat standing to his right. "I'd like to introduce you to Dr. Jade Reilly, one of our finest minds and without a doubt one of the great young geneticists whose work will take humanity into a new age of medical technology. She's part of the team that developed Consurge. Jade is here to give you an overview of the development of the drug, and will discuss with you what you can expect during the trial." He smiled. "We know that this program is a little more than you'd expect from your run-of-the-mill drug trial, but I don't think I need to tell you that this is no run-of-the-mill drug! In fact, we're so confident about the benefits of this drug that we want you to tell everyone about Consurge. Get the word out! Tell people what the future promises! There's no stepping back from here."

He stopped, allowing the crowd's excitement to peak, before taking a breath and smiling again. "So now, I'll leave you in Jade's very capable hands. Good day."

Dr. Johnson exited the room as quickly as he entered, leaving Dr. Reilly to continue. She began by extending a warm, glowing smile to the audience.

Oh, please, Jade Reilly, look this way. Anoint me with your gaze.

"Welcome everyone, and good morning. We're extremely excited to have you here. As you'll soon find, Drax has developed some truly ground-breaking medical technology, and we're very happy to be sharing it with you."

A British accent! I'm hooked!

"Before I discuss what you can expect during the drug trial, we're going to play a short introductory video."

She picked up a remote control from a small table, pushed a button, and within seconds, the windows in the auditorium tinted to complete opacity.

So cool! I've so gotta get that in my car! Oh wait, I don't own a car. Or a bike...

Camden's melancholy monologue was soon stifled as he focused on the unhappy people on screen and the polished narration emanating from the speakers.

"Does it seem", the video began, *"like you never have enough time in the day? Do you find yourself waking up tired every morning, never getting enough sleep? What if you could have more time each day to spend with your family, to catch up at school or at work, or to just relax? Imagine the possibilities.*

"Drax Pharmaceuticals is pleased to announce the development of Consurge, a revolutionary new drug designed to reduce the body's need

for sleep. Consurge, Latin for 'Awake', has been developed through extensive and groundbreaking scientific research over the past several years. We are pleased to present this brief video highlighting the exciting innovations that have led to the production of Consurge."

The video cut from a room full of serious-looking scientists to a guy who looked like he hadn't slept in weeks.

"Ordinarily, lack of sleep can have detrimental effects on the body, such as depression, obesity, heart disease, aching muscles, increased blood pressure, irritability, and many others. Consurge is proven to reduce the bodies need for sleep, while at the same time overcoming the negative effects of sleep deprivation. How is this possible?"

She sounds like a smug Siri. Camden was still drinking in every word.

"Genetic research has made rapid advancement in recent years. Extensive study has been carried out by universities and private firms in the field of sleep deprivation. For example, a study conducted by Wake Forest University in two thousand and seven found that a nasal spray containing the hormone orexin-A reversed the effects of sleep deprivation in monkeys. Other drugs, called eugeroics, have also been developed to promote wakefulness. However, concerns about addiction and cellular breakdown remain. Further, the mechanism by which these drugs act on the brain is not thoroughly understood. No significant progress had been made in overcoming the long-term consequences of extensive sleep deprivation in humans..."

The voice paused, measuring out the perfect amount of dramatic effect: *"Until now."*

"In two thousand seventeen, Drax Pharmaceuticals identified previously unknown reciprocal links between specific areas of the hypothalamus, including the ventrolateral preoptic nucleus, and arousal centers in the brainstem. These and other links act as a 'switch' in the brain, inducing either sleep or wakefulness. This discovery led to the development of the patented compounds now used in Consurge to control this 'switch.'

"To further explain how Consurge works, it's helpful to understand what happens to the body during sleep." Here the video changed again, from a cross-section of the brain to a 3-D image of the entire body, various biological systems being highlighted by glowing light. "Sleep is normally a time the body undergoes repair and detoxification. Hormones are released that promote the growth, maintenance and repair of muscles and bones. Protein production is increased, aiding the immune system.

"These and many other functions necessary for a healthy body occur during sleep. Consurge does not prevent the body from carrying out these vital functions. Rather, Consurge works by allowing these necessary processes to happen continually, throughout the day, instead of being confined to just one period during the night. Therefore, the health of the body is maintained.

"Importantly, studies also demonstrate that Consurge is not addictive, and when the drug is discontinued, sleep resumes as normal."

Finally, the video whirled back to a wide shot of the entire Drax team. They all seemed remarkably photogenic. Jade Reilly stood at the front, beaming.

"We are confident that Consurge will help you to get more out of life. Never again will sleep get in the way of living the life you deserve. So, spend more time with your family, catch up with school, work, or just relax. Consurge - Awaken to a full life."

As the video ended and the windows cleared, those in the audience turned to one another with wide eyes and smiles. An immediate buzz of conversation began. Camden too sat awestruck – not only by the presentation but by the presenter.

The heavenly vision in the lab coat continued speaking quickly and assertively: "I hope you all enjoyed the video. Now, we'd like to let you know what you can expect during the next month. First of all, I'll give you some background information. Phases one and two of these trials were conducted as randomized, double-blind, placebo controlled experiments. This meant that each study subject was randomly assigned to receive either treatment or a placebo, and that neither the subjects involved nor the researchers knew which study treatment they received. However, these previous studies demonstrated that because the effects of the drug were unmistakable, further placebo tests were not deemed appropriate or necessary."

She placed her hands comfortably in her lab coat and began to amble around the room. "One thousand people will be participating in this trial for one month. Ten groups of fifty will be administered today and ten groups tomorrow. Following this presentation and tour, you'll all have your blood drawn by one of our friendly staff. As you know, you'll then be required to come in every weekend for the next month for a checkup.

"You'll also be required to keep a daily online journal of the drug's effects. In the paperwork that you received at reception, you'll find a username and password you can use to log in to our website. Please follow the instructions there to chronicle your daily progress during the drug trial.

"Okay. So if you'd like to follow me, I'll give you a brief tour of the lab where Consurge was developed. Right this way please."

The room rose as one and filed out, following Jade. Camden and his two acquaintances trailed behind the rest of the group, Camden lost in deeply pleasant daydreams involving a life with less sleep, perfect grades and a red-headed companion. The other two were muttering to each other, eyes swiveling, scanning their surroundings.

Descending a flight of stairs, the group emerged into a laboratory with a handful of intently focused technicians in white lab coats. One person was burning up his keyboard at a minimum of a hundred words a minute. Another was shaking a test tube full of a mysterious violet solution under an ultraviolet lamp. As Camden stared, the liquid turned colorless, and the technician made a quiet mark in a notebook.

Jade invited everyone to gather around a machine which she said isolated specific drugs from blood samples. She waved her arm wide. "This lab is where the magic happens. Does anyone have any questions?"

Yeah, Why do I have to be stuck here in the back with these two morons?

As she set about answering the first question from a woman in the front, his mind raced.

Okay Camden, now's your chance. Think of a question. Something clever. Let her know you exist. Impress her with your erudition. Dredge up something, anything, just so this goddess notices you and remembers you. Show her that you're not some waste of space like these two guys next to you...

Camden turned.

Wait a minute. Where are they?

He glanced over his shoulder at a rapidly closing door in the corner.

Where do they think they're going?

Camden followed, opened the door and stuck his head around the corner into a room full of boxes. His two friends were busy stuffing their backpacks full of bottles.

Camden raised his voice. "What do you guys think you're doing?"

"Look at this," whispered the one.

"It's boxes of the stuff!" whispered the other.

"You can't just take it!" said Camden.

"You bet we can. This stuff'll cost us a fortune when it goes on the market!" said the one.

"We'll only have a month's supply during the trial. Then we'll have to pay for it through the nose!" said the other.

They scampered to their feet and pushed past Camden and through the door.

He heard Jade continue: "Any further questions?"

Camden caught up with the men and firmly grabbed one of them on the shoulder. "You've gotta put that stuff back or I'll—"

The man wrenched Camden's hand from off his shoulder and squeezed his knuckles into a vice grip. Camden winced. He soon found his face pulled close to the badly-shaven, weather-beaten features of someone who now wished him nothing but ill.

"Or you'll what?"

Camden grimaced in pain but said nothing. The man's eyes, he now saw, were bloodshot. He held his breath.

"That's what I thought."

"Okay," came the pleasant voice of Jade, apparently oblivious to the commotion not twenty feet away, "if there are no more questions, that concludes the tour and orientation. So if you'd like to follow me, I'll take you downstairs to the waiting room where you'll be called when it's your turn."

Minutes later, Camden slumped down into a chair in the waiting room, trying to the shake life back into his mangled fingers. Hopefully, those reprobates hadn't caused any permanent damage.

I tell you what, I'd like to give those guys a piece of my mind.

No sooner had the thought crossed his mind when the two 'gentlemen' squeezed in on each side.

"I hope we made ourselves clear earlier," said the one.

"There's a lot worse things than broken fingers," said the other.

"I get the picture," said Camden, evenly. He didn't let his emotions show, though inside his rage was burning brightly.

Who do these morons think they are? How dare they threaten me! I have rights. They can't talk to me like this. They need to know they can't just push people around like this. And I'm gonna tell them! I'm gonna stand up and say–

"Camden Walker," flooded the voice over the intercom. "Room twenty-three." Camden promptly rose to attention, spun around to address the two deviants, then firmly and decisively walked away.

At the end of the hallway, the door to room 23 was wide open. Camden could feel the sweat starting to build in his underarms. This was the part he'd been dreading all morning. Needles. Well, one needle. But one was enough. 'Your blood will be drawn by one of our friendly staff,' Jade had said.

I don't care who you are, nobody is friendly enough to–

"Hello, I'm Jade. You must be Camden."

!!!

Just breathe. Play it cool. There must be a dozen nurses working here. What are the odds I get her? Wait, is this a dream?

Pull yourself together. Close your mouth! You don't want her to think you're some weirdo fixating over a beautiful woman he's only just met. My goodness, look at that hair, those green eyes, those lips...

Wait a minute, how long have I been standing here mute?

"That's me," he grinned coyly.

Jade smiled automatically back at him, before turning to her clipboard. "Please have a seat. I'll take your picture and then get your blood work started."

Her countenance radiated intelligence and confidence, and yet warmth and kindness. Camden felt lost in a perfect world.

"Okay," she said, picking up a camera from the table, "if you face me, I'll get a couple of pictures for your file. No need to smile."

Okay, Camden, you've been given another chance. Think of something witty to say. Something charming. Don't blow it.

Finished, she put the camera back down. The pictures immediately appeared on the computer screen.

"You remind me of someone," he blurted.

She turned from the screen, her smile now a little quizzical. "Oh yeah, who's that?"

"Did you ever see Batman: The Animated Series?"

She giggled. Camden's stomach did a loop-de-loop. "I can't say that I have."

"It's from the nineties."

She chuckled. "A bit before my time I think."

"Well, for me too. But you can find anything on YouTube."

"I see."

"You remind me of Poison Ivy."

Her eyebrows rose almost up to her scalp. "Is that so? Isn't she a villain?"

You could've said anything in the world and you compare the girl to a supervillain. Very smooth. You should be teaching classes in this...

"Oh yeah – I mean – well – not when she's in her green leotard –" Camden could feel the blood rushing to his face. "But

47

when she's in her lab. You look a lot like her. And – and she's a genius!"

She grinned, apparently amused. "Poison Ivy? Interesting. So, are you afraid I'm going to poison you, Camden?"

"Are you?"

She held up a syringe like a scene from a horror movie and smiled menacingly.

"You really know how to put your patients at ease," said Camden.

She laughed, one great, strident "Ha!"

"Now," she said, leaning towards him as he sat back in the chair, "didn't Poison Ivy have a thing for Bruce Wayne?"

"I thought you didn't see it?"

"I didn't. But... I do remember the film with George Clooney." Her eyes went a little dreamy at the mention of the name, though none of that delicacy was extended to Camden's arm, and he winced as she tied him for the blood draw.

"Just to warn you," he said gingerly, "I have a hard time with needles."

"No problem. I'll be gentle."

"Also, I know it's a bit weird, but I have to look at it. I have to know when it's gonna happen."

She mused for a moment. "That's unusual."

"Don't worry; I'll keep you talking during the blood draw."

She grinned. "That's what I'm supposed to say. Now, you'll feel a slight poke."

Camden shivered as the needle entered his forearm. It was never pain, really – more a deep sense of discomfort, of violation.

"So, how long have you been working here?" asked Camden, gritting his teeth slightly. He could feel the small bite of metal and was trying desperately hard not to move his arm.

"Oh, about a year now," said Jade airily. "First job out of Uni."

"Really? Your first job? Dr. Johnson seems very impressed with you."

"You could say I landed on my feet."

"Yeah? Very cool." Next subject, next subject! "Where did you go to school?"

"In London. I applied for the job here and they took me on."

"Cool. My mom lived in London for a year when she was in college. That's why she named me Camden, after Camden Town."

At this, she met his eyes with a look of excitement. "I love Camden! The town, I mean." She gave him a wink and his heart almost shut down.

"Right. Are your parents in England?"

"Yep. They're not far from London actually, where my mum is from."

"And the red hair?"

"Dad's from Ireland." She leaned her head to the side allowing her hair to cascade to the front of her shoulder. For a brief moment, Camden almost forgot there was a needle in his arm.

The second vial now filled with blood, Jade pulled out the needle and bandaged his arm. "Right, that's your blood work finished. Just a few more things."

Camden tried to slowly let out a deep sigh of relief without her noticing. He had the feeling she did anyway. She next opened the cupboard above the sink and pulled out a small box from among the dozens stacked there.

"Here's your EEG sleep monitor and enough sensors for forty days. You'll need to wear this every night for us to monitor the electrical activity in your brain. Just follow the instructions on the leaflet to send the information to us through our website. Make sure you charge it every day."

"Roger that. I've never used one before but I know how they work. We sell these at WestCo Medical Supplies."

"Is that right? I think that's who we bought them from."

"Yeah, you guys have been one of our best customers for a while. I'm glad it's all going to a good cause."

Jade nodded at that. "Do you see yourself at WestCo for a while?"

Camden shrugged, noting his arm was stiff. "It's just part-time until I finish med school – or something better comes along."

Jade raised her eyebrows. "Oh, you're in med school?"

Looks like that night at Murphy's Pub wasn't a total waste after all. Thank you, Sam!

"That's great," she said. "Where do you go?"

"University of Seattle. I'm in my second year."

"What field do you plan to specialise in?"

"You know what, I'm not really sure yet. There are lots of interesting avenues. Medical research would be amazing, for example" – he waved his arm, indicating the lab through the window – "but to be honest with you, I'm struggling to find the time to fit in all the studying."

"Consurge should help with that."

"That's the idea."

Jade motioned to Camden to stand, and held the door open for him.

Now's your chance, Camden. It's now or never. "So, uh... you must be working a lot of hours with the launch of this drug."

Jade gave another perfect smile. "Yes, it'll be another late night tonight. The price of breakthroughs."

"Oh, right..." Camden paused, made eye contact and smiled. "So I guess that means I can't ask you out for dinner tonight."

"Dinner?" In spite of herself, she let out a giggle. "Well, I'm not sure my boyfriend would like that."

Camden's heart sunk. "Oh, you have a boyfriend."

She burst out with a beautiful laugh. "Actually, no. Sorry. I'm just mean like that."

Camden pursed his lips. "Wicked." Jade grinned at him.

"I'm flattered, really. But we're not supposed to date test subjects. Walter says it might cloud our judgement."

"Who said anything about a date? I have to eat, you have to eat. We just happened to be eating together. Besides, I know a great little place I think you'd like."

"You know what I like?"

"Good. It's settled then."

Jade's eyebrows shot up. "I haven't agreed yet. What if I say no?"

"Then I'll express to your boss my aversion to being referred to as a 'test subject'."

"Hmm, yes, that was a poor choice of words. Very well. Where is this place I'll supposedly like?"

YES!

"How about I meet you at the Gum Wall. Do you know where that is?"

She tucked her hair behind her ear in a thoughtful manner. "The famous brick wall in Post Alley near Pike Place Market covered in millions of pieces of multi-coloured used chewing gum?"

"That's it."

"No, I don't know where it is."

Camden rolled his eyes and smiled at her.

"But I can't get there before eight," she said.

"Perfect. And bring your dancing shoes."

CHAPTER FIVE

"*Kells Irish Restaurant and Pub.*"

Jade grinned as she caught sight of the sign above the door.

"Well you are *Irish*, right?" said Camden.

"I love it."

Camden's heart was singing in his chest. After meeting at the Gum Wall, the pair climbed the steps under the glowing red lights of the Public Market sign and past the old brick cafes and shops of Post Alley. Jade looked astonishing, wearing an all-black set of jeans, suede coat, and high Chelsea boots. Her red hair fell down her back like a velvet waterfall. She'd laughed at his stories about skateboarding and the mishaps he and his friends had suffered; he'd listened carefully to stories of her work and the incredible breakthroughs they were close to making. And now, they'd arrived at *Kells*.

Despite the Saturday night hordes, they managed to find a quiet table in the corner. Camden soon flagged down the waiter who took their order: two pints of Guinness and two bowls of Irish stew. He felt a ridiculous sort of giddiness that they'd ordered the same thing; like in sixth grade when Rebecca Hamilton said she also liked "I'm Yours" from Jason Mraz and they had held hands for the rest of the day.

The two slowly worked through their meals, chatting all the while, until finally they were left nursing their second Guinness apiece, sitting in a pleasant haze. The *Red Rose Café* played in the background while several musicians gathered on stage; one opened an accordion case, another pulled out a fiddle. Camden couldn't remember being this happy in quite some time.

Now's the time to get a little more personal. Surely she's comfortable now. Heck, I'm almost falling asleep, I'm so relaxed.

"So, how do you like living in Seattle?" asked Camden, hefting himself forward and dropping his elbows on the table.

Jade remained lounged in her chair. She'd long removed her coat to reveal a Lynyrd Skynyrd t-shirt, and stared hazily at the ceiling while thinking.

"Overall, it's great. The city has a good vibe. But sometimes I think the people could be a bit friendlier."

"Ah yes, the Seattle Freeze."

"The what?"

"The city has a reputation for being a bit impersonal."

"I guess that's true – but not any more than London. In London, you could get hit by a car and everyone would just walk on by. Things are really disimproving there."

Camden's head jerked. "What did you just say?"

"Hmm? Oh, I said things are disimproving in London."

"Disimproving?"

"Yes, why?"

"That's not a word!"

"Sure it is."

"There's no *way* that's a real word."

"Of course it's a real word. Look it up."

"I don't need to look it up."

She gave him a grin and carried on. "Suit yourself. But, going back to your earlier question, I do like that Seattle's on the water. And I like being close to the mountains as well."

There you go. Something you can work with.

"That's cool. What do you like to do in the mountains?"

"Well, I've been hiking a few times and snowboarding a couple times."

"Awesome. Where have you been hiking?"

"I'll show you."

Jade pulled out her phone and held it so they could both see. The pair leaned in as she swiped through a gorgeous gallery of scenic mountain lakes, valleys, and forests. Camden suddenly realized how close he was to Jade's face. His eyes soon shifted from the phone to the contours of her gorgeous visage and her beautiful green eyes.

It didn't take long for Jade to feel his gaze upon her and she turned to meet it. Camden quickly looked down at his food and leaned back in his chair.

"Beautiful – the pictures. They're great." Camden scratched the back of his neck nervously, and let his gaze scan the room.

Jade winked at him and took a sip of her Guinness. *Okay, so she's not creeped out. That's good. Keep it under control.*

"Who's in the pictures?" he asked.

"Some friends from work. *Ha!* Friends with a car. Because I live and work in the city, I decided not to get a car."

"Oh yeah, uh, me too." *You can tell her you're broke if there's a second date.* "So where have you been snowboarding?" he asked.

"Once to Steven's Pass" – she flicked to a photograph of a blinding white slope – "and once to Alpental."

"Cool. I grew up skiing at Alpental. A lot of good memories there. I know every inch of that mountain."

"I'm sure." She tucked her phone back into her coat pocket. "Sadly, we don't have mountains like that in England. Plenty of pretty green hills. We like to call them mountains, but they're nothing like the Cascades."

"What was it like growing up in England?"

"It was okay, I guess. Beautiful countryside. National healthcare. Horrible customer service. Washing machines in the kitchen. Separate hot and cold water taps. You need a licence to watch telly."

"What?!" Camden had never heard anything so disgraceful in his life.

She carried on. "Interesting history. Bland food. Manor houses. Stately gardens. Basically, it's full of a lot of people who sound like me and talk like me. I'm not sure if they all think like me, mind."

"Do they all look like you?"

She raised a slender finger and pointed at him. "Ah, Camden. Would you like that?"

Camden suddenly found himself violently hot under the collar. Jade giggled and drained the remnants of her drink.

"Well, it – it would be an interesting place to go on vacation," said Camden, desperately trying to divert attention away from him by motioning to the waiter for another round of drinks.

Jade snorted, and then leaned forward in one fluid movement, eyes suddenly bright and focused. "Camden, tell me this: why are Americans obsessed with the English accent?"

"Dunno. I guess we think it sounds educated, sophisticated."

"Hmm. If you say so. There's this amusing American tendency to believe we've all been educated in castles and have tea with the queen each week. Mind you, not all English accents would be considered 'sophisticated'."

"I suppose it's the same here."

"True. I'm constantly amazed at how many differences there are in American English versus, well, you know, proper English."

"Careful now!" said Camden, menacingly pointing his finger. Jade brushed an amused eye over the offending digit.

"For example, the other day I figured out a maths problem at work and somebody said to me, 'Wow! That was quite good.'" Her voice reared with her best American accent.

"So?" *And it's 'math' problem, but I'll ignore it.*

"I'll tell you. You see, in England, adding 'quite' in that context can turn a compliment into a sarcastic insult. Approving of someone's work in England is a fraught process. The most positive word can immediately be viewed as an insult."

Camden laughed.

Good to be in a country that doesn't have any problems with direct communication, albeit often the rapid, gunpowder-propelled type...

"So what about the Irish side of your family?" he asked. "Do you still have relatives in Ireland?"

"I have a lot of family there. Mostly in County Cork, where my aunt and uncle live."

"Have you been there?"

She smiled wistfully. "Oh, yes. Many times. I used to spend the summers there when I was young. It was such a contrast to London. London's all grey concrete and traffic. Cork is far more pleasant – all greenery and mist. I love it. My aunt and uncle have a sweet old place in the country. They're lovely. Uncle O'Donovan's a farmer. No airs or pretentions about them at all."

Camden tried to imagine it. Rolling green hills, narrow roads winding through small villages of stone cottages. Chickens in the yard, perhaps. The occasional pig. Geese splashing through a stream. "What's it like, living in Ireland?"

"It's great – apart from the weather. You're kept indoors more often than you'd like, considering what's around you; cliffs, beaches, castles."

"I'd love to see it."

"You do have to develop patience though. There's a more laid-back approach to most things. Bus timetables are more of a suggestion."

"Some stereotypes are true, huh?"

Jade nodded in agreement from behind her pint of Guinness. "Enough about me. What about you? Have you travelled much?"

"Does Canada count?"

"Hmm... I suppose. You mean you've never been anywhere else?"

"Well, Mom never had the money for us to go anywhere more exotic. My dad died when I was two, so my mom had to support me on her own. No savings, I don't think. Just a lot of hard work and rationing."

"Oh." Jade paused. For the first time that evening, Camden saw her looking confused, unsure. She took a sip of her drink and put it down, not looking at him. "I'm sorry to hear that. It sounds rough. Must have made your childhood difficult."

"Thanks. Yeah, but I think more about my mom. She hasn't had an easy ride. She's fighting cancer now as well."

"Oh dear."

"She's positive, though. She's really strong. Always has been. I try to look after her as much as I can."

"I'm sure she appreciates it."

"It means I'm often back home on the weekends, trying to make sure she's looked after. Problem is, most of the best care is something we can't afford. And I feel bad sometimes because I can't give enough time to everything, you know? When I focus on school, she gets neglected. When I focus on her, school gets neglected."

"Consurge will help with that."

"I hope so."

"If it can't help you, in your situation, then we've failed in our goals." Jade suddenly sat up a bit straighter, her gaze a bit sharper. "You're also working part-time as well, right?"

Camden shuffled in his seat. He didn't want to talk about work. He wanted to talk about Jade. "Yep, twenty hours a week. Nothing special. The money's not great, but I can walk there from my apartment, which is handy." *I am not going to tell her my bike was stolen.*

"Do you have a flatmate? Or are you all alone in a big apartment?" There was now a teasing tone to Jade's voice which Camden found extremely pleasant.

"Yeah, his name's Jeremy. He's a good friend. A real techie. Although he hates being called that. He's studying advanced computer sciences, as well as a couple of other things I don't even understand. You should see his room. Nothing but laptops, tablets, phones, cameras. Not whole, of course – most of them he takes apart with a screwdriver the second they're through the door. He just loves seeing what's inside stuff."

"Interesting, that's the way I think. I think I might like him."

Hmm. I'd better make sure they never meet.

"I always think" – and at this moment, she placed her hand on the table, palm lifted, fingertips straight down, a semi-sphere – "what's underneath this rock? Is there something down there in the earth where, if I'm willing to get my hands dirty, will benefit me? Perhaps benefit everyone? How far do I have to dig? Will I be able to dig far enough? Could I live with myself if I didn't?"

Camden didn't know how to respond. He liked to think of himself as the inquisitive type, but he'd never quite heard anyone talk like this before. She'd stared at her own hand, flexing her fingers the whole time. It had been almost poetic.

"What about you?" he asked mildly.   "Do you live with anyone?"

She nodded.   "Actually, you would've met her this morning. Do you remember the receptionist?"

"I do."   He easily recalled the pretty Indian woman with the gorgeous voice.   Drax clearly made a point of hiring people who could charm with merely an accent.

"That's Chetana.   She's great.   She moved here from Mumbai around the time I moved from London.   We've got an apartment in Pioneer Square."

"Cool, I love it there."

As their plates were taken away and they drained their glasses for the third time, the lyrics of "I'm into Something Good" kept repeating in Camden's mind.   Jade had it all.   Beauty, intelligence, wit.   She was clearly a deep thinker, a philosopher, a muse.

The band, which had begun with a few slow ballads, chose this moment to kick into full swing, guitars jangling and fiddles reverberating through the packed room.   Camden could see Jade eyeing the packed dance floor, the vibe of healthy competition spurring on the crowd.

"Do you wanna dance?" Camden shouted over the music.

She pulled him up from the table.

The jigs and reels filled the air with an irresistible energy that demanded dancing.   Camden and Jade jumped and clapped to their hearts' delight, allowing the music to overcome them while just about managing to avoid crushing people's feet.   They swayed together to the waltzes and sang along to the classics, Camden thoroughly impressed at Jade's knowledge of the lyrics and her ability to hit the high notes.

As the band finished the final notes of 'Whiskey in the Jar', Camden shouted to Jade.   "I'll be right back!"

He pushed his way through the throng, and after a brief word with the lead singer made his way back through the crowd, satisfied.

"What did you say to him?" asked Jade, noticeably intrigued.

Camden smiled and leaned into her ear. "Special request. Just for you. A classic with a twist."

The band eased into a version of "Dicey Reilly", – the tale of Dublin's infamous inebriate – but with one key difference: "Dicey Reilly" had been replaced with 'Jade' Reilly. Jade landed a playful thump on Camden's arm then joined the audience as they double-clapped in all the right places.

By the time the song finished and they'd collapsed in their chairs, Jade was practically weeping with laughter. A deep well of tension seemed to have released in her, and she hiccupped giddily, trying to catch her breath. She leaned to her side and shot Camden a slightly hazy, evil eye. "So that's what you think of me? You think I'm a drunk?"

Camden laughed. "No! I don't think that. I don't know you well enough yet!"

She smacked him again, her wild swipe catching him on the elbow.

"Okay, fine, I deserved that."

Jade's hand waved around a little in the space between them, and he reached out to it. His forearm brushed her fingers, the tips of which began running up and down his skin. He looked at her, but she was gazing into nothingness, her hand seeming to act of its own accord. It was a small moment of delicacy in the midst of a heaving, groaning, sweating crowd.

She then stopped, pulled her hand back, and turned to face him, eyes clear once more. "You know the Irish songs really well! I'm impressed. You kept up with me."

"Well, I've never been to Ireland, but I love the music. I do have to admit, though, that I only got into Irish music because of the Dropkick Murphys."

"Ha! Well, there's a lot more to love about Ireland than just the music. You must go, someday. You're made for it."

"It's on my bucket list."

Eventually, Jade reminded Camden that another 500 people were scheduled to go through the Consurge orientation tomorrow and that she had to begin work at the crack of dawn. Soon, the pair found themselves standing outside the pub with their coats on. Camden was shifting his weight from foot to foot, and not just because of the cold. This evening had been brilliant, better than even his wildest dreams could have predicted, and right now, all he could think about was the infinite number of ways he could screw it up.

He waited for Jade to say something. She was adjusting her hat atop her head, taking her time. Finally, she looked at him, an amused expression on her face.

"So." She grinned.

"*So*," replied Camden, nodding.

Another pause. Jade's smile grew wider. "I had a nice time tonight."

Okay, Camden. Don't panic. Don't make her think you're too interested – don't make her think you're uninterested. Walk the line!

"Yeah, me too. It was great." Camden rocked back on his heels, screwing up his courage. "So... can I see you again?"

"Would you like that?" said Jade, mischievously.

She wants you to beg? Go for it. "I would like that very much, yes. We could both go out for dinner again, another night, and again, just happen to be in the same place at the same time at the same table."

Jade pretended to get a notebook out of her pocket, flipping through some imaginary pages. "Hmm... hmm... oh! Do you know?" She flipped the fictional notebook shut. Camden's heart sank. "I am free. Next week. Friday evening."

His heart rose once more. "Excellent." Drunk on his own exultation, he continued, "And if this time 'round worked so well, maybe you'll let me do the same again. You choose the time, and I'll take you somewhere you'll like."

She gave him a wide, flirtatious smile. "That, I think, sounds delightful."

Now! Now! Do it now!

Camden stepped forward – concentrating furiously, balancing himself on his front leg, trying desperately hard not to arrive with too much force – and delicately kissed her on the cheek. He stepped back. One smooth movement. His inner voice gave him a standing ovation.

Jade smiled.

He knew for a fact that he'd be skipping all the way home, whistling a merry tune. He couldn't remember feeling this good for a long time, if ever. Even if he never saw her again, for whatever reason – no one would ever be able to take this feeling away from him.

On the bus ride home, a message from Jade popped up on his phone: *"Thanks again for a fun evening. You're 'quite' a good dancer. ;-)"*

CHAPTER SIX

"Here's to better grades."

Upon awakening Monday morning, Camden's first thought was of Jade. Following closely behind, however, was Consurge.

He rubbed the sleep from his eyes, swung his body to the edge of the bed and reached for the pale orange bottle on his bedside table. The pills were large, half blue, half red. He wondered at the choice of colors. Was it deliberate? Blue was often associated with sleep, red with wakefulness. He'd read about this before: the placebo effect in humans was so strong, so unexpectedly powerful, that drugs would have a significantly greater effect on the body depending on the color of the capsules. Of course, this was no placebo.

He swallowed his first dose and waited, half expecting to somehow feel instantly different.

"Don't be stupid," he muttered to himself under his breath.

That night, as bedtime approached, Camden opened his laptop to the Drax Pharmaceuticals website, logged in, and recorded his first entry of the Consurge trial.

DAY 1 (Monday, November 2nd): No noticeable effect from the drug. Going to bed at 10 p.m.

He fitted the EEG monitor to his head, turned it on, and turned off the light. Maybe he'd dream of Jade.

By the end of the next day, his bed called him again at 10 p.m., but perhaps he didn't feel quite as tired as normal. Maybe it was his imagination.

DAY 3 (Wednesday, November 4th): Going to bed at 10:30 p.m., but don't feel too tired. I was able to concentrate well in class first thing in the morning.

Camden hurried through the week, impatient both for Consurge to start having a notable effect and for his Friday evening date with Jade. Williams hadn't said a word to him personally all week, Jeremy was his usual mix of passive-aggressive and curious, and other than the Monday study session,

Sam and Johnny were busy with their band. So he kept himself to himself, scribbling papers in the library, packing delivery carts at work, and all the time dreaming of a vigorous Celtic melody, of flying red hair and waving arms, of Chelsea boots stomping on the floor.

Finally, Friday arrived. Camden had reserved a window booth at a fancy restaurant on Pier 66 overlooking the city skyline and waterfront. The view almost made up for the prices.

"An Irish pub one week and a swanky restaurant the next," said Jade, as they met up by the entrance. "Pretty soon there'll be nowhere to go but down."

Camden opened the door for her. "Yeah, and we'll end up shoveling down noodles out of paper boxes while sharing a cigarette on the curb."

"Ahh, I can taste the grease now!" said Jade, smacking her lips. She giggled and meandered inside as he followed.

The maître d' showed them to their booth. Camden tempted fate by feeling proud: it was a gorgeous room, a gorgeous booth, and a gorgeous view. Jade was also looking suitably gorgeous in a floral smock and black leggings. Camden knew he was on her turf this time, and deliberately so: he wanted to impress her by showing he was more than a one-trick Connemara pony.

They sat – *ohh, that's comfy* – and Jade picked up the menu.

"Impressive," she said, eyeing the selection.

"Only the finest, for you," he replied, his faux-seductive tone drawing a grin from Jade.

"Well, *monsieur*, in that case, and since you're paying, I'll have the Dungeness crab cakes with ginger-plum sauce and beurre blanc."

Camden swallowed.

"That's as a starter, of course. Then I'll move on to a whole North Atlantic live lobster, with..." She flicked over to the wine list. "Yes, a bottle of Trimbach Gewürztraminer should do fine. Won't it, Camden?" She pinned him with her most arrow-like smirk.

Camden breathed in. "Okay, what I meant was, 'only the finest on a starving student income'."

Jade laughed. "Don't worry, I'm only teasing. I'll have the roasted acorn squash risotto. That should do me wonderfully." She closed her menu.

Camden wiped his brow.

The waiter delivered their starters along with two glasses of water.

"How are things going with the trial?" asked Jade.

"Yeah, good. I mean, I assume so. I'm not feeling weird or anything. Last night I went to bed at eleven and I wasn't really all that tired."

"I know," she said sheepishly. "I read your entry today."

He raised his eyebrows. "You can read my entries? Those are my innermost thoughts! How am I supposed to keep any secrets from you?"

She burst out laughing. "Yes, your 'innermost thoughts'." She flicked her fingers in air-quotes. "'I'm tired'; 'I'm a bit less tired'. I do hope there's more to your mind than that, otherwise, I might stop finding you interesting."

Camden chuckled, concealing his inner voice's panic attack: *I'm interesting! She finds me interesting!*

"It does feel like the drug's making a bit of a difference," he said, wrenching himself back to the conversation. "Class first thing in the morning today wasn't as much of a haze. Maybe just a mist."

"I'm glad. Alertness is recognised as the first stage in the process. We'll track that and see how it extends into the rest of the day."

The waiter took away their empty plates and Jade picked up the wine list, giving him a coy look.

"Are we on a budget?"

Camden, anxious not to derail a very pleasant evening, gave an airy wave. "By all means, try to wow me."

This drew a split-second look of impressed surprise from Jade, followed by a smirk. She turned a few pages and singled out an entry to the attending sommelier. "A glass of the Chateau Sainte Michelle Chardonnay, please. Thank you."

"Same for me," said Camden.

The lady nodded and slipped away.

The waiter delivered their main courses: Jade's risotto, Camden's halibut cakes.

"Tuck in," said Jade.

"What?"

"Bon appétit."

"Oh. Thanks, you too."

"*Mmmm*, molto buono," said Jade, taking a bite.

Camden assumed this was positive so he carried on. "So, how's your week been?"

Her eyes widened and she tilted her head back, mouth full of risotto and mushrooms. "Very, very busy. Today we had another lecture from Walter in the auditorium."

He couldn't quite tell from her tone whether this was something she had enjoyed or something that irritated her. "What did he say?"

She sighed. *Okay, the latter.* "It's not so much what he says, but how he says it. He 'enlightened' us" – air-quotes again, this time awkwardly as she was holding her knife and fork – "with the theory that sleep is an evolutionary artifact."

"Huh. What does that mean, exactly?"

"Well, he went on about different animals and their sleep patterns. Did you know that giraffes only sleep for twenty to thirty minutes a day?"

"No. That's insane."

"I know! And apparently, when dolphins give birth they're continuously active for months at a time, with *no* possibility of extended periods of sleep. And they never show any obvious signs of impairment during that entire time. It's very interesting actually. So the argument is that sleep in some animals – like humans – is just evolution's way to limit our activity."

Camden mulled this over. "That *is* interesting. Do you think there's something to it?"

Jade shrugged. "Maybe. I don't know. I just know that sometimes he can be so zealous – so full of himself. He's got no problem with self-esteem, that man."

This didn't surprise Camden. His one experience of Johnson in person was that of someone whose ego could fill a stadium. "You know, maybe he's just passionate about Consurge."

"I guess... I suppose I shouldn't be too hard on him. There's no way we'd be anywhere close to where we are without him. He's gotten all the funding together; he's hired a whole bunch of really brilliant people. And, he has done a lot for me this past year."

Hmm. "Yeah? Like what?"

"He took me under his wing really; looked after me. I've got a serious career ahead of me because of him."

"I see. It sounds like he's into you." *Please don't let him be into you.*

She laughed. "Well, he did ask me out a few months ago."

"Did he, now? But you said no?"

"Well you know Camden, he *is* very sophisticated, and he has a lot of money, several expensive cars, eats in places like this three or four times a week. And in a year's time, he's going to be awarded the Nobel Prize for Medicine."

"If you're trying to make me jealous, it's working."

Jade grinned. "But he's way too old for me. Besides, I don't think I could handle that level of hubris in a relationship. I told him I was flattered, but I wasn't interested."

"Good choice."

She took a sip of wine. "I'm glad you approve."

"Speaking of Walter, where did the name 'Drax' come from anyway? I can't imagine your boss is the kind of guy who likes Guardians of the Galaxy."

"*Ha.* I asked Walter the same question. He told me the name came from his oldest grandson."

"Really."

"Yep." Jade swallowed a mouthful and put down her fork. "His grandson was eleven at the time. Walter was looking for a name for his new company and one day his grandson came up to him with a comic book in hand. The grandson explained that Drax the Destroyer was a human who had special powers to combat evil, and that was like his granddad's new company. Walter liked it and the name stuck."

"Cute. I think."

Jade picked up her fork and smiled. "I guess. I'm still not sure I believe it, though."

The meal ended and Camden paid, wincing at the final amount. That being so, he was still very much prepared to make such a commitment to the evening.

Now it was time to take Jade somewhere a little quieter. Wrapped up in their coats and scarves, they meandered along the waterfront for a post-meal stroll, trying to clear the food-induced fog from their minds. The moored boats gently rocked in the glistening harbor. The taste of salt water and the aroma of fish and chips wafted through the air. Jade wrapped her arm around Camden's, leaning onto him as they walked. Her head just about reached his shoulder. It was deeply soothing.

"You could've ordered dessert, you know," said Camden.

Jade shrugged. "Don't worry. I'm not bothered. Besides, you need your money for books!"

He spied a small restaurant along the pier, with a large, jolly sign out front. It advertised a much-loved homemade delicacy, and Camden wasn't going to let a silly thing like the biting wind get in the way of enjoying it.

"How about an ice cream?"

"Ice cream?" said Jade, eyeing the sign. "It's November!"

"So?"

Jade acquiesced. "Go on, then."

They hopped up on a low wall overlooking the eclectic and weathered Pier 57, swinging their legs, shivering and giggling as they licked their frozen treat. Iconic and whimsical though the pier was, it was obvious in places it was over a century old.

"Have you ever been up the Great Wheel?" asked Camden. They could see it clearly in the moonlight at the end of the pier: a glowing white structure, curving up into the sky.

"The only Ferris wheel I've been on is the London Eye."

"The gondolas are heated…"

Her face lit up like a school girl. Camden hopped off the wall, took her by the hand and tugged her down. The pair raced over hand in hand to the promise of a cozy cabin in the sky.

From the top of the Ferris wheel, the lights from the city sparkled on the bay below. The pair sat side by side watching as a ferry slowly pulled away from the docks.

"It's beautiful," said Jade.

"I hoped you'd like it."

Jade pointed. "Hey, look! You can see the top of the Drax building from here."

Camden could just make out the curved glass roof in the distance. "Awesome."

"Well, Camden. What can I say? Two out of two."

Jade reached out and gently held Camden's hand, sending an electric current through his body. His hands were sweaty, but somehow he knew she didn't mind. Camden turned to find her emerald eyes already fixed on his. Until this moment, he'd never really realized how vibrant green her eyes were. Jade green. Did her parents have a feeling her eyes would be green? Was it just a coincidence? Suddenly, Camden found himself wanting to know everything about the beauty sitting beside him. And more than anything, he wanted to feel her lips on his.

He wasn't sure his heart had ever beaten so fast in his life. Reaching out, he gently caressed her face, and slowly leaned in. The warmth of her mouth sent a jolt flooding through his body, currents running the length of his spine and making his fingertips tingle. Jade placed her hand on Camden's neck as he lost himself in her soft lips.

The pair slowly pulled away and smiled. Camden tenderly wrapped his arm around Jade as she snuggled into his chest. There they settled as the city spread out before them.

Unfortunately, as much as Camden willed for the moment to last forever, the wheel eventually returned them to the wooden planks of Pier 57. Her kiss had left his knees in a jellylike condition. Even so, he was ready to paint the town. Feeding himself on the adrenaline coursing through his body, he turned to Jade with wide eyes. "So what should we do now? How about the Space Needle? Did you know the whole floor is glass? You can look straight down on the Seattle Center."

By now, however, Jade's eyelids were protesting. "I'd love to Camden, but I really need to get back home."

"Already! Oh, come on, stay out with me a bit longer. It's only ten-thirty!"

He grabbed her hands and started dancing around the pier. Jade laughed helplessly as she was spun around by him, her protestations being drowned out by her breathlessness. Eventually, she pulled herself free and doubled over, hands on knees, catching her breath.

Composed, she stood up, tucking her hair behind her ears and crossing her arms. "*You* may not be tired, but I have to get some sleep. I have to *work* tomorrow!"

"I suppose..."

"Don't fret. I'll be seeing you very soon."

"Oh, you wanna go out tomorrow night?"

She rolled her eyes. "You've got your first checkup in the morning, remember?"

Camden brightened up. "Oh, yeah!"

"And I made sure you're scheduled with me."

"I never thought I'd actually look forward to a blood draw."

Jade smirked. "Yeah, well, we try to make it as pleasant as possible."

She walked up to him, his face still displaying a wide-mouthed grin of pure elation, and kissed him tenderly on the lips.

"Goodnight," she said. "Thank you for this evening. It was most wonderful."

Camden sauntered home.

Time was nothing. Space was nothing. As he leaned against the bus window, as he stepped slowly up the stairs in his apartment building, as he collapsed into his desk chair, all he could think about was Jade.

Day 5 (Friday, November 6th): Going to bed at 11:30 p.m. I feel on top of the world. Floating on cloud nine. Thanks for a wonderful evening. ;-)

CHAPTER SEVEN

"So, what were you doing with your extra time last night?"

Over the past week, Camden and Jade had nearly worn out their phones exchanging text messages. One night after his shift at WestCo, Jade had taken Camden to a cinema in the University District to see an obscure independent film which he didn't understand. At least he'd been able to sip on a beer during the movie. Another evening Camden had taken Jade on a stroll around Green Lake. He'd treasured every moment.

A grand total of two hours – one solitary study session – had been spent with Johnny and Sam studying neurology. Instead, Jade had offered to help with his studies and Camden had no intention of refusing. Today, Friday, Jade had met Camden after work at the university's Hendon Library, though the Gothic-style building felt more like a church than anything else. Perhaps it was his affinity for all things Irish, but Camden always upon entering, felt an odd compulsion to walk up to one of the librarians and begin confessing.

He raised his head from his book. "Hmm? My extra time?"

Jade pulled up the post on her phone and read quietly. *"Day eleven: Going to bed at two-thirty am! Could've probably stayed up longer. No negative side effects noticeable. In fact, overall mood has improved. I feel fresh and rested every morning."*

He grinned. "I see you're still spying on me."

"Not spying," said Jade, tartly. "Just checking up on you. Actually, I'm amazed and really quite irritated, at the sheer number of people who haven't been updating their journals or wearing their night-time monitors. It's almost like the contracts they signed don't matter." She put her phone down on the table and stretched out her arms like a cat. "Well, I'm sure they'll realise their errors when we take a similarly lax approach to paying them at the end of the month."

Ouch! Drax means business. Those poor idiots don't realize who they're dealing with.

"That would be an unpleasant surprise."

"There's a lot at stake here, Camden. Lots of money, lots of prestige. We've got to make sure this all goes the way we want it."

"I get the picture."

"So – what were you doing with all your extra time in the night?"

"I was researching my paper on inductive reasoning. And, it was amazing actually – I didn't even feel drowsy. I've gotten so much study done these past few days," he looked up at her and grinned, "despite all the time I've spent with you. And, well... okay, maybe it's just my imagination, because I want this to happen, but I seem to be taking it in faster as well. I'll test myself on what I've just read and it all comes back to me so clearly. I feel like it'll have a massive impact on my grades."

Jade smiled sweetly. "I'm really happy to hear it. You deserve to do well. You're exactly the kind of person we want to help."

"Thanks, Jade." He closed his book. *Theoretic causes of hypothyroidism include high levels of human chorionic gonadotrophin, a pituitary adenoma (non-cancerous) and thyroiditis. Thyroid cancer itself has an unexpectedly low correlation with hypothyroidism, though not so low to not be considered a potential cause.*

"How's your mum doing?" asked Jade, breaking into his perfect mental recitation.

"Oh, my mom? Yeah, she's in good spirits. I've been able to spend a bit more time with her the past couple weeks. She's been really happy about that."

"Have you told her about the drug trial?"

"Yeah. She's really excited. The cancer means she's got so little energy most days. All she can manage really is the kitchen, the bathroom, and bed. She told me that if – when she beats the cancer, she wants to go on Consurge herself. Make up for the lost time."

Jade's eyebrows shot up at the news. "That's great. What a fantastic reason to take Consurge – if you're recovering from an illness and want to live a normal life. We already know about the applications for the elderly and dementia sufferers... I'll mention it to someone at work. What a brilliant idea."

"Cool. I told my mom about you, ya know. She wants to meet you. I know she'd really like you. And you and I could go for a hike in the woods near where she lives."

"Where you grew up?"

"I'll show you the best trails. And the best trees to climb."

Camden turned his attention happily back to his book. A daydream began to stir in his mind: racing through the woods of Saint Edward Park down to Lake Washington; strolling hand in hand peacefully along the waterfront; stopping to soak in the view, his arm around her waist. They stare into each other's eyes for a moment. They kiss tenderly.

After a few moments of happy contemplation, however, something elbowed its way to the forefront of his mind. A small, niggling thought that he'd ignored up until now, but for some reason was refusing to stay quiet.

"Are you okay?" asked Jade, noticing his change of expression.

"Can I ask you a question?"

"Of course."

"I've been going to sleep every night about a half an hour later than the night before. It makes me wonder... well, how far will it go? I mean, does it level off? The video at the orientation said Consurge would *reduce* the body's need for sleep. Reduce by how much, exactly?"

She gave him a wry smile, one without a great deal of humor in it. "I'm not allowed to speak about the potential effects of a drug to a test subject during a trial."

"There you go again with that 'test subject' business!"

"Oh no, Camden. This time it was intentional. I'm being very serious. I could prejudice the entire trial if I start feeding you information. We're not even supposed to be dating, remember."

"Aw, c'mon. What about the previous trials?"

"I'm not at liberty to talk about the results of previous trials either."

Camden threw up his hands. "Oh, you're terrible!" he said, a little louder than he'd meant. A guy at the next table glared at him, and he calmly retracted his arms. "Over dinner, you already told me about feeling alert. How is this different?"

Jade lowered her voice. "This is very different. Before, I was confirming something you already felt and that fell within expected parameters – and to be honest, I probably shouldn't have even said that. I'm certainly not going to ruin the objectivity of this trial just to satisfy your curiosity. I'm sorry. I have a job and a reputation that are very precious to me."

"You and your principles," said Camden, in a jokey, lighthearted tone that he didn't entirely feel. Jade smiled vaguely back at him and nodded pointedly at his book.

Don't worry. Every good relationship has its boundaries. You respect her work, and she'll respect you.

Over the weekend, apart from his medical checkup and a brief visit to his mom, Camden forced himself to study. This was no small sacrifice as Jade had invited him on a boat trip to the San Juan islands with some friends. It was worth it.

Monday morning in Professor Williams' class, Camden sat with his back straight. The professor strode to the front of the class, the fug of cigarette smoke emanating from him in every direction. He slapped his briefcase down on the chair and surveyed the room through bloodshot eyes.

Man, Williams looks rough. He looks like he's slept less than I have.

"Okay, everyone. Good to see you're all here. I hope your weekends were better than mine – I *really* do. Let's review page three-seventeen of our textbook. It refers to the concept of abstract thought. Everybody needs abstract thought, don't they? Can't be stuck in reality the whole time. So, who can tell me: in what part of the brain does abstract thought cause significant activity?"

Camden's hand shot up.

The professor was clearly caught unawares. "Yes, Camden. You got there first."

"The inferior frontal gyrus and middle temporal gyrus."

"Yes, good stuff. Now-"

"That is, of course," Camden continued, cutting over the professor's follow-up, "compared with concrete concepts which cause greater activity in the posterior cingulate, presumes, fusiform gyrus, and parahippocampal gyrus."

Williams gave him an amused look, softening his weary face.

"Okay, yes, that's excellent too. Thank you. That actually covers my next question, so... let's move on to page three-eighteen."

Camden turned to find Johnny and Sam gaping at him with wide eyes. He smiled. Camden had been building up the confidence to get to this point over the whole of the previous week. The newfound clarity of his mind enabled words to leap from the page and into his long-term memory with an ease and fluidity that he'd never imagined possible. And there they sat, waiting to be accessed once more.

After class, Camden gathered his things and threw them into his bag. He stood to see Professor Williams ambling up the stairs, hands in his pockets, a warm smile on his face. The professor leaned against the seat at the end of the row and rubbed his forehead with his palm. Camden wandered over and waited to hear what the older man had to say.

"So, Camden," said Williams, after a moment. "How are things going? Something really seems to have spurred you on."

"Really good, professor. I've been studying a lot lately."

Williams nodded slowly. "I can tell. Your paper on inductive reasoning shows a marked improvement in quality from your last paper. An exemplary breadth of research. I can tell that you're comprehending the subjects better."

Hey, look at that. Approval from Williams, no less. That's definitely worth pinning to my wall. "Thanks, professor. I'm chuffed."

Williams blinked. "You're what?"

"Sorry. I have a British girlfriend now. She's teaching me new words all the time."

It wasn't often the professor looked lost, but this was clearly outside his area of expertise. "Well, okay then. I'm happy that your vocabulary's getting exercised as well. Anyway, well done on your answers. Let's see some more of that, eh?"

Williams glanced around, to make sure it was just the two of them left in the room. "So," he said in a low voice, "how's the trial going?"

"I went to bed at four o'clock this morning," said Camden, dropping his voice to match the professor's. "I literally slept for only *two hours*, but that's all I needed. I was up at six like I'd just had the best sleep of my life. It's been like this for a few days now. I got loads of extra study in over the weekend. So yeah, the trials are going well – *really* well. I'd massively recommend the stuff."

The professor nodded fervently. "I'm sure you would. If it works as well on everyone else, we could have something really special on our hands. Special on a civilizational level. And of course, if you carry on like this in my class, you'll soon pull yourself away from the edge of the cliff."

"Yeah. These last two weeks have been incredible."

"Well, two weeks are two weeks. Let's not count our chickens yet. But keep up the good work. Well done."

"Thanks, professor."

Camden hoisted his bag onto his back and walked away, a spring in his step. Williams had always been good for him, but that was the first time the old man had ever been *impressed*. It made him feel heady with excitement and pride, like his chest was filling up with air, ready to lift him off the ground and into the clouds.

DAY 19 (Friday, November 20th): Only slept 15 minutes last night! Going "to bed" at 5:45 a.m. again today. I feel healthy, strong, alert, and energetic. Retention of information continues to improve.

Sunday evening, Camden and Jade were wading through several plates of Thai food in a small restaurant in Pioneer Square, the heart of Seattle's old town.

"I *love*," said Camden, shoveling another forkful of pad thai into his mouth, "how close this place is to your apartment."

Jade, prevented from replying by the vast quantity of noodles pressing down on her tongue and spilling out of her lips, nodded vigorously in return. She swallowed hard and drained her bottle of Singha.

"I tell you what – I might be finished," she said, rubbing her hand over her stomach. She'd already undone the belt on her jeans and sat back heavily in her chair.

Not one to miss such an opportunity, Camden reached forward. "Don't worry, babe, I got this." He scooped the remaining rice noodles and chicken onto his plate and held his fork aloft in gleeful anticipation.

"My hero," said Jade, waving her hand at him limply.

As Camden continued to gorge himself, Jade heaved herself forward.

"I saw your entry yesterday morning," she said.

Camden looked up, cheeks bulging like a chipmunk. "Yeah, it's incredible, huh. I've only needed fifteen minutes of sleep for the last three nights."

"That's great."

"Mhhhm!" *Why does she have this grin on her face like she knows something but isn't telling? I wonder if I can pry it out of her.*

He swallowed heavily, anxious not to let the conversation get away from him. "Actually, that's something I've been wondering about." Jade gave him a suspicious look, but he plowed on. "As impossible as it seems, I was beginning to think I wouldn't need any sleep at all, but, well, it seems to have plateaued at fifteen minutes. Is it gonna stay that way?"

She laughed. "We never said Consurge would *eliminate* your body's need for sleep – only reduce it. Greatly reduce it."

"So you're saying it *has* plateaued?"

Jade shrugged. "I don't mind telling you now. We're well into the trial."

"I'm listening."

"Part of the reason the body needs sleep," began Jade, looking up at the ceiling as she talked, "is for your brain to consolidate memories; affixing them to your long-term memory. Some of it can happen while you're awake, but a lot of your conscious emotional stimuli are processed and stored while the mind is unconscious. And *this*" – her face formed, for a moment, a look of extreme irritation – "is something that Consurge can't do. Not *yet*, anyway. But believe me, it's the next frontier we're going to overcome. For now, though, the brain still needs to go offline in order for memories to be properly consolidated. With Consurge, the brain takes about fifteen to twenty minutes each night to settle down, process everything, and then get back up to full conscious capacity." She smiled proudly. "It's what we refer to in the lab as a 'Drax Power Nap'."

"You're enjoying this, aren't you? Knowing something that I don't. Seeing me trying to figure it out."

"Camden, love, this isn't the only thing I know that you don't. But I must admit, it's been nice to watch your journey. I like to see smart people trying to figure things out. It's why I hire them."

"Are you offering me a job?"

Jade smiled but said nothing.

Interesting. I must remember to bring this up again, next time we've eaten too much Thai food.

"Well," said Camden, "I'm glad you've found it entertaining. In any case, it's resuscitating my medical career. Professor Williams told me the other day just how good my work has become, and that if I carry on this way, I'll definitely turn things around."

Jade's eyes went wide. "Wonderful! That's such good news. If Williams is that impressed, that's hard evidence of your improvement."

But Camden soon felt the happiness and pride inside him begin to deflate, like a balloon slowly losing air. He gradually slumped and began to push his food around with his chopsticks.

"Did I say something wrong?" asked Jade, cautiously.

"No! No. It's fine." Camden took a deep breath. "But it does make me think about the next couple of weeks, though."

"What do you mean?"

"Well, I mean that there are only ten days left of the trial. What's gonna happen then? I'm honestly afraid I'll lose the progress I've made..." His eyes dropped. "I'm afraid I'll end up back where I was."

She reached out and touched his hand. "Camden, listen to me. You shouldn't think about it that way. Consider the trial an opportunity to catch up – an opportunity you've taken, mind. Taken with both hands."

"I'm trying to."

"It's true that the effects will wear off once the trial concludes. But now you can *keep up* instead of getting behind again."

This cheered him a little. "I hope so, babe. You make it sound so simple."

Jade, seeing that Camden was visibly unconvinced tried to brighten up the mood. "Don't worry! Consurge will be available before you know it."

"If I can afford it..."

Jade crossed her arms, looking proud of herself. "Believe me, the cost of the medication isn't something that should bother you. We're not making this drug for the rich – we're making it for everyone. If you can afford Sudafed, you can afford Consurge. I mean, I'm not in charge of pricing, but one overhears things."

"Oooh. Sounds exciting. Overheard anything else?"

Jade gave him a grin that he was certain he'd seen before, on a Cheshire Cat. "Yes, and I'm going to keep it *all to myself*. But don't fuss. You'll only be off Consurge for... maybe eight months at the most; provided the trial is a success and the FDA approval comes when expected."

"Eight months... Seems like an eternity. How long will it take me to start sleeping again?"

"It's different for everyone. You'll return to a regular sleep schedule faster than you exited it, I can tell you that much for sure. That's why it's a thirty-day drug trial with a ten-day monitoring period."

Camden slurped up the last of his pad thai and managed a smile. "I tell you what; one thing's for sure. Drax is gonna make an absolute *killing* with this drug."

CHAPTER EIGHT

One day. One day, I'm gonna hold somebody's life in my hands and I'd better recognize it when I see it.

One week on, Consurge flowing through his veins and fifteen minutes of sleep each night giving him all the rest he required, Camden had become a scholastic hermit. Desperate to get as far ahead as possible before the end of the trial, only lectures and work could draw him from his room. He felt wonderfully alone during his hours of study, like a single monk on a grand island monastery, surrounded by hundreds of years of learning; the weight of what was still to be known so comforting on his shoulders. He devoured books like once upon a time he'd devoured comics: *Guide to Neuroscience, Atlas of the Human Circulatory System, Clinical Anesthesia* – done, done, done. He'd even begun tracing the drawings in Grey's Anatomy, trying to commit to memory every nerve, every blood vessel, every divide of organ and muscle tissue.

It hadn't gone unnoticed by his professors. Ellis in his Renal/Genitourinary class, Courtois in Reproductive Studies, Samiir in Health Care Ethics and, of course, Williams in Neurological Disorders had all commented on his progress and expressed a desire to see him in their classes the following year should he continue to make such rapid improvement. His participation in class discussions was starting to draw envious looks from his peers, even from Johnny and Sam. And he'd even begun some of the coursework not due until February and March.

Unfortunately, the by-product of this was less time with Jade. Although this wasn't entirely his fault. She'd been scooped up by Drax to work late every day, and her texts had taken on a clipped, sharp tone around which Camden knew to tread lightly. The one time he hadn't – texting her, '*It must suck to be needing Consurge and I'm the one who has it*' – had drawn such a venomous reply that Camden had to switch his phone off to avoid the words burning through the screen. Jade had apologized the following morning, but he was certainly looking forward to the time when the two of them could just get away for a bit. Maybe go on vacation, away from the pressure and the deadlines.

This evening, therefore, was something to treasure. It was Sunday, only two days before the end of the Consurge trial, and Camden felt in a celebratory mood. Jade was coming over to introduce him to *The Quiet Man*, one of her favorite Irish films, and Camden had given the apartment the clean it had always wanted yet never received. He'd rushed through the last few pages of his paper on cauterizing blood vessels – *I cannot wait to replace that mental image with anything not involving blood and seared flesh* – and had vacuumed, wiped, dusted and tidied until the apartment looked like something out of a catalog. He'd even cleaned the espresso machine in the kitchen, something he hadn't touched since about midway through the Consurge trial.

Seven o'clock arrived and the doorbell rang just as Camden stood in the kitchen mixing a pitcher of gin and fresh lemonade. He tried to rinse his hands as quickly as possible, but his roommate made it to the door first.

Oh no...

Jade stood in the hallway, an enormous white scarf encircling her neck and chin, her cheeks pink with cold. The rest of her body was wrapped in a huge black coat, and she stood stiffly.

Jeremy leaned on the door frame, crossed his arms and blocked her way. "Ahh, the mad scientist is back."

Jade laughed. "You really have apprehensions about my work, don't you?"

"Apprehensions? That's one way to put it. I think what you're doing is dangerous and foolish."

She smiled. This wasn't the first time Jeremy had voiced his opinions to her. "Does that mean you won't let me in?"

Jeremy softened, grinning back at her. "Please come in."

He took her coat and followed her into the living room where Camden was waiting to embrace her. Jeremy, however, wasn't finished.

"Tell me something, Ms. Reilly."

She turned, still in Camden's arms. "Are we going to have another debate, Jeremy?"

"Discussion."

"Oh goodie. Well, let's not waste any time then. Camden is going to fix me a drink, and you're going to hit me with your best shot. And once I've wiped the floor with you, I'm going to enjoy my evening!"

Oh boy.

She threw herself down onto the sofa with a satisfied sigh and put her feet up. *Red socks. I like them.*

Jeremy grumpily stood, weighing up what to say. Camden, finding the whole process a little embarrassing, slid across to the kitchen, eager to impress Jade with his homemade lemonade.

"I think what you're doing," Jeremy began, "is messing with a fundamental natural process. And whenever people get it into their heads that that's the next step, nothing good ever comes of it. Creating problems where there aren't any problems."

"Interesting, interesting. You're smart, aren't you, Jeremy?"

The comment was simultaneously complementary and condescending.

"Huh? The problem's there, whether I'm smart or not."

"I only ask – oh, *thank you*, babe." She took the tall glass, resplendent with mint leaves and sliced cucumber, and took a deep swig. She nodded in satisfaction. "Oh, that's strong. I like it. Anyway, I was saying" – she turned again to Jeremy – "if you're a smart person, you shouldn't need me to make you understand why what you're saying is foolish. Our work is simply the next step in a long list of medical advances, like so many before us."

"Listen," said Jeremy, leaning forward, "you don't need to talk me through medical advances. I wear glasses. I take painkillers when I need them. I've got a couple of pins in my leg holding my knee together."

"So why are you interrupting my evening?" asked Jade, sweetly.

"Let's try this as a theory." Jeremy paused, evidently having decided that now was the acceptable time to sit down. He dragged a stool over and plonked himself on it, his head now level with Jade's, and continued. "Here's the thing. Everything I've just described is where something in my body has gone wrong. My eyesight's weaker than it should be, I have pain in certain places that doesn't teach me anything, which I therefore want to block out, and I broke my leg playing football. The body isn't designed for that."

Jade continued to sip her drink. "I'm with you."

"Your company, and whoever's funding you, thinks that sleep is a mistake as well. Thinks that it's something we need to correct, like setting a broken bone or digging cancer out of someone. It's *really, really* not. That's where you've gone wrong."

There was a pause.

"Well... I respectfully disagree with you," said Jade, giving him a pleasant look. "And so would many others. One of my favourite quotes is from Thomas Edison, who called sleep 'an absurdity, a bad habit.' If you were given the opportunity to add years to your life otherwise lost by sleep, that would be something only a fool would turn down."

The atmosphere in the room had grown noticeably chillier, despite Camden's valiant attempt to save things by putting out a bowl of chips and salsa on the table.

"I certainly wouldn't sprint at it like a toddler looking at a display of candy. Let me ask," said Jeremy, changing the topic bluntly, "your boss doesn't believe in God if I recall correctly. Do you?"

Oh, Jeremy. Really? You attack her work, and now you're moving on to religion. You're determined to spoil this evening.

Jade had taken a moment to consider this. "I would say," she began, carefully, "that I am not averse to the possibility that a higher power is in existence. Beyond that, I do not care to share with you this evening."

"Okay, well, that's something. Let's take your vague acceptance of a possibility – *air quotes* – and run with it for a bit. Do you believe that this higher power made a mistake when he designed us with the need to sleep?"

"Jeremy, I'm indulging you by talking about my work. However, I certainly did not plan to come here this evening and debate theology with you."

"Discuss."

"*Discuss* theology with you. But, fine. You answer me this: do *you* believe in God?"

Jeremy gave a short nod.

"That's fine, I'm not attacking you. But here's something I will say. You specialise in computers. Those computers don't stay the same, do they? You build them, you replace bits as and where you need to, you upgrade. Perhaps you could look at it that way. We're carrying on where he, or she, left off, as it were."

"You think what he's designed needs improving?"

For the first time that evening, Jade's smile grew broad and genuine. "Well, Jeremy, what makes you so sure that God got it right the first time?"

"Unbelievable. So now you've put yourself in the place of God?"

Camden could see that this was the moment to intervene. It had remained even-tempered until now, despite the chilly atmosphere, but he didn't want the occasion to devolve into an all-out argument between his girlfriend and his roommate. Not least because it slightly troubled him just how readily he'd take Jade's side. "Okay, okay, kids. You've had your fun, but that's enough for one evening. You can duke it out again another time. Now, Jeremy, if you don't mind, my girlfriend and I are going to watch a movie."

Jeremy gave a slight bow. "I bid you a pleasant evening." As he exited, Jade blew a kiss at him.

Camden settled himself with a sigh. "I'm sorry about that. I didn't expect him to get all up in your face like that."

"Oh, Camden," said Jade, dismissively. "I think I'm capable of defending myself. Besides, we're going to get no end of much the same once Consurge hits the market. I might as well get my practise in now."

Finally, they could focus on the film. Besides, something had been bothering him, leaving him with a faint anxiety at the end of every study session. He wanted a good opportunity to bring it up, and couldn't have possibly done so with his roommate hanging over them.

An hour later, the movie was paused on an emotional Maureen O'Hara glaring at John Wayne from behind the half-door of an Irish cottage. Jade had declared a desire for popcorn and had disappeared into the kitchen. Camden, tipsy on cheap gin and good lemonade, already missed her warm weight on him.

Jade emerged, carrying an enormous stainless-steel bowl. She sat cross-legged at the other end of the sofa, hugging the popcorn between her thighs.

"Any of that for me, babe?" asked Camden. He received a handful thrown at him by a giggling Jade in return.

"I honestly can't believe you've never seen this film," she said, mouth bulging as she stared at the frozen image on the screen.

"I like it." Camden was being honest. It was funny and sweet and appealing. He was rather surprised that Jade liked it though. Until now, her taste in movies had edged toward the more unconventional end of the spectrum. He'd enjoyed *Amelie* very much, but the Coen brothers hadn't been his thing and the less said about Darren Aronofsky the better. Maybe she'd found a kindred spirit in the fiery redhead on screen.

"And just think," he continued, "if you were on Consurge, we could watch movies all night!"

Jade nodded in agreement, hastily swallowing. "Actually," she said, once she'd choked down her popcorn, "as soon as it's available in pharmacies, I'm planning to start."

"Oh!" *Oh?* "That'd be great. It's hard enough not seeing you in the day, but it's terrible at night. I can't even call you 'cause you're asleep."

She cocked her head affectionately. "So, test subject, how do you feel these days?"

"Physically, never better. Honestly, you'd think I'm sleeping eight hours a night."

"And emotionally?"

"Fine, as far as I can tell. Although some of the adjustments are weird. Sometimes I forget what day it is."

Jade snorted. "You could always look at your phone."

"Well, yeah, I know that. I just mean that there isn't this clear distinction between one day and the next anymore."

"Makes sense."

"I'm starting to develop a different perspective on things as well."

"Hm." Jade leaned over, scanning him with her gaze. "How do you mean?"

"Well, for example, yesterday somebody said 'Good morning' to me. I just thought to myself, *What does that actually mean, 'Good morning'?* Just because it's gotten dark for a few hours people greet each other with this renewed enthusiasm each day. Just because the earth's turned on its axis for a few hours. It's become a bit humorous to me. I mean, nothing else has really changed, has it? To them, every day is new. But to me, time just carries on."

"Interesting."

"Yeah, people will think, 'Things will be better tomorrow'. I don't see why that means anything anymore. All that's happened is a bit of time has gone by – why should anything be different? And the other thing is that, even though I don't get particularly tired – unless I've been exercising, or something like that – I still need to relax mentally, you know? I'll watch a movie or go for a walk in the park. I can't just study twenty-four hours a day. I need some time when my mind can rest."

"I'm going to make a note of that. We might have to produce some literature on it. Tell me: do you miss sleep?"

Camden considered. He hadn't really thought about it much before now. "Good question. *Not really* would be my answer, I think. I guess it's because I'm not fatigued. Although" – *and this is going to sound weird* – "I do miss dreaming. I don't know why. But it's like there's a little something reminding me that I haven't dreamed in a while. But anyway, it's a small price to pay. I'm sure I can live with it."

"I'd agree with that," said Jade, slightly distracted as she tapped away at her phone.

Camden seized the opportunity to neatly transfer the bowl of popcorn into his own lap. "How's your work going?"

"Busy, which I'm sure will come as no surprise. We've been preparing the final report for submission to the FDA to get Consurge approved. We've done about as much as we can for now, but we're stuck until we have the results of this trial. Tuesday's the last day, so come Wednesday, we'll be working *very* long days. We'll need to analyze the results and finish the New Drug Application. Walter said he wants the submission made December thirtieth. So we've basically got a month." She held her head in her hands for a moment, before composing herself. "So, yes. It's going to be blood-on-the-walls crazy."

"And there I was thinking your *current* schedule was ridiculous," said Camden, feeling an awkward mix of sympathy and disappointment. "I get the feeling I'm not gonna be seeing much of you."

"Sorry, babe. We started going out at an awkward time."

"How long will it take for the FDA to make a decision?"

"Usually, it takes ten months, but we applied for Priority Review which is six months. So Walter's hoping Consurge will be approved by the end of June, pending our phase three trials being a success" – she traced Camden's outline with a dramatic flourish of her index finger – "and you seem to have everything in order, which bodes well. Plus, Walter doesn't lack for connections, so I think it'll go through."

"That's fantastic. The sooner it's on the market the better."

"Walter's already got the Drax marketing machine fired up. There'll be a massive advertising campaign the moment Consurge is approved. Then, hopefully, it'll be on the market by July twenty-ninth. The pills are already there – we've manufactured millions. All ready to be shipped to pharmacies."

"Wow. That many? You think they'll all go?"

"Walter's very confident. We've spent a *lot* of money on our marketing people. When the approval comes through, the first thing I'm doing is popping open a bottle of champagne."

"And I'll be there to celebrate with you."

But for some reason, Camden's upbeat tone didn't seem to be having the desired effect. Jade was staring into the distance, suddenly a million miles away.

"You... okay?" asked Camden, slightly alarmed.

Jade shook her head and turned her attention back to the television. "Go on, babe, hit play. I love this part."

Camden, unsure what he'd just seen, poked the remote at the screen, and the image unfroze. They saw Mary-Kate Danaher, still in her wedding dress, locking herself in the bedroom, sending a clear message to Sean Thornton on their wedding night. The tall American kicked open the door, pulled the covers off the bed, grabbed his bride, and spun her around.

Camden sneaked a glance at Jade, seeing her mouthing John Wayne's next line. *"There'll be no locks or bolts between us, Mary-Kate, except those in your mercenary little heart!"*

Wayne then forcefully kissed his bride as she acquiesced to his embrace. Scooping up his now docile wife into his arms, he launched her onto the bed, the timbers collapsing under her weight. The scene appeared set to consummate the marriage – but as dramatically as he'd entered the room, John Wayne slammed the door behind him, leaving his bride crying on the bed.

"It's good, isn't it?" said Jade.

"Very good."

Camden, however, was just as pleased watching her reaction to the movie as he was with the movie itself. The scene appeared to have shaken her from her pensive stare, and her face shone once more.

As the credits rolled, they sat nestled together, Jade comfortable against Camden's chest as he wrapped his arms around her front. But the question that had been pressing against his lips all evening refused to leave him alone, and Camden knew he couldn't put it off any longer.

"Hey, uh, I have something to ask you."

"Ah, Camden," said Jade, not shifting from her position. "Don't you think it's a bit early for a marriage proposal?"

Don't freak out. Don't freak out. "Maybe it is, maybe it isn't," he said, in a bright attempt at humor.

Jade sat upright and smiled. "What's up, babe?"

"Professor Williams said he's never seen such a turnaround in any of his students."

"That's great. Is there a problem?"

"Jade. I'll be honest with you. I'm freaked out that when the drug trial ends on Tuesday, it's all gonna slip through my hands."

"Camden, babe." She took both of his hands in hers. "We've *talked* about this. The past month, you've gotten yourself ahead. *Stay* ahead, and by the time Consurge hits the market, you'll still be in a good place."

Camden shook his head frantically and stared pleadingly at her. "No, Jade, you don't understand. I'm freaked out I'm gonna crash and burn. There has to be something else we can do. I need... to keep this going..."

There was a brief pause, then Jade's nostrils flared as she realized what he was asking. "Oh, no. *No, no, no.* You can't ask me to do that. You can't ask me to steal from the company."

"Oh, c'mon!" Camden threw up his hands into the air, pulling them out of Jade's grasp. "You said yourself they have millions of pills. Who's going to miss a few dozen?"

"*That is not the point!*" Jade rose from the sofa. "Besides, I'd have to falsify data!"

"What do you mean?"

"The ten-day monitoring period! After coming off Consurge we're meant to record how quickly people resume normal sleep patterns. I'd have to fabricate figures for you!"

"Jade. Can't you see how important this is to me? I've gone from waking up every morning wishing I was dead to feeling so *in control.* I know that means something to you, that I do well, that I succeed. Doesn't it?"

"Don't try guilting me into this!"

"Jade, Jade, I'm sorry, I am. I didn't mean for it to come across like that. Look, it's just enough Consurge until it comes out at the drug store and I can pay for it properly. That's it!"

A long silence ensued. Jade's face gave obvious evidence of the mental battle occurring within. Camden didn't even dare to blink, every fiber of his body pleading with her.

Eventually, she pointed straight between his eyes.

"If anyone finds out," she said quietly, "I lose my job, and I'm nothing. I just want you to know that."

"I'll be as quiet as the grave, I promise!" said Camden, trying to not make his elation obvious. "No one will find out."

She gave a deep sigh. "Only until it's available at the pharmacy."

Camden jumped up, smiling from ear to ear. "You're the best, Jade! You're the best, you're the best, you're the best."

She gave him a weary smile and wrapped her arms loosely around his neck. "Say it again."

"The very best!"

CHAPTER NINE

Kill the desk lamp!

Camden had stuffed a towel at the base of his bedroom door to block the light, but he couldn't risk it. He was accustomed to hearing it now, between 2-3 a.m.: the faint sound of Jeremy's door handle turning. The routine was becoming second nature; hear Jeremy going to the bathroom, wait for the toilet to flush, wait for the bedroom door to click shut, turn the desk lamp back on.

As far as Jeremy knew, Camden had stopped taking Consurge a month ago and was now fast asleep. Camden had to be as cautious as possible, knowing that one mug knocked to the floorboards would be enough to stir Jeremy. The last thing Camden wanted to do was jeopardize Jade and her career. The second-last thing he wanted was another lecture from Jeremy about the evils of 'Big Pharma' and their attempts to mess with the sanctity of the natural order.

It was worth the hassle. Camden had never felt so alive. He was even beginning to surpass others in his classes. He felt in control – like a path was laid before him, and he simply had to tread carefully and correctly from this point forward. Every new success spurred him on.

He turned the light back on and resumed his studies. However, reading about the inner workings of the digestive tract was either making him hungry or nauseous. He couldn't decide. He just knew one thing at that moment: studying for days on end without seeing Jade was certainly losing its charm. Sure, texting and chatting on the phone for a few minutes at a time filled the gap like a piece of buttered toast, but it wasn't substantial. He hadn't seen Jade since the ten-day monitoring period for Consurge ended over two weeks ago. Outrageously, Walter Johnson had compelled his employees to work over the Christmas holidays.

I didn't realize it was possible to miss someone this much! Who knew that love could be painful!

At that exact moment, his phone vibrated. A text message! From Jade!

"New Drug Application just submitted to FDA! Now we wait six months... x."

"Best news in weeks!!" he replied. *"Now I get you back!! Get some sleep. :-)"*

The next several months took Camden from 'strength to strength' – a British idiom Jade delighted in using, both about him and about Drax's projected stock value. In addition to teaching him her favorite expressions, Jade continued to help Camden with his studies. Her experience in what she gleefully called "the real world" was proving invaluable; Camden didn't mind enduring some gentle mockery about his lack of travel and his continued need to attend lectures in exchange for the obscure and extremely interesting medical case studies Jade was able to produce for him.

A new bike gleamed in the corner of Camden's room, a splurge from part of the money he'd received after the Consurge trial. A Celtic silver necklace also graced Jade's neck, purchased with another part of the earnings. He thought it only fitting considering all that she'd done for him. Camden's mom was also benefitting – being so far ahead of his syllabus meant his Sundays could now be spent with her, and her doctors had announced that her cancer seemed to be in remission. Even his boss at WestCo had noticed him going the extra mile, and had, in hope rather than expectation, offered Camden a guaranteed full-time superior role once he'd graduated.

Five months ago I would've snapped your hand off, Nicole. Today, though. Thanks but no thanks. I've got my eyes set on bigger things.

While he'd been cautious about asking Jade about job opportunities at Drax, the subject had emerged more than once. Toward the end of April, her recommendation had been to spend a few years learning on the job at a teaching hospital, preferably somewhere in a fast-paced, stressful environment. *If you can manage that,* she'd intimated, *we'll throw money at you.*

By the end of May, Camden turned his attention to final exams, now less than two weeks away.

Time for me to 'swot up' for the exams. Thanks, Jade. I didn't even know how to speak before I met you. Now, I'm singing.

CHAPTER TEN

The clock is laughing in my face...

It was Friday, June 18th, and the sun was melting the road tar. Camden's usual haunt at this time and in this weather would be swimming in Lake Washington, or catching air at his local skatepark, or testing the natural human capacity for ice cream at Molly Moon's in Wallingford. It was, after all, summer vacation, and he deserved some downtime. However, on this day, at precisely 11:59 a.m., Camden sat in his room, in front of his computer, entirely stationary. Not a video game, not a YouTube compilation, not even a Soundgarden track broke the silence and the stillness.

His exam results were being released in one minute.

The previous Friday, he'd emerged from his final exam with his head held high. Each test had come with its own set of challenges, of tests to his memory and speed of his writing, but each time he had risen to the occasion. The muscles in his hand had ached for several days, and an entire week of second-guessing his answers had passed, threatening to bleed the joy from everything he'd done. Every text to Jade, every dart thrown at the board, every plate of scrambled eggs eaten had been overshadowed by *what if, what if, what if...* This was the culmination of months of hard work and sacrifice, rigorous self-control and, Jade aside, monkish isolation. His future plans rested on the outcome of these exams. *What if...*

12:00 p.m. *Click!* As he scanned the screen, Camden's eyes grew bigger and bigger. He sighed and shook his head, his arms falling to his sides.

Just then, the phone rang. Jade knew well what day and time it was and had declared herself just as excited for the results as Camden himself.

"Hi, babe," he said.

"Come on, lovely. Don't leave me in the dark. How did you do?" came the tense voice from the other end of the line.

"How did I do with what?"

"Oh, you tease! You're awful!" shrieked the reply. "Just tell me, please!"

"I don't believe it," said Camden, his voice gathering to an elated peak. "I've passed every exam with distinctions! And I'm bang near the top of the class."

The scream coming from his phone almost blew out its speaker. As far as Camden could discern from the cacophony, Jade was celebrating at the top of her voice by slamming her phone against her leg; the gaps between the thumps filled with the sounds of her whooping and cheering. It gave Camden a feeling of great satisfaction that she was reacting in the same way to his exam results as she had to the approval of Consurge.

Just then, his phone beeped.

"Jade! Jade! I'm getting another call. Can I call you back?"

The cacophony concluded.

"Sure. Love you, babe. I'm so proud of you. Well done."

"Thanks. Love you too."

The number was one he didn't recognize.

"Hello?"

"Camden, this is Professor Williams."

Camden's skin suddenly went cold, and his heart dropped into his stomach.

"Oh! *Haha.* Hello, professor. What a glorious day! How are you?"

He heard a chuckle. "You've seen your exam results, then."

"Yeah!" *Too high-pitched.* "Yeah, absolutely. I'm super happy. They're way better than I could have hoped." His heart thudded in his chest.

"I'm not surprised you're so pleased. Anybody would be with results like those. Listen, Camden, do you have a few minutes to come to my office? There's something I'd like to chat about."

"Sure."

"Marvelous. I'll be waiting here for you."

Click

'Something I'd like to chat about?' Something definitely went wrong. The exam board is waiting to tell me I actually failed every class and they're arresting me for illegal use of stimulants and that I'm nothing but a phony.

The walk to Williams' office gave his brain time to stew. He walked quickly, just to get it over with as soon as possible. He had no idea why he'd suddenly begun panicking so heavily, but he supposed that such a high of elation should naturally be followed by a crash of equivalent depth.

Camden hesitated for a moment before approaching the professor's door, but he knew that if there was a problem, Williams was as complicit as anything. Surely, if nothing else, the two were on the same side.

To Camden's relief, the professor was alone, surrounded only by his library of medical books and his collection of classical music records. William's stood and stretched out his hand, a beaming smile on his face. Camden tried to conceal a large sigh of relief as he shook Williams' hand firmly. The older man was clearly in a fine mood.

"Well done, Camden. Well done, indeed."

"Thanks, professor. I couldn't be happier."

If anything, the professor seemed the more pleased. "Your hard work has been an example to all of us. It's shown us new ways medical science can benefit everyone, and even lift humanity to a new plane."

"Well, when you put it that way... I mean... I have you to thank."

"Indeed!" said the professor, hardly listening. "Camden, just think: imagine if the greatest minds we know, or those now with the brightest potential, went through the same process you did. Imagine the leaps! Not just catching up on schoolwork or passing exams – though again, congratulations – but slicing through the Gordian knots that have held us back for so long. Give this kind of potential to Elias Corey – ah, might be a bit late for him – or Federico Faggin, or Shirley Ann Jackson, and just sit back and watch!"

The professor grasped Camden's hand again, squeezing it. "And you were there at the beginning of it. You're the apple falling on the head of Isaac Newton! The dirty washing-up of Alexander Fleming! The first step!"

Huh. Apples and dirty washing-up. Way to kill my buzz.

"But I didn't just ask you to come in to congratulate you," continued the professor, happily ploughing on. Camden's heart stopped for a moment, but he didn't have time to reply.

"I've been speaking to Dr. Herman at the University Hospital about you these past few weeks. Dr. Herman is a brain surgeon and a good friend of mine. Much smarter than I am. He's saved enough people to start his own religion. Anyway, he's been very impressed with your progress, and after seeing your exam results, he told me that a role has opened up in the hospital."

"He's offering me a job?"

"Well, he wants to interview you. It's an administrative role, and the pay isn't great, but you'd have the chance to work around doctors and get experience in the hospital environment. It's ten hours a day, Tuesday through Thursday over the summer. What do you think?"

"It sounds amazing! I'm really grateful, professor."

"I know you are, Camden. You're welcome. I'm glad to see you doing well. You can go and see Dr. Herman today for an interview if you like. He's expecting you."

Camden smiled broadly. "I'm on my way."

Is that a hemp necklace?

Camden had expected Dr. Herman to be cut from the same cloth as Williams. Well, perhaps more expensive cloth, considering how much better paid he likely was. But the same design, at least. Older, greying, slightly dour and wry. Thoughtful and understanding, but hard to impress.

However, Dr. Herman didn't fit Camden's doctor stereotype in any way. Certainly not the long dark hair tied back in a ponytail, or the sideburns down to his jaw, or the tie-dyed shirt unabashedly hidden under his scrubs. In fact, he looked more like someone who'd staggered here from Woodstock, having stolen a lab technician's jacket en route.

"Very pleased to meet you, Camden," said the doctor as he stood up. He was tall and muscular, composed and unhurried. "I've heard many good things."

What is he, six-four? I can finally look someone in the eye for a change.

"Nice to meet you, Dr. Herman."

"Ah, call me Josef. Everybody does."

His office matched his clothing. Photographs adorned all four walls, displaying what looked like travels to every corner of the globe. The doctor's many degrees were all crammed into one single square, above which hung both a copy of the Bill of Rights and a Native American dream-catcher. A bean-bag chair sat in the carpeted corner, next to a yoga mat. A huge poster of Jimi Hendrix dominated the wall behind his desk, the iconic shot of him kneeling over his flaming guitar, and Camden found it extremely difficult to focus on anything else.

"I, uh, like your poster of Hendrix," said Camden, nodding slowly.

"Thanks, yes. I put that up the first day I got here."

"Does it put people at ease?"

Herman laughed. "Maybe, maybe. But it makes me feel good to have it there. Good Jimi. Wonderful man. I was at his funeral, you know."

"No way!"

"I was only small, but I remember it. Man..." The doctor's face became wistful, and Camden half-expected this giant of his field, this lauded titan of medicine, to pick up the guitar sitting in the corner and start playing Purple Haze.

"So," continued the doctor, "Williams told you about the job?"

"A little, yeah. It sounds great."

"Good," said Herman. The man's natural speaking voice was deep and slow, quite the opposite of Williams' quick rasp. Camden found it remarkably comforting. "Did you bring your resume? Your exam results speak for themselves, but I always like to see a background."

Camden handed the doctor his tablet. He scrolled down, muttering as he read. Camden knew full well there wasn't much there to interest him. He'd be getting this job on the strength of the last eight months alone.

"Gardening... Taco Bell... WestCo Medical Supplies... Inglemoor High School... University of Seattle." Herman handed the tablet back to Camden. "Nothing on there to count against you. I always admire people who are able to work and study at the same time. It requires willpower and determination. We need to make sure people like that become doctors, not lawyers or all the rest who take more than they give."

Camden wasn't sure what to say and therefore said nothing.

"But I run away with my thoughts. Tell me, Camden, what made you want to work in medicine in the first place...?"

After conversing with Herman for half an hour and being cheerfully promised a job beginning in eleven days' time, Camden headed for his next stop: WestCo Medical Supplies. He wanted to talk to management before his 3:30 p.m. shift started.

Fortunately, Nicole was available and very understanding of Camden's new opportunity. While the well-wishing was delivered a little more formally and a lot more mournfully than Camden felt comfortable with, he was glad that there would be no complications. Everybody liked a clean break.

Outside Nicole's office, an effervescent Krista was waiting for him. "Oooh, a meeting with the boss! Did you get a promotion? I bet you got a promotion." She took a cheerful swipe at his arm, and he caught her fist.

"Actually, I've just handed in my notice."

Her eyes widened, and she shook her hand free from his. "Your notice! No! You can't do that. You didn't ask my permission!"

She looked honestly distressed, and Camden racked his brain to quickly think of something to say. "Ahh, Krista, don't be upset. I've really enjoyed working with you. You're great. But I got a job at the hospital!"

"Aww..." She put her fingers to her mouth and pulled down the side of her lips, creating her sad-clown look. "I'm happy for you but sad for us. We'll miss you." She reached out and gave him a hug, wrapping one arm around his neck and the other around his ribs. It was surprisingly gentle and warm, and Camden did his best to return the feeling.

"I'll miss you guys as well. But hey, I'm still here for another week."

"Oh really?" Her eyes glinted madly, and she cackled. "We're gonna give a week you'll never forget." Camden remembered the last time a colleague had left at short notice, and *someone* had filled their locker with whipped cream. *Ah well. That's the price of moving onward and upward in the world.*

"So, what does the future hold for *you*?" he asked, as they walked slowly along the corridor towards the break room.

Krista shifted a little. "Ya know, to tell you the truth, I'm not sure I'll be here much longer either."

He turned. "What? Why not? I thought this place was working out for you."

"Yeah, *buuuuut*," she said, lowering her voice to a whisper, "they're just rumors, but I've heard talk the company isn't doing so hot."

"Huh?" This surprised him. "That's the first I've heard of it. People keep getting sick, right? Hospitals keep needing stock."

"I don't know about the business stuff, but some people are saying the company could go under... Maybe you're getting out at the right time."

Camden donned his white lab coat and picked up his clipboard, ready for his shift. "No, WestCo's been around for decades. It's a well-established company. I'm sure that wouldn't happen, Krista."

"Huh. I hope you're right."

CHAPTER ELEVEN

"Camden! Welcome to the circus."

"Good morning, Dr. Herman."

"Josef, please. Nobody calls me doctor."

"Sorry, Doc- Josef. Dr. Josef."

Camden's first day of work at the University Hospital evoked a nervous excitement that was clearly bubbling over. The doctor now known as Josef began by leading Camden on a tour of the Neurology Clinic, a collection of offices and laboratories that had been polished to a shine.

"I hope you're ready for the chaos," said Josef.

Camden gave a playful salute. "Ready, sir."

Josef's response was a slow nod and a smile. "Good man. Let me introduce you to Betty, our receptionist. She'll show you what needs to be done."

Betty sat at the front desk of the clinic – clearly her domain. She had short curly hair, wore purple glasses and bright red lipstick, and gave him a firm smile as he approached. Had Camden to guess her age – which he certainly wasn't going to do out loud – he'd have put her at a youthful fifty. Notably plump, Betty gave off an air of no-nonsense orderliness. Camden's immediate impression was of someone who knew the exact contents of each filing cabinet, who had put it there, when they'd done so, and what they'd done wrong. He resolved to be as polite and friendly as humanly possible.

"So," she said, "you're my new charge." She heaved herself up from her desk and beckoned him with a finger. "Let's take you back in the file room, dear – away from people. We don't want others to see you mess up on your first day, do we?" She gave him a friendly wink.

"No, ma'am. Very kind of you."

"Ma'am." She rolled her eyes. "That's what leaving birthday cards out in the open gets me."

By the end of the day, Camden was beginning to feel more comfortable with his new job. Sorting through paperwork, making coffee, photocopying forms, and – for something totally different – stocking shelves with medical supplies; whatever the task, he was just happy to be working at the hospital. There was a pleasing efficiency to the place. People seemed to be enjoying their work, and Camden fed off the positivity.

The next day, during his lunch break, exactly six months after the New Drug Application for Consurge had been submitted to the FDA, Camden received a phone call from Jade. She was nearly shrieking with joy. "It's been approved, Camden! It's been approved! Can you believe it! We're through! It's actually happening!"

"Congratulations! You've worked so hard, babe. So what happens next?"

Jade, judging by the sounds echoing down the phone line, was leaping around her office in a frenzy. He waited patiently for this to conclude.

"Okay," said a breathless Jade, "the market will get absolutely saturated with advertising. You'll see Consurge everywhere – television, billboards, online, radio, *everywhere*. Walter's even bought out Times Square. That's just the next couple of days. We're expecting a massive rush to get prescriptions. Consurge should be available in pharmacies by July twenty-ninth."

"You're not wasting any time, huh."

"A lot of money went into this, Camden. There are a lot of investors who need to be made happy. The faster we placate them, the faster we move on to even bigger things. No time to waste."

"Absolutely. I can't wait to see what you come up with next. If this was your debut, your sophomore is going to be insane! You should be really proud of yourself."

"Thanks, babe. I'm excited too." She lowered her voice. "And it means that from the first of next month, you can get Consurge in the same way as everyone else: by demanding your doctor give you some. I won't have to feel like an underhanded scoundrel anymore."

He smiled. "Thank goodness for 'Ask your doctor'."

"It also means we can spend more time together! I've already made an appointment with my doctor to get a prescription."

"Awesome! So how much is it gonna cost?"

There was a bit of a pause. "Well, Walter settled on thirty dollars for a month's supply."

"Thirty dollars? I thought you said it'd be similar to Sudafed."

"Well, that's what I heard at the time. Things changed. Believe me, Walter wanted it higher, but others managed to talk him down."

"I see."

"Hey. Compared to Modafinil, it's a steal."

Thursday morning, after awakening from his Drax Power Nap, Camden brewed himself a cup of tea – a habit he had acquired from Jade – and opened the CNN website.

She was right.

He read the top story from behind his mug and smiled. *"FDA approves anti-sleep drug."* He checked NBC, ABC, Fox News, The Los Angeles Times, The New York Times, and even the BBC. All of them led with Consurge. Next, he navigated to YouTube. The 30-second advertisement before a 'Best Fails' compilation he clicked on invited him to *'Awaken to a full life'*. He ran to the living room, grabbed the remote and turned on the television. During the commercial break for Good Morning America, slick television doctors extolled the benefits of the new wonder drug. As he left his apartment to bike to work, a bus rolled by with a poster inviting the public to *'Ask your doctor if Consurge is right for you'*. Even the billboard on Pacific Street by the hospital showed happy families getting more from life.

The line was being cast.

Everywhere Camden went that day, the topic of conversation was the same: this drug would be a game-changer and people wanted in on the action. Two young mothers at a bus stop discussing how they could spend more time with their husbands while the kids slept. Fellow students making appointments then and there with their physicians, desperate for prescriptions from the moment of the drug's release. Supervisors at work arguing about new shifts, paying people to work through the night and increasing their demand capacity. At the pub, where he allowed himself a quiet drink in order to process the day, a couple of exhausted-looking businessmen discussing a possible reprieve from their eighty-hour work weeks.

Camden could feel their excitement. Of course, there were always fears to be had: if life without sleep became the new normal, would everyone just fill up the available time once more and again find themselves running out of hours in the day? Running short on resources did seem the thing humans did best. And also – and this he had the good grace to feel guilty about – did he feel that he would soon be less unique in some way? His edge over everyone else would soon to be wiped out. It was almost like he had to share his superpower with the rest of the world; a great leveling, and no longer would he hold his advantage. But it was okay. He knew how much Consurge would help people, and that was the main thing.

Friday night, Camden strode down the tree-lined streets of Pioneer Square toward Jade's apartment. Even before he'd met Jade, Camden had always looked for an excuse to visit this part of the city. The 19th-century brick buildings radiated a character all their own. Camden could just imagine the thousands of prospectors passing through, preparing supplies for the long trip to Alaska, hoping to strike it rich in the gold rush. So many dreams, such a small chance of striking a fortune. An old sign still hung above the door to Jade's apartment block: 'State Hotel. Rooms 75¢.'

The inside of her apartment echoed the character of the neighborhood. Exposed brick walls, high ceilings supported by ancient timbers, and hardwood floors made from trees felled by the early pioneers. The kind of distressed design that cost more than if someone chose to add carpets and wallpaper. Camden sprawled himself on the couch while Jade prepared snacks in the kitchen.

"How's work going?" she asked.

He raised his head from the cushions. "So far, so good. They haven't fired me yet."

She stuck her head around the corner and gave him a coy glance. "It's only been a week. Sample size is too small to be conclusive."

"Thanks for that. I'll let you know if next week becomes statistically significant."

"What's been the hardest part so far?"

Camden gave a wide grin. "The hardest part has been resisting the urge to say '*Hello-o-o nurse!*' all day long."

"What?"

"Animaniacs!"

Jade returned with a blank stare.

"Oh come on," he said. "Nineties cartoon show. There was this cute nurse that Yakko and Wakko were in love with and they... never mind."

Jade was still staring at him suspiciously. "More time wasted on YouTube, I see."

"You missed out."

"I'm *sure*. Moving on. Are you getting accustomed to the hospital routine?"

"I guess. It's a bit hectic at times."

"Get used to it, babe. You don't even have any responsibility yet."

He frowned. "I know. I'm getting there. Sometimes there's some serious drama, though. We had one guy come in screaming, complaining of burning pain in his head. It's not easy to watch. I mean – I can handle being around it, and I'd have no problems treating them, but man, I just think about being in their shoes."

Camden shivered. He could comfort himself knowing that everyone who'd come into the clinic had been treated, but he still couldn't quite get the images out of his mind: the motorbike rider whose head had been smashed in, or the young girl who suffered a grand mal seizure in the waiting room. He contorted his face into an exaggerated grimace and tried to lighten the mood. "It freaks me out, the thought of people probing and testing me."

Jade set out some chips and tzatziki on the coffee table. "Haven't you ever been in hospital as a patient?"

"No. I've never needed to go. I've always been healthy."

Jade paused, laden chip halfway to mouth. "Wow. Never? You're lucky. You're among the few."

Camden shrugged. "I know. And I'd like to keep it that way for as long as possible."

CHAPTER TWELVE

"What's been your experience with Consurge, sir?"

Two months later, toward the end of August, CNN reported that "seemingly half the country is talking about Consurge and the other half is taking it." The drug was still some way from release outside of the US – Jade had voiced several grumpy comments about the bureaucracy involved in exporting any sort of medication to the European Union – but that hadn't stopped the rest of the globe pricking up its ears. Camden and Jade snuggled up in front of the television in Camden's apartment ready for the long-anticipated Friday evening CNN special. As a prelude, a reporter in Times Square, New York was interviewing passersby. Early data, the reporter had explained, indicated that Consurge usage was three times higher in big cities than elsewhere.

An older man, sporting a beard and a hi-vis jacket, waved at the camera. *"For me, it's been a lifesaver. I work the night shift three days a week and the day shift two days a week. Before I was on Consurge, my body was all outta whack. But now, it's not a problem."*

Another woman was literally crying tears of joy. *"I'm a caregiver to my mom – she's terminal, she don't got long left. Before I started Consurge, there weren't no time for myself. I was always exhausted... overwhelmed. Now, I can catch up on life at night while mom sleeps. I'm so grateful. Thank you so much!"*

"And you, sir. What's your opinion of Consurge?"

A young man wearing a baseball cap and a huge puffa jacket gave the camera a dismissive look. *"Consurge? Naah. Why would I go on Consurge? Not sleep?! I love sleeping! It's the best part of the day!"*

"What about you sir. Have you used Consurge?"

An older, tanned businessman in a neat suit gave a curt nod. *"I've been on Consurge since July twenty-ninth. I travel around the world for business, and in the past one of the biggest challenges was jet lag. Now I can maximize my time. I never feel behind schedule anymore."*

"How about you, ma'am? What are your thoughts on Consurge?"

A middle-aged lady gave the reporter an unconvinced look. *"It does sound interesting. But I think I'll wait and see how it goes. I might try it in a couple of years. To be honest, I'm not really sure what I'd fill the extra time with."*

The reporter next approached a man with dreadlocks and a marijuana leaf on his shirt. Camden giggled in anticipation. Jade snorted irritably.

"What do you think of Consurge, sir?"

"Issa bad idea, man. Iss affecting the global consciousness." He turned to the camera with bloodshot eyes. *"Don' touch the stuff!"*

They both chuckled.

A quiet voice came from behind the couch. "He may be crazy, but he's saner than the rest of you."

Camden picked up a cushion and threw it at his roommate. "Jeremy, get lost!" He hadn't heard Jeremy come home, and the last thing he wanted was for such a celebratory evening to be ruined by Jeremy's pedantry.

"Suit yourself," came the glum reply from the kitchen. "I still can't believe you went back on that stuff."

Camden and Jade exchanged knowing glances. Camden made an enquiring expression: *Do you want me to get rid of him?* Jade wrinkled her nose and shrugged: *Nah. He's harmless.* They turned back to the television, just in time for the main event to begin

"Here it is!" cried Jade, sitting bolt upright.

Back in the studio, the moderator's opening words set the scene for the conflagration.

"The motto of the city of Valencia, Spain, is 'Vivir sin dormir', or, 'Live without sleep'. However, that motto is no longer limited to Valencia. Since it was made available only a month ago, approximately four million people in the United States are now taking a new wonder drug called Consurge, allowing them to sleep for only a few minutes every night with no reported side effects. Despite Consurge being released at a premium price point, demand for the drug has skyrocketed, and Drax Pharmaceuticals has quickly become one of the most successful pharmaceutical companies in history.

"However, as you'll see tonight, the drug has also ignited a series of furious debates. Proponents of the drug have pointed to a decrease in occupational and automobile injuries relating to sleep deprivation, along with a decrease in reported cases of depression and an upturn in consumer spending during the month of August. Must be all those late nights.

"However, not everyone is happy. Critics of the drug highlight various economic impacts, including decreased demand for caffeine products and energy drinks, along with a notable decrease in hotel bookings. It seems that some tourists would rather paint the town than spring for a hotel room.

"With us to discuss the rise of Consurge is Dr. Walter Johnson, owner of Drax Pharmaceuticals, and Derek Hart, Professor of Business Ethics at Harvard Business School."

Slim, handsome and in his early forties, Dr. Hart sat eyeing the older man from the opposite end of the table. The anchor turned to her left: *"Professor Hart, perhaps we could start with you. You're a strong opponent of Consurge. Tell us what objections you have to this drug."*

Professor Hart adjusted his glasses and laid his hands flat on the table. *"Well, there are many. First of all, it's impossible to argue against the creation of an artificial imbalance in society. For example, two people work at the same company. One person decides to take Consurge and he excels. The other falls behind, through no fault of his own. Why should he, despite his abilities, be left behind?"*

Walter Johnson gave a broad, reptilian smile. "Oooh," muttered Jade. "He's in a mood."

"No one is stopping him from taking Consurge as well. The drug is reasonably priced. Many companies are arranging to have it included as part of their health insurance."

The professor rolled his eyes. *"Of course. But why should he feel pressured to take a drug to keep up with his colleague? Maybe he doesn't want to pump chemicals into his body."*

"Consurge has consistently been proven safe," replied Walter immediately. *"There's no need to worry about the effect on the body. And whatever ethical dilemma you may think this creates, no one can*

stand in the way of progress. If an individual falls behind his colleague because he refuses to take advantage of what's on offer, then how is he different from the person phased out for not knowing how to operate a telephone or a computer?"

Professor Hart shook his finger, as though scolding an infant. *"No, no. That's a facile comparison. Consurge isn't a skill to be introduced and added to a repertoire. It's a fundamental reconditioning of the way the body works. History's taught us that when humans tamper with natural processes, things never work out well."*

"I get the funniest feeling I've heard this argument before," whispered Camden. Jade shushed him with a wave of her hand.

"Define tampering with natural processes?" demanded Johnson, keeping a smile plastered to his face. *"Is it tampering with natural processes to use penicillin to prevent the spread of 'natural' bacteria? Isn't polio 'natural'? Or hemorrhage at childbirth?"*

"That's a completely improper comparison. Penicillin prevents a person from dying. Consurge is altering the very nature of human existence."

"As defined by whom? Is using Accutane to save a teenage kid from permanent physical and emotional scaring unethical because it's altering a natural process?"

The moderator raised her hands. *"Gentlemen, gentlemen, please! I want to explore this idea of a two-tiered society a bit more. Professor Hart, can you elaborate on this?"*

"Yes, of course. Let's take professional sports as an example. Why are performance enhancing steroids banned from the Olympics? Because they create an unfair advantage for those taking them. What happens in a university when students are allowed to take Consurge? It creates the same unfair advantage."

"That's a totally unfair analogy," exclaimed Walter. *"A person who takes steroids starts from a base level and artificially enhances their abilities. Consurge isn't artificially enhancing the brain, or anything else. It simply gives a person more time in the day to develop their existing abilities. There's a major difference."*

"Very well," said the moderator, *"you've both made your point. Next, I'd like to discuss some questions from our viewers. First of all, Nick*

Watson from Detroit, Michigan writes: 'I work at a company that produces sleeping aids. There's a real fear that our entire business will go under. Sales have already dropped in the last several weeks with people switching from sleeping aids to Consurge. Dr. Johnson, how can you justify the destruction of a five-billion-dollar-a-year American industry?'"

Walter was rapidly tapping his finger on the desk.

Jade grinned. "You see that? He does that when he's anxious. He's formulating his words, trying to think of the most diplomatic thing to say."

"Will he succeed?"

"Yeah, he's been prepping for days."

"Dr. Johnson?" prompted the moderator. *"How would you respond?"*

Johnson calmly angled himself toward the camera. *"Mr. Watson,"* he said, slowly and clearly, *"I'm very sorry there's uncertainty in your company. I'm sure that it must be stressful, and I do sympathize with you. Having built up a company from its foundation, I'm well aware of the pressures involved in looking after staff and trying to get ahead in a competitive marketplace. However, and I'm sure you'll agree with me here: none of us can stand in the way of advancing technology. If my company hadn't developed Consurge, someone else would have. It's the same in any field. When cassettes were replaced by compact discs, thousands of companies were affected. And I'm sure horse-breeders were furious about the invention of the automobile. But that's the price of progress. We can't look back. We have to make bold decisions and work toward the future."*

Professor Hart rolled his eyes again. *"Heartless. Absolutely heartless."*

Johnson glared across the table.

The moderator continued. *"Next we have Jane Preston from Hoboken, New Jersey. She says: 'I've noticed more and more stores open twenty-four hours since Consurge came on the market. People are shopping at Bed Bath & Beyond at two in the morning and others are working extra shifts to accommodate them. Do you think that having all this extra time in the day is fostering a sense of greed and excessive consumerism in our society?' Very interesting. Thank you, Jane. Professor Hart, let's start with you."*

"Absolutely. People need to fill their extra time with something. It's nice to think that everyone will spend the extra time with their family or do volunteer work or something noble. But the consumerist reality of our society means that a lot of people will simply use that extra time for themselves. They'll see it purely as an opportunity for indulgence."

"Dr. Johnson?"

"I honestly think that Professor Hart should be ashamed. Millions of people in this country alone are struggling financially – just keeping their head above water. Some without the basic necessities of life. All they want is an opportunity to provide for their families. Consurge gives them that opportunity, allowing them to work and feel a level of security the professor here clearly already enjoys, and the professor thinks it's immoral!"

And so the debate continued for half an hour. Neither side seemed clearly victorious. One thing, however, was indisputable. Every day, Consurge sales were increasing exponentially across the nation, and the rest of the world was waiting at the doorstep.

CHAPTER THIRTEEN

Has there ever been a more perfect summer's day in Seattle?

A quiet packed lunch at Gas Works Park never let Camden down. The view from his bench on Kite Hill overlooked a glistening Lake Union below with the city in the distance. A gentle breeze caressed his face. A small circle of hippies played guitars by the water. Families were flying kites.

With no better setting for quiet reflection, Camden found himself ruminating on events of the past few months. Jade had been on Consurge for about a month now, which had allowed them to spend even more time together. Yesterday, he'd found himself staring in the window of a jewelry shop looking at engagement rings, wondering which one she might like and if it was too soon to even contemplate popping the question. At the hospital, where he'd worked for almost two months now, he'd received praise, not only from 'Matron' Betty but also from Dr. Herman. Betty had commented on his orderliness and willingness to please and Josef had commended him on his questions during their weekly chats. "Sign of a growing mind," he'd said. To top it all off, even his mom was starting to feel better and looked forward to beginning her own course of Consurge.

He looked around and smiled. Gas Works was an unusual park, but perhaps that's why he liked it. A large, rusty gasification plant from the early 1900's rose up from the middle of the green grass, its twisted towers and pipes a testament to a bygone era. It wasn't beautiful, but it was eclectic, just like this part of Seattle.

Normally, he'd come here on a Friday or Monday when Jade was at work, but after yesterday's CNN special, it meant she had to work the weekend to deal with the fallout.

I really must bring her here one day.

No sooner had the thought crossed his mind when he raised his eyes from his sandwich and gazed down the hill.

No. It couldn't be.

Camden shook his head and squinted.

I must be seeing things.

Jade and her boss, Walter Johnson, were strolling along the water's edge, only a stone's throw away.

But that wasn't the problem.

As much as Camden fought against what his eyes fed his brain, it didn't change the fact that Jade was holding Walter's hand!

Camden's body stiffened. Alarm bells sounded in his head.

The pair seemed so peaceful together. So comfortable with each other. Eventually, they paused to soak in the view. Walter's arm found its way around Jade's shoulder. It soon slipped south to her waist. Where it was heading next, Camden didn't want to know. Walter leaned in and whispered something in Jade's ear. She pulled away with a wide smile and gave him a playful smack on the chest, before leaning against him once more.

What did he say to her?! A horrible fascination gripped him. *There must be some explanation.*

Walter reached into his jacket pocket and pulled out a long narrow box. He opened it, pulling out a necklace of clear gems that sparkled brilliantly in the mid-day sun. Jade raised her hands to her mouth, kicking up a leg behind her in excitement.

Really, a leg kick?

Gently, Walter lifted her hair and secured the necklace. They caressed each other's face for a moment, forehead touching forehead.

No. She wouldn't. She couldn't...

She leaned in.

She did...

Her kiss didn't go unanswered. His left hand under her head, his right hand found its way around her waist and pulled her in. A tender kiss soon accelerated into a passionate embrace.

Camden's hands tightened around the bench, his nails digging into the wood. He wanted to explode. He wanted to drop kick the old geezer into Lake Union. But instead, like a victim of locked-in syndrome, he sat frozen, screaming on the inside.

The two lovebirds continued their stroll along the waterfront without a care in the world, seemingly oblivious to the world around them. Jade held on to Johnson's upper arm with both hands, her head resting on his shoulder. As Camden watched them walk away, waves of nausea built up inside him.

Five minutes turned into ten. Anger soon yielded to dejection. His grip on the bench gradually loosened, leaving nail marks in the wood. He stared blankly into the water, the built-up feelings of rage and frustration slowly settling, leaving him instead feeling hollow and thin. The repulsive scene of the kiss replayed in his mind, torturing him further with each viewing.

Where did I go wrong? Why would she cheat on me? Has our entire relationship just been a... a study? Did I push her too hard to give me Consurge? Was it Walter's money? A promotion? Or was she forced to make a choice? Am I the disposable one?

His head sank into his hands. His breathing was sharp and ragged, and he hugged himself tightly around the chest to try and settle it. He'd never been in this situation before; this level of betrayal, this kind of hideous revelation.

There was only one thing to do: bury his head in the sand.

CHAPTER FOURTEEN

"Forget about her, man. Girls are nothing but trouble!"

Jeremy, Sam, and Johnny had spent the evening at Murphy's Pub trying, unsuccessfully, to console Camden. For all the drinks they'd bought him and all the abuse they'd heaped on Jade and her fresh choice of man, Camden wasn't sure if it was helping him forget his troubles or wallow in them. Given they'd spent two hours talking about literally nothing but Jade's infidelity, he was deeply regretting the whole evening.

Johnny took a sip of his beer. "Dude, I know what you're going through."

Camden rolled his eyes. "You think so, huh?"

"Of course. Happens to the best of men. We've all dealt with break-ups; all had our hearts broken."

"I suppose." *You really don't, Johnny. But keep talking. It's all just... words.*

"It's true," said Sam. "I remember this one chick." He gesticulated toward the heavens as though calling out to a vindictive god. "Man, I was *crazy* about her. Like she'd walked straight out of my dreams. We dated for two months until she broke up with me over Facebook."

"Ouch." *At least she was unambiguous.*

"She told me my forehead was too big."

Johnny snickered. Sam rubbed his forehead.

"The truth was she had a thing for my teacher."

Jeremy was clearly not happy with this method of comforting the afflicted. "You guys aren't helping anything," he muttered across the table. "Can you at least try to be positive?"

"Hmm, positive," said Sam. "Okay. How about this: It's good to have you back. We haven't seen you in weeks. You never did anything but hang out with that girl!"

Jeremy raised his eyebrows slightly. "Marginally better..."

Camden sank deeper into the booth. "What's the point? Maybe I should just take a hike into the mountains and stay there..."

Jeremy draped his arm around Camden's neck. "C'mon man. You just need time. It might take a while, but the pain will ease."

"Never mind her," said Johnny, giving Camden a pat on the back, "you've got us, don't you?"

Sam burst out with a loud laugh. "You're supposed to make him feel better, not worse."

Camden sighed. "Can we just talk about something else, please?"

After a long pause, Sam spoke up. "Hey Camden, did we tell you we started on Consurge!"

"That's great," said Camden, brightening slightly. "How's it been?"

Johnny's eyes lit up. "Best thing we ever did, man."

"Threw the Modafinil in the garbage," said Sam.

Jeremy laughed. "Traded one poison for another, hey?"

Camden ignored him. "Glad to hear it. So, what have you been doing with all your time? No, wait, let me guess. The band?"

"Yep," said Johnny, nodding vigorously. "We're ten songs deep this month alone. You'll love the new material. You'll have to come hear us play this weekend."

"We never had the time to practice before," said Sam. "You should see Johnny on the banjo now! The folk punk world won't know what hit it! We might even have a shot at the Battle of the Bands this year."

"Unless they're all on Consurge as well," said Jeremy.

Camden caught Sam motioning something to the barmaid. Moments later, a Dropkick Murphys song shattered the quiet pub air. The rowdy, furious sounds of Irish punk finally caused Camden to crack a smile. It was one of his favorite songs, and he knew exactly what they were doing.

Sam jumped up onto his chair and bellowed along with the opening lyrics, shouting wild lines about solidarity and friendship. Johnny leaped up also and took over the next verse, even fuller and louder than his brother. Others in the pub started to stare and smile, but he knew the brothers didn't mind. And as cheesy as the whole thing was, neither did Camden. As the chorus approached, Johnny and Sam pulled up Camden and Jeremy to sing along, jumping in unison with their arms locked in a huddle. Jeremy knew none of the words, but he was happy to join the fray.

Finally, the song finished and the group collapsed in their seats, grasping their drinks once more.

"Feel better?" asked Sam.

Camden smiled wearily. "I do. Thanks, guys."

The voluptuous barmaid appeared by the table to clear away the empty glasses and flashed them all a wide smile. "Well, gentlemen, that was quite the performance."

Sam gave Camden a quick wink and then piped up. "Thanks. It's for our boy Camden, here. His girlfriend has been untrue."

Camden dropped his head and rubbed his temples.

"Oh no," she said. "That's terrible. You poor thing."

Sam put on his best sad face. "Yeah, he could really use some comfort now." Jeremy shut his eyes, and Camden groaned internally.

She put her hand on Camden's shoulder. "Tell you what, lovely. Let me bring you a pint – on the house."

"Oh, well, thanks very much," said Camden.

As the barmaid left to pour Camden's pint, Sam rubbed his hands together in satisfaction. "How about that, eh? I think she likes you!"

Camden gripped the bridge of his nose between thumb and forefinger. "Look, Sam, I appreciate all of this, I really do. But I'm not ready to move on. Another relationship is the *last* thing I need right now."

"What *can* we do for you?" asked Johnny. "How can we help you?"

"I'd like you to erase the memory of my girlfriend making out with her boss. Can you do that for me?"

CHAPTER FIFTEEN

Ugh... I don't think those enchiladas are sitting so well...

Camden had occupied an entire booth at his local Mexican restaurant, a colorful place not far from where he used to work. The Friday lunch special had been meant for two people, but in a fit of nihilistic frustration, he had managed every taco, tamale, and burrito on his own. Anything to take his mind off Jade's betrayal almost a week ago now.

The restaurant was quieter now, the lunch rush having concluded, and Camden rubbed a hand over his bloated, gurgling stomach.

Ooooof...

I may have made a mistake.

He staggered from the restaurant and started his walk home, hoping that the fresh air would clear his system. Unfortunately, the heat from the sidewalk and the fumes from the gridlocked cars produced the opposite effect: He was starting to feel light-headed and his legs were becoming shaky. He leaned against a wall, sucking in air, trying to stay calm.

Must find a bathroom!

He stared ahead desperately. And then it clicked: only two blocks away was WestCo, and he could definitely find someone to let him into the employee restroom. Placing one foot carefully in front of another, holding his protesting digestive system together through willpower alone, he stumbled forward until he reached the WestCo side door, the employee entrance, which would take him directly to the basement, and precious relief.

He banged on the glass, trying to get someone's attention. Camden hadn't seen any of his former workmates since he quit over two months ago, and he looked forward to catching up. Unfortunately, the circumstances weren't ideal.

"*Camden!*" Krista screamed as she caught sight of him, and hurled the door open, nearly jumping into his arms. "We've missed you! You've been gone so long! We thought you'd died!"

Aaaaaaaahhhh... Camden almost fell to the floor, unable to bear both Krista's weight and the pressure from his abdomen.

"I've... missed you too... Krista," he managed, sweat dripping down his forehead and into his eyes.

She reached up and rubbed his cheeks with both hands. "Hey, I like the new unshaven look. Very sexy."

Yeah, sure, that's what I was going for...

She frowned dramatically, putting her hands on her hips. "So why don't you come visit us, huh? You don't care about us anymore?"

He attempted a smile, which came out more like a grimace. "Well... haha... you know, life's busy..."

"Hey Camden!" she shouted out of the blue. "Guess what! I started on Consurge a few weeks ago. It's amazing!"

Camden's focus, however, was fixed on the stairs leading down to the restroom. "Oh, yeah, cool. Um, that's really good." But before he could escape, Nicole appeared from around the corner. Then Mark. Then the interrogation began: *'What about Jade? How's your new job? Is your mom better? How's school going? You wanna come to a party tonight? Could you get something from the hospital for me?'*

Camden, his fragile state of mind failing to deal with the onslaught, panicked.

"*Alrightalrightalright* I'm *really* sorry guys, but I *really need* to use the bathroom. Just be a couple minutes-"

As he raced away, he heard loud laughing, and a "*Don't fall in!*" from Krista.

To his surprise, a new sign was proudly displayed on the bathroom door:

ALL GENDER RESTROOM
Anyone can use this restroom regardless of gender identity or expression.

Wow. WestCo has become so 'progressive!'

Inside, Julie was casually touching up her makeup in the mirror.

Okay... This is not awkward at all!

"Oh, hey, Camden! Good to see you," she said, smiling at his reflection, obviously accustomed to the new arrangement. Camden, thoroughly unaccustomed, gave an awkward grin in return. "Hey," was all he could choke out.

The restroom had just one cubicle, and, as he had a big job to do, he promptly closed the stall door behind him. However, to add to his frustration, the lock on the door was broken.

"Cheapskates," he muttered under his breath.

"Did you say something?" asked Julie.

"No, no. Just prepping myself."

Leaning forward to hold the door shut with one hand, he precariously perched on the toilet seat. As much as he tried to keep it subtle, the unavoidable sounds and scents of nature soon filled the confined space.

Julie chuckled. "Nice one, Camden. Too many beans, eh?"

He hung his head.

"Thanks for the commentary, Julie."

Seriously, whose idea was an all-gender restroom, anyway! Don't people know what happens in restrooms?

Before long, someone else entered the restroom. Camden coughed on purpose to make his presence known but to no avail. The door pushed open, and for a split second Camden and Julie exchanged glances in the mirror. Camden quickly pushed back, slamming the door closed.

He heard a man apologize and Julie giggle.

"I'll wait here until you're done," said the man.

Camden peered through the crack in the door. It was Robert, waiting attentively, no doubt bursting as Camden had been. Just then, two others came in, chatting away like it was the local bar.

By this point, Camden was hurrying to finish up, a job that was far easier with two hands. But as much as he tried to hold the door closed with his knee, the door wasn't cooperating. All four bystanders, thoroughly amused at his predicament, seemed unable to look away and unable to contain their laughter.

"Come on Camden, don't take all day. There's a line out here!"

He hadn't been so embarrassed since Timmy Bartlett took a picture of him over the restroom stall in fifth grade and pinned it to the school noticeboard. "Hold your horses!"

Camden burst out of the stall and exploded at the four of them.

"What's your *problem*?! Show a bit of decency."

This only made them laugh more, pouring gasoline on an already-flaming dumpster. Robert pushed past him into the stall and Camden headed for the sink, washing his hands furiously next to a snickering Julie. He stormed out.

Steps away from the main exit, and moments away from escaping his humiliation, he felt two arms wrap around him from behind. Something inside him snapped and he whipped around.

"Krista, *what is it?*"

His reaction caused her to start. She looked at him through wide, offended eyes. "Wow, Mr. Grumpy Pants."

"Sorry. I'm sorry."

"Um, I was wondering if you still have a key to the store. One of our keys is missing. I've been meaning to phone you about it, *buuuuuut...*" She looked around guiltily. "I keep forgetting."

"I'm pretty sure I gave my key back, Krista. I know I don't have one on me, that's for sure. But I'll check when I get home, okay?"

She jumped to kiss him on the cheek. "You're the best Camden."

This brought about a half smile. He could always rely on Krista to cheer him up. He missed her. Maybe he'd give her a call over the weekend, see if she wanted to hang out.

"I'll definitely swing by on Monday either way and say hi, okay? Since you 'never' hear from me anymore."

She winked at him. "Awesome! Thanks, Camden. Be good!"

CHAPTER SIXTEEN

Maybe it's better if I come off Consurge...

Camden lay on his bed early Saturday morning, fresh from a Drax Power Nap, contemplating the bottle of pills in his hand. A melancholy Ash song played on his stereo and the curtains drifted gently.

The week had dragged on. It had felt insubstantial, weightless, dust-dry. Work, eat, listen to music, play video games. One time to Murphy's Pub with his friends, and one time to a Mexican restaurant yesterday which had ended in disaster. The stubble on his face would soon graduate into a beard. What was the point of shaving? He hadn't even touched his textbooks. Just seven dead days, and he was about to begin an eighth.

Better to be unconscious for eight hours a day than to be in pain for twenty-four...

The ground beneath his feet had fallen away and he'd been left with nothing to hold on to. He was drifting, like a leaf thrown off the side of a building, slowly descending, buffeted from side to side. He'd loved a woman with every fiber of his being only to realize he'd been delusional. Hypnotized, hoodwinked, who knew? In an instant of time, his reality had vanished. She had thrown him to the side of the road like a piece of trash and he was still lying in the gutter...

Don't be stupid.

He opened the bottle and popped his daily dose.

I'm not giving up my future for some backstabbing girl.

Camden rolled out of bed, thumping to the floor. He jumped to his feet, took a deep breath, and began to do a series of squat thrusts, arms held straight out in front of him. He then fell over forward, his palms absorbing the impact, and forced himself into a furious sequence of push-ups.

Around twenty minutes later, after working up a good sweat, he made himself a cup of tea and checked his phone. Another text message from Jade was waiting for him.

"Are you okay? Why won't you return my calls or texts? I can see you're online. Is something wrong? Please call me when you get this."

Jade had called or texted every day for the last week, but he couldn't bring himself to answer or respond. Why bother? It wouldn't change anything.

Just then, there was a knock at the door. He looked through the peephole.

Speak of the devil.

Jade's hair was tied back and her mouth was set. Despite the enormous sunglasses covering most of the top half of her face, Camden could see through them to the outline of her eyes. It looked like she'd been crying.

He tried to hold off the rising feeling of panic. *Maybe she's sorry for what she did. Maybe I should talk to her. Maybe there's some explanation.*

"Camden! I know you're in there. Please open the door. Let's talk about this. Whatever's going on we can work it out."

Explanation!? What explanation could there possibly be? Jade made out with someone else, simple as that. And that's only the time I caught them. Who knows what else she's doing with him...

He shivered at the thought. Slowly, he backed away from the door, sat at the table, and took a sip of his tea. The bell rang a couple more times until Jade seemed to admit defeat, and then there was quiet. He picked up his phone and deleted her text messages along with all her contact information, a vindictive pleasure whipping around his chest with every confirming beep.

Five minutes later his phone beeped again.

Can't she take a hint!

It was his mom.

"Can you pick up some potato chips on your way, dear? See you soon!"

Oh no...

He'd completely forgotten. His mom had been planning a family reunion at her house for months now. Everyone would be there. Relatives were even flying in from Europe. Uncles, aunts, cousins, nephews, nieces: people he hadn't seen in years, if ever.

Camden buried his head in his hands. He hadn't told his mom about Jade's unfaithfulness yet. Showing her off to the family at an event like this would've been perfect – make everyone drop to their knees in envy.

But now...

Socializing was the last thing he wanted to do. Making inane small talk over light beer, the whole time trying to avoid any mention of his personal life. He could hear the incessant questioning now:

"Where's this girl we've heard so much about? Didn't you bring her?"

Maybe he could tell them she got hit by a bus and he'd spent several days tearfully by her bedside until she breathed her last. That would be less painful than telling them that she betrayed him for an old man, and had a pleasing romanticism to it.

"Forget it," he said out loud. "I can't deal with that."

He grabbed his skis from his room, along with his ski boots and a change of clothes. He marched outside, strapped the skis to the roof of the car, threw everything else in the trunk, and within ten minutes was burning rubber eastbound on Interstate 90, MxPx blasting on the stereo, shaking the whole dash.

I feel better already.

This would be just what he needed. To get away from it all. To recharge his batteries. To come back feeling fresh.

An hour later, the mountain scenery looking impossibly gorgeous in the sun, he pulled into the Alpental parking lot and strapped on his ski boots. He looked up at the craggy mountain, towering ahead of him, gleaming in the blue sky: his destination, his goal. He was going to own it.

About to shut the door, he realized his phone was still in his pocket. Camden never skied with his phone. Too distracting. He pulled it out, ready to chuck it into the glovebox, then hesitated.

Maybe I should at least call mom. I don't want her to worry.

Then he imagined the conversation.

"You ditched your family to go skiing? I'm so disappointed in you, Camden."

He threw the phone in the car and shut the door.

I'll take the heat later...

Carving through trees, bouncing over moguls, swiping from side to side along the great, vertiginous slopes; a feeling of gratification overcame him, alongside a deep desire to race up the mountain and begin the whole adventure again. The brisk air filled his lungs and his quadriceps burned. The muscle memory of his feet never failed to clip the snow at just the right angle, his ankles locking together as he twisted and turned through the snow. He drunk deeply of the thrill of being airborne, launching himself from ledges, seeing the deep drifts laid out beneath him, before thumping down in a spray of powder and flying away once more. Nothing compared to it.

After a hearty lunch at the lodge, Camden jumped on the Edelweiss chairlift, bound for the top once more. Up there was another world. Up there he felt at peace. He knew every run, every chute, every jump. The steeper the better; the more heart-stopping the initial approach, the more satisfying the landing. Of course, he was also well aware of the dangers. He could still pop his sternum from the fall he took over that hundred foot cliff two years ago.

As the chairlift steepened over the first rise, Camden's ears picked up the faint sound of a plane. He smiled and looked up into the clear sky trying to spot the aircraft.

Must be nice, off to some exotic holiday destination. I could sure use a vacation...

He still couldn't locate the plane, but the sound was growing steadily louder. Perplexed, he strained his ears. Surely no pilot flew this close to the mountains.

The woman in the chair in front of him had noticed as well, and he could see her looking into the sky. Within seconds, the noise was on top of them: a horrendous, deafening roar bellowing from just the other side of the rise in front. Soon the chair began to quiver. Within seconds, the vibration threatened to shake him off. He grasped the pole connecting him to the cable, clinging desperately with both hands.

How could a plane fly so low! Don't they know they can start an ava—

A huge wall of snow crashed over the rise above, slamming him into the chair, smashing the air from his chest and pitching him around like a wind chime in a hurricane. The force of the snow ripped the skis from his boots, his goggles and hat from his head. Numbness spread over his face, battered by unrelenting white waves of snow.

This is the end...

But just as he was wishing he'd called his mother, and heard her voice one last time, the pressure on his face and body relented.

Camden, his ears ringing, so shaken he could barely make sense of his surrounding, continued to swing in the chair, dangling above the gnarled snow. Besides the shock, it was strangely peaceful, like the water of a pool after someone jumps in. He wiped the snow from his face.

Oh no...

The chair in front of him was swinging empty.

He heard shouts from behind and turned around to see a crowd scrambling up the mountain. Looking down, it was now only a twenty-foot drop to the freshly churned slope below. He twisted around. *No bones broken, I think.* He dangled off the chair for a moment, took a deep breath, and let go. Landing clumsily on the snow, which was much harder than he'd anticipated, he raised himself up then slid awkwardly down the slope, bumping and rolling, crying out at the top of his lungs.

Finally, a muffled scream caught the edge of his audible range. He turned. A solitary wiggling black mitten poked out from the snow. Camden yelled, raced over, and began digging furiously. He'd kept his gloves, thankfully, and shoveled great mounds of snow away from his fellow victim.

As he cleared the snow from a woman's head and away from her mouth, she gasped for air, revealing a bright pink face covered in evil-looking lacerations. Moments later, two ski patrol arrived on snowmobiles. They carefully extricated the woman while Camden collapsed on his back, his head hitting the snow hard, his breath condensing in the cold air above him.

This was not the sort of exhilaration I had in mind today...

An hour later, after being given the all-clear by a visibly-shaken member of Alpental First Aid, along with a new pair of skis and a free season's pass in exchange for not opening a lawsuit, Camden lumbered back to the car. For several minutes, he sat motionless in the driver's seat breathing slowly, trying to process.

I just... got hit... by an avalanche... in Alpental... Nobody's going to believe me.

He looked in the rearview mirror. His face had faired remarkably well compared to the woman in the chair in front of him; only a few small cuts and some redness that would soon fade. After a while, he reached over and retrieved his phone from the glovebox. As expected, he had three missed calls from his mom. There were also three text messages.

9:34: *"Camden, where are you? Are you okay? Love, Mom."*

12:07: *"Tried calling you three times. Worried about you dear. We're starting lunch now. Everyone asking about you and Jade."*

Time to face the music.

Writing his reply, Camden forced himself to not only apologize for his absence, but to also describe Jade's betrayal and the shock to the system it had been. He hoped, knowing this was the first time he'd pulled something like this, that she would understand his absence and forgive him.

The third text message was from an unknown number.

"I love you and I miss you. Please call me. Please."

Delete.

CHAPTER SEVENTEEN

At least she hasn't called me to complain. That's definitely a good sign.

The following afternoon, Camden watched the landmarks pass by on the bus bound for his mom's house in Finn Hill. He'd traveled this route so many times he could tick off the landmarks as he went, and passed the time by trying to find something new.

It was all just a distraction from the inevitable. That morning, he could think of nothing else but how his mom would react to his blowing off the family reunion. Not that Deanna Walker was a harsh woman; all his life, she'd been warm-hearted and kind. Her eccentricities, such as her curious habit of using one towel to dry the dishes and a different one to dry her hands, never distracted from the care and sympathy she offered, and he knew that she would always be on his side, willing to hear anything he had to say. Even when the cancer had been at its worst, confining her to her bed and chemotherapy draining her of what little money she'd put aside, she would always insist on others being helped first, and resolutely refused to complain about her situation.

So it was with trepidation that he stepped off the bus and walked the short distance to the old, small, one-story house, the grass in the yard growing a little long.

I'll have to mow that. Not today. Maybe next weekend.

He took a few more steps up to the door, composed himself, and knocked. The faint outline of a woman appeared through the frosted glass; the familiar shape of his mom: tall, thin, her short hair slowly growing back. The guilt and the nerves began to rise, and his heartbeat quickened as she turned the lock.

Camden was about to open his mouth, to voice an apology, or something, any attempt to get the hardest part of the day over and done with as soon as possible, but in that instant, the air was crushed from his lungs as his mom wrapped him in her arms.

"Come in, come in. I've made lunch."

O... kay. Suspicious...

She beamed at him and waved him into the house. "Can I get you a drink? Something to start you off. Maybe a beer? I'm sure I've got something cold in the fridge from yesterday."

"Uh... yeah. Sure, that would be great."

He sat down on the couch and she brought him a cold bottle. He inspected the label. *Brookman's IPA.*

Where have I heard...? Suddenly, he remembered. Brookman's was a new, small craft brewery in Fremont, and he'd been meaning to visit them for some months now. Everyone who'd tried their beers had been evangelical about them.

His mom sat herself down on the couch alongside him, clearly desperate to talk. She looked bright-eyed and was practically fidgeting with excitement.

"So, Camden, guess what."

He took a sip of the beer. *Nice!* "What's up?"

"I had my first night of fifteen minutes' sleep last night!" She giggled breathily, the first time Camden had heard her do that in about two years. "I'm absolutely in love with Consurge. I already feel fresher and stronger, and my head is so much clearer. I'll be able to catch up on so many things that I let slide during the treatment."

"Mom, that's brilliant. I'm really happy for you."

She clapped her hands and locked her fingers, beaming the whole time. "So, how was your morning?"

"Fine... I guess."

Camden desperately wanted to clear the air. His mom's happiness was, if anything, even worse than disappointment. At least if she told him off, he'd know where he stood.

"Look, I'm sorry about yesterday, Mom. I just needed some time on my own. After everything with Jade, I – I just couldn't face people."

She looked at him sideways and squinted.

"Dear, I'm... Well, I'm very sorry if you felt yesterday went badly, but Camden, really, I don't think anyone else felt that way. Everyone said what a lovely time they had, and how glad they were to see you."

???

Camden scratched the back of his head. "Um, what are you talking about, Mom?"

"I just mean, you don't have to apologize about anything, dear. You were good company."

He tried again, half laughing. "Mom, don't you remember? I didn't make it. I drove up to Alpental and went skiing. I'm apologizing because I didn't come. And for ignoring your text messages."

He didn't want to mention the avalanche. She'd never approve of his going skiing ever again.

"You... drove up to Alpental?" she asked, after a pause.

"Yeah. I... Like I said in the text, I broke up with Jade. Well, sort of. I needed to be alone, try and work through things. So I went skiing, okay. But I should've come and I'm sorry." The words were coming easier now. "She cheated on me, Mom. With her boss. I saw them at the park. Clear as day. No shame. I'm sorry I didn't tell you sooner. I should have explained everything. I should've let you in. But, well, I just bottled it up and that was a mistake."

He breathed out. He felt a little calmer, even though he knew it must hurt his mom to find out about Jade this way. His mom, however, was still staring at him.

"Camden, dear, you told me all about Jade yesterday. Don't you remember? We had a long chat about it when everyone else was in the den. They were playing Monopoly..." She shook her head, as though questioning herself. "No, that's right. We were in the kitchen. You were drinking one of those beers that you brought, these nice IPAs that went down so well with everyone, and you told me about Jade and that Walter fellow.

"And I got so angry," she continued, "and I said I'd stop taking Consurge if that was the kind of man who's behind it. Remember? But you told me not to ruin my future just because of one... well, I'm not going to repeat the word you used." She gave him a wink. "But no, you told me to keep it up, and so I will. I haven't felt this good since before you were born. No offense, dear."

"So," he began, carefully, "you're saying I was here yesterday?"

"Yes, of course. Uncle Matt gave you a lift back to the city."

Man, she's worse than I thought. Has someone switched her meds? Are they reacting badly with Consurge? Maybe I should ask Jade.

"Mom, I'm sorry, but I think I know what I did with my day." He laughed. "I'd know if I was skiing or not. It's a pretty hard thing to forget!"

"And I think I'd remember if my own son was here yesterday or not!" she returned hotly.

"Are you *sure* that, maybe with everyone else here, you didn't just *think* I was here too."

The suspicion in her eyes was rising.

"Is this some sort of practical joke, Camden? Are you filming this? Am I going to end up on YouTube as 'Mother begins to doubt her own sanity'?"

"What?!" Camden was appalled at the suggestion. "No! Of course not! But this isn't right. Have you hit your head? Have you changed your medication recently?"

"No, and no. You're starting to worry me, dear. Have you hit *your* head?"

"No! And you're worrying *me*!"

There was a brief moment where the two looked at each other, suspicion becoming concern. His mom then reached for her tablet on the coffee table, swiped through a few photographs, and handed it to Camden.

"Does this jog your memory?"

Camden looked, unimpressed with the sarcasm in his mom's voice. The picture was clearly taken in the backyard. Into it was squeezed about fifty of his relatives, smiling and laughing. In the very back was a head sticking out above everyone else's.

What the...?

"Is this a joke?" he said. "I don't remember this. When was this taken?"

"Yesterday, of course! When else do I have fifty people come round for the day?"

Camden checked the date on the picture: *Saturday, September 4.*

He handed the tablet back to her. "Okay, I get it. Uncle Brendan Photoshopped me into the picture, didn't he? Nicely done."

"What? No! I don't know why you're playing games with me, dear, but it's starting to upset me."

"Mom, I'm not playing games!" He stood up, frustration and fear writhing within him. His mom had been ill for a long time, but she'd never been psychotic. This was new, and it was bad. The second he left here, he'd have to call Doc Josef and try to get her an appointment for Monday.

"Listen," he said, making one last attempt. "I'm telling you, I was at Alpental yesterday!"

"Dear..." his mom replied, patiently as ever, "it's the end of summer. You couldn't go skiing now if you *wanted* to!"

There was a still moment as he stood there, his mom looking up at him. Camden heard an odd ringing in his ears and felt the blood drain from his face.

"Are you feeling okay, dear?" asked his mom. "You've turned pale."

There's no snow in the mountains this time of year...

His legs suddenly felt unstable beneath him.

He decided to do what anyone else would do under the circumstances: lie.

He took a breath, and with every ounce of willpower he had, forced a smile onto his face. "Yeah, Mom, you got me," he said, trying his best to keep each word calm and light. "I'm... I'm only messing, Mom. I – I wanted to see how you were doing with the Consurge and the lack of sleep. Check your cognitive abilities. Ha! Well done, you passed. But, yeah, no, everything's perfectly normal. And, uh, it was a great party, wasn't it? I really loved it."

He downed the remainder of his beer, trying to think of how to cut the afternoon short. For a few moments, his mom continued looking at him with a mixture of concern and suspicion, but her face slowly cleared, and a weary look replaced the anxiety.

"That's a very odd game to play with your mother, dear. And I'd expect something a little more medical if you wanted to test my health. You will be a doctor one day, after all."

She got up to tidy the table.

"Alpental," she laughed, papers in her hands. "You don't even own a car!"

On the bus ride home, his mind full of fog and static, every attempt he made to reason things through, any attempt at clarification, was being met with more confusion, more dead ends, more unshakeable half-realities. He knew he'd gone skiing yesterday, but at the same time, it was physically impossible. The family photo was one thing – Uncle Brendan was a Photoshop wizard. But the fact that it was summer? The fact he didn't own a car? After a fruitless trip home, and staggering back up the stairs to his apartment, the only solution he'd settled on was one beloved of mankind since the dawn of time: he would firmly and ruthlessly ignore the problem until it went away.

CHAPTER EIGHTEEN

"University Book Shop?!"

Camden stood on the sidewalk with his mouth open, staring up at the glimmering sign.

After he'd arrived home from his mom's place on Sunday, Camden, Sam, Johnny, and Jeremy, had spent the evening exhausting themselves by playing round after round of ping-pong at the apartment. And, because they were all on Consurge except Jeremy, they had decided to waste away the hours into the early morning with a Star Wars marathon before the brothers crashed on the couch for a Drax Power Nap.

By Monday lunchtime, Camden's stomach had demanded attention. However, after Friday's gastronomic Katrina, he'd decided to give the local Mexican restaurant a miss and instead opted for a falafel at the nearby Lebanese restaurant. The results had been significantly better. No need to sprint to WestCo in order to paint the pan.

However, despite his fear that Julie, Robert, and the others would relive the bathroom stall disaster, Camden had pointed himself in the direction of WestCo Pharmaceuticals again. That morning, he'd looked high and low for the missing key that Krista had asked him about. Nothing. He was sure he gave it back when he quit, but he'd promised he would stop by and tell her either way.

I wonder if she's still dating the cheek tattoo guy...

However, as he reached to open the front door, an advertisement in the window jumped out at him.

'Book club every Thursday night. Everyone welcome.'

Strange. Why would WestCo run a...

He stopped, stood back, and looked up at the sign above the door.

Book Shop? Am I in the right place?

He turned around, looking back across the street.

Yep, across the street from Trader Joe's and the Mazda dealership.

Cautiously, he opened the door and carefully assessed his surroundings. A number of college students were perusing a thick wall of academic books, headed by a banner stating 'Newest Arrivals'. A barista in the corner was constructing something tall and topped with whipped cream. Several businesswomen sat around a table, typing feverishly, occasionally firing questions at each other. A soothing indie song was playing in the background.

Have I entered an alternate reality?

"Can I help you, sir?"

Camden jumped, then slowly turned. Behind him stood a man wearing a flannel shirt and trendy glasses. The hipster was about his same age, though a good foot shorter. Camden had to bend down slightly to see the name on the man's badge: 'Barry, customer care'.

Camden motioned with his arm. "What's all *this*?"

Barry looked around, as though seeing the place for the first time. "This is... a bookshop, sir."

"What happened to WestCo!"

"Hmm..." The man looked simultaneously puzzled and annoyed. "What's WestCo?"

Camden clenched his fist inside his pocket. "WestCo Medical supplies – Barry."

Barry considered, stroking his stubble with an elaborate hand motion. Camden wanted to punch him. "Yeah, I don't know the name so much, but apparently the place that was here before was some kind of hospital store or something. I dunno. I only started working here a couple weeks ago."

A couple what?

Camden laughed. "A couple weeks ago? That's impossible. I was just here on Friday! They didn't say anything about a bookshop taking over."

"They? They, who?"

Camden closed his eyes, groping around inside his head for the last vestiges of patience. "WestCo!"

Barry laughed again, his impossibly-cheerful smile still locked in place. "Are you feeling well, sir?"

He raised his finger at the employee. "Besides, how could a place be converted over a weekend?"

"Umm, I think the medical store place went out of business a couple months ago. We opened this about a month ago."

"A month ago? That's not possible."

Camden's stomach churned. Sweat was beginning to bead on his temple. His heart rate was speeding up to the point of causing him physical pain. He tried to control his breathing, but it was coming more sharply, the tendons in his throat constricting like iron rods.

I need to get out of here.

"Hey, man, are you okay?" Barry was staring at him, concerned. Their conversation was beginning to attract the glances of other customers. "You don't look so good. You want some water? You can sit down in the break room if you want, it's always quiet in there. I can bring you a book if you want to chill for a bit."

Camden put a hand on the shelf next to him, desperately trying to steady himself.

"No, Barry, it's fine," he said, by this point barely managing to breathe at all. "I'm just- I'm just going to- 'scuse me..."

He pushed past Barry and stumbled to the door without a backward glance, hand on his chest, sweat dripping down his face. In his haste, he almost ran straight out into the street but caught himself.

Back home, Camden immediately flung his clothes to the bathroom floor and ran the shower. Cold water poured over him, chilling him to his core, but at least it had the desired effect: his heart-rate slowed, his breathing came more easily. Camden's legs continued to feel like jelly, though, and it was only by pressing himself against the wall that he could stagger the short distance to the kitchen.

He poured himself a large whiskey and knocked it back in one motion. He coughed and spluttered and waited for it to take hold.

He needed a diagnosis, and fast.

Camden maneuvered himself to his bedroom, seated himself heavily in front of his computer and did what any good doctor would do: went straight to WebMD.

'Symptom Checker'

'Male aged 18-24'

'1. Choose Symptoms'

'Head'

'Scalp'

'Scalp symptoms: Agitation... anxiety... confusion... delusions... difficulty sleeping...'

He chuckled.

'...disorientation... fear of air...'

What?!

'...feeling of being detached from reality... forgetfulness... memory problems...'

Bingo.

'2. Your Choice'

'Memory problems'

'3. Possible Conditions'

'Alcohol withdrawal...'

Definitely not.

'...medication reaction or side-effect...'

He stopped. His eyes slowly shifted over to the small bottle of pills on his bedside table.

"Naaaa."

There was no way. He'd been on Consurge for ten months now. Not a single problem. Millions of other people were on Consurge with no major reported side-effects. If there was a problem, he'd have heard about it by now. Surely Jade would have told him about...

He refocused on the screen.

'...postconcussive syndrome... head injury... brain tumor...'

He stopped again and slowly raised his head from the screen. His memory, apparently so unreliable, suddenly produced a recollection of perfect clarity. A lecture in Professor Williams' class, months ago.

Irresistibly, his eyes were drawn back to the bottle. He reached to the shelf, pulling from it his neurology textbook. His shaking hands found the index. *Sleep Deprivation*, page 242. His finger scanned down the page.

'Effects of Sleep Deprivation'

He read each one out loud.

"Obesity – no. Diabetes – don't think so. Blurred vision – no. Increased stroke risk – hard to tell. Decreased Performance and Alertness – no. Development of false memory–"

A chill rippled through his body; an eerie, cold spasm, like icy water dripping down his spine. He sat there, the open book in front of him, staring into space.

At that moment, there was only one person he wanted to see.

CHAPTER NINETEEN

"Give me one good reason not to shut the door in your face?"

Chetana stood like a sentinel, loyally guarding the entrance to her and Jade's apartment. Camden knew she didn't want her friend to be hurt any further. His panicked eyes and sweat-caked t-shirt weren't making a great case for his stability.

"I've come to apologize."

Her eyebrows raised, unconvinced. "Hmm."

"Can I please come in?"

She folded her arms. "So you've decided to talk, have you?"

"Listen, Chetana. I made a mistake. I just want the opportunity to explain myself."

She flashed him a look of utter contempt. "I'd say you were given no shortage of those. What kind of a man ignores his girlfriend for over a week with no explanation?"

Jade appeared at the end of the hallway behind Chetana. Camden could see her face clearly: she looked much the same as the first time he'd met her at the Drax orientation. But there was no affection in her eyes as they met his; just a coolness as she scanned him, appraised him.

Camden allowed desperation to win out over patience. "There's something wrong with me, Jade!"

Chetana snorted. "You came here to tell her *that*? Tell her something she *doesn't* know."

"I'm serious, Jade," he called, trying to ignore her roommate. "I'm freaking out, here. Can I *please* come in?"

Chetana turned for Jade's approval. Jade gave a quiet nod, her face still blank. Chetana rolled her eyes as she turned back to Camden.

"I was just leaving," said Chetana, disdain dripping from every word. She gathered her coat as Camden stepped inside, gave him a final dirty look, and closed the door behind her.

Awkwardly removing his shoes, he followed Jade into the lounge where she had positioned herself on the couch.

"Well, haha, I guess we both have roommates who don't care for us," was his attempt at an icebreaker. Jade continued simply to stare, her expression neutral.

Camden joined her on the couch and took a deep breath. He was well aware that this was his only opportunity, so he needed to make it count. Starting from the beginning, he related his experience of seeing her and Walter Johnson at Gas Works Park, followed by his experiences with the WestCo bathroom fiasco and the avalanche. He then, keeping his voice as steady as he could, related the revelations, first from his mom and the second from the bookshop. He quickly continued to his self-diagnosis earlier that day and the panicked realization that something was clearly very wrong.

While he spoke, he was acutely aware of Jade's expression. It started blank, moving to skeptical and angry when he mentioned Johnson, through to an element of academic curiosity, to confusion, and ending with a look of mild alarm.

"I don't know what's going on, Jade. But I tell you, I'm remembering things that didn't actually happen as clearly as I'm talking to you now."

He reached out and took her hand. She didn't resist. "I stopped talking to you because I saw you and Johnson going at it like... Jade, I swear, it was like being stabbed in the heart. I'm sorry. I must have put you through a lot, just cutting you out like that, and that was wrong. I hope you can forgive me."

He could see the tears welling in her eyes. She brushed them away with an impatient hand. "I... Yes, of course I forgive you, Camden. You know I care about you. But if only you'd spoken to me!"

"I'm so sorry. I really am."

"And Walter? *Honestly.*" She stuck out her tongue. "Megalomaniac. Not my type at all. You're my type, Camden. You're the one I'm in love with."

"I love you too, babe."

They embraced tightly on the sofa, Camden's arms tight across her back as she gripped a handful of his hair. After a moment, they broke apart.

Jade gave a choked laugh. "And even if it is under these – very bizarre – circumstances, I'm glad there's an explanation, of sorts. That's the first time anyone's ever treated me that way. It was horrible!"

Relief surged through Camden. Just having Jade back, and at his side, meant everything. He suddenly had back both his strength and his resolve.

He could see the resolve building in her eyes as well as she wiped away the tears. "We need to figure out what's going on."

She swept up from the sofa and marched towards the coat rack, Camden following in her slipstream.

"What's the plan?" he asked.

"We need," said Jade, firmly pinning her hair back, "to go to the lab."

"What, now?"

"Right now."

"Working late tonight Ms. Reilly?"

"Just giving a friend of mine a tour, Bill."

The security guard in the Seattle Investments Tower lobby, Jade had explained, was used to seeing her at this time of night, though she was usually leaving. He ran an eye over Camden.

"At nine p.m. on a Monday night?"

Jade smiled, not breaking her stride. "His plane leaves early in the morning."

The guard chuckled. "Just giving you a hard time, Ms. Reilly. You have a nice night."

In the laboratory, Jade slipped on her lab coat and set her face, mouth narrowed to a grim slit. "You ready for some tests, love?"

He shivered. "You know there's nothing I like more..."

Ordering Camden to lie on the same examination table he'd sat on the first time they'd met, she drew blood, then spinal fluid, then bone marrow. Each needle felt more painful than the last, although Jade said it was only in his mind.

"Time for an MRI," she said, handing him some headphones. "What do you want to listen to? Tchaikovsky or Beethoven?" His answer of "Postal Service" was quickly vetoed citing potential overstimulation.

Finally, she wired his scalp with electrodes and recorded the results on her computer.

After two hours of tests, an exhausted-looking Jade sat, hunched over her microscope, staring into the distance.

"So, what do you think?" asked Camden. *Surely* there was something in one of the results that would point them in the right direction. He'd been through too much discomfort that night to fancy disappointment.

Jade puffed out her cheeks in frustration and shook her head. "I'm afraid I don't know what to tell you. I've run all of the basic tests and there's nothing obviously wrong with you. Everything checks out fine."

This wasn't how he'd imagined the tests ending up. "But I'm not fine!"

"I know, love. I know."

"Come on. You must have *some* ideas!"

Camden immediately regretted his tone. Jade, however, chose to ignore it, in favor of rubbing her eyes with her fingertips.

She took a deep breath. "Okay," she continued. "First of all, what do we know? We know that you're having false memories. That's a start. False memories involve a person remembering events differently from the way they actually happened. Right?"

"Right."

"But you're going beyond that. It's like your brain is *replacing* what really happened with something completely different, and have you no recollection of your actual experiences."

Camden nodded in agreement. "Okay, good. Where does that lead us?"

Jade drummed her fingers on the table. "I've read, in one or two places, about more dramatic cases, wherein people remember events that never happened at all. Entire hallucinogenic episodes."

"Great..."

"In fact, some false memories involve treating *dreams* as if they were playbacks of real experiences."

"Dreams?"

"Effectively, the brain dreams while someone's awake. Normally, dreams feel real while you're in them, but your mind lets them go once you regain consciousness. But if someone dreams whilst awake, how can you wake up from it, and how can you know where the dream ends?"

They paused for a moment, digesting this.

"But," said Camden, slowly, "I haven't been dreaming since I've been on Consurge."

"That's true. That's because you're only sleeping for a fraction of your usual cycle. Dreams generally occur in REM sleep. That doesn't start until about ninety minutes after someone falls asleep. But because you're on Consurge, you never get there. Neither do I anymore. It's possible..." Jade hesitated, then continued, "that your brain is compensating somehow."

"Go on."

But Jade didn't seem inclined to do so. She kept fidgeting, running her hands over each other. Eventually, she stood up and began pacing. "For some reason, Consurge stimulates the dopaminergic pathways in the brain."

"Dopaminergic? Those are... neural pathways that transmit dopamine to the brain, right?"

Jade nodded. "When the pathways are stimulated, the frequency and vividness of dreams increase." She continued to stride around the lab, tapping her forehead. "But of course, for someone on Consurge, dreams are never produced."

"So is it a problem?"

"Well, some in the lab brought it up as a talking point during the stage two trials, but – well, it didn't seem to be a problem at the time. There was never any evidence that the dopamine levels were doing anything other than spiking and settling down again. Not everyone was happy, though."

"What did they say?"

Jade sighed and rolled her eyes. "I don't remember all the details. Something about the fact that our understanding of dreams is always changing and we don't fully understand the function and content of dreams, blah blah blah... They said that if we didn't understand why the pathways were being stimulated, should we continue with the drug? It all seemed very preachy, mind you. You have to understand, we were entering uncharted areas of science. If we let every tiny roadblock slow us down completely, we'd still be years behind where we currently are."

"I suppose..."

The ensuing silence was the longest of the evening. Finally, Camden raised his eyes to meet hers. "Jade. Tell me something. No one on Consurge has ever reported something like this... have they?"

A variety of emotions morphed over her face once more: fear, confusion, frustration, determination.

"Not that I'm aware of..."

"So why has no one else had this problem?"

Her eyes suddenly became empty. "Maybe... Maybe because no one else in the world has been on Consurge as long as you have..."

Camden swallowed. "You think it's having a cumulative effect?"

"I don't know. The stage two trial lasted for a month. The FDA wanted the stage three trial to go for two months, but Walter convinced them that one month was enough. There didn't appear to be any evidence that it mattered how long a person was taking Consurge. Mind you, even two months wouldn't have resulted in your effects..." She drifted off.

"Do you think something's wrong with the dru-?"

"We can't say that for sure," said Jade immediately. "We need to run more tests and make a thorough investigation. Eliminate as many variables as possible."

Camden stood up. "I'm not sure I like the idea of being studied like a lab rat."

"Camden, sit down. It'll only be me running the investigation. This isn't something I'm going to share around, not until I have some more hard data. Until then it's important to keep these events to ourselves."

Camden sat, unconvinced. He didn't like this. Jade had plenty of reasons to keep bad press on Consurge from getting out. He hoped that wasn't her priority.

"So what do I do now?" he asked.

"I don't want to say it love, but, maybe you should go off Consurge for a fortnight. See if the false memories stop. I'll run daily tests on you, and you keep me informed of your mental state."

"I was afraid you'd suggest that."

"It's just until we find out what's going on. You can always start taking it again once we figure this out. Besides, you're on summer holidays now. You don't have to worry as much about studying." She paused for a moment. "I think I'll stop taking it for a while as well – just until we know what's going on."

This surprised Camden, but he quickly pressed on to his next concern. "But how will I know if the false memories have stopped? Maybe I've had loads already that I'm not even aware of."

"I guess we'll have to wait and see. Maybe run through the day's events with me every night. I might be able to tell if something's out of place."

"What about my job at the hospital? What if... what if I put someone's life in danger?" His breathing was starting to come more sharply, and his chest constricted. Jade gripped his hand.

"Camden. Just breathe. Don't panic."

"I'm not sure... I can keep... working there in good conscience."

"Listen – *listen*." The commanding tone of her voice forced him to focus. "Now is not the time for rash decisions. I hope that, once you start sleeping again, the false memories will go away."

"How long will it take before I start sleeping?"

"Not long. A few days. It's different for everyone."

Camden could tell that Jade was mulling something else over in her mind.

"What are you thinking?"

"I'm just wondering if I should tell Walter about this. If this happens to other people, we could have a problem on our hands."

Camden shook his head resolutely.

"No. Don't tell him. Not yet. Besides, you'd get fired for giving me Consurge. Let's just wait and see for a couple weeks like you say. Okay?"

"Okay," Jade said reluctantly.

It was past midnight when Camden arrived home. Emotionally shattered, he landed on his bed with a bounce, wincing from the still fresh needle holes in his back. He stared at the ceiling. A mixture of emotions swirled in his brain, chief among them being ecstasy from his reconciliation with Jade. But close behind was fear. Fear of what was happening to his body, fear of what would happen to his schooling if he went off Consurge long-term, fear of falling behind everyone else again.

What if...

He reached out, picked up the bottle of Consurge on the bedside table and hesitated. Finally, in an extreme moment of will, he placed it in the drawer and shut it decisively.

"Two weeks."

CHAPTER TWENTY

'How's it going? I'm starting to get sleepy already. You? x'

Jade's text message found Camden late the following night at home, watching 'telly' as she called it. Despite his concern that he'd start to get sleepy, Camden had reported to work at the hospital that day as usual. The last thing he needed was to give a bad impression to the doctors or draw any negative attention. Fortunately, it had been smooth sailing.

'Not yet,' he replied.

He'd decided to keep notes of everything he did during the day, in order to compare his account to those of others. It was a mundane collection of errands – restocking, ordering, delivering – but thus far, no one had called him to demand to know why he hadn't done this or that. It was a start.

By Thursday afternoon, however, Camden was left scratching his head. Like Jade, he'd stopped taking Consurge three days ago, yet unlike Jade, his sleep had remained at fifteen minutes a night. In fact, he wasn't even drowsy.

Surely this can't be normal...

"It's different for everyone," Jade had said. "Sometimes it takes more than a few days."

On the bright side, however, he seemed to have gone three days without any false memories. He'd kept as calm as possible until the end of his shift when he was only a few filed papers away from heading home. Nearly ready to clock off, he felt a tap on his shoulder.

"Ah. Hello Josef."

The doctor, who was normally in good spirits, seemed even more jovial than usual. "How's life treating you, Camden?"

He forced a grin. "Well, you know. It doesn't do any good to complain."

"You look tired, my boy. Have you been getting enough sleep?"

How do I answer that?!

The doctor didn't know he'd been on Consurge, and given the present circumstances it was probably best it stayed that way.

"Well, to be honest with you, no. I haven't. But I don't think it's affecting my work though. I'm focused while I'm here."

The doctor winked. *Winked?* "No, your work is always fine."

Camden let out a sigh of relief.

"As for me," the doctor continued, "I haven't been sleeping at all. And I feel great!"

Camden tried to turn his grimace into a grin. "You took the plunge, huh?"

"Yes!" Herman raised a double thumbs-up. "I've been on Consurge for three weeks now and I love it. Why should I keep prescribing it for others and not give it a try myself?"

"I can see the logic."

"You know that sometimes I have to work eighteen-hour shifts and perform surgery when I should be in bed? It's not safe for anybody. But now – now it's copacetic."

"That's... really good." Camden said, unenthusiastically.

"It *is* good! Hey, maybe *you* should try Consurge!"

Camden bit his lip. He had to choose his words carefully. "Ahh, you think so?"

"Why not?" The tall doctor spread his palms wide. "You never know what it might do for you."

"Yeah, you never know..."

The doctor placed his hand on Camden's shoulder. "Camden, maybe you should take a vacation. You haven't taken any of your vacation days since you joined us. Take a few. Enjoy a bit of time away. It'll do you good."

"Yeah. Yeah, that's a good idea."

The doctor turned to leave with a smile. "I'll see you next week, shall I?"

"That's the plan."

Camden dumped the last of his files and jumped in the elevator, desperate to leave the building. He crossed the street briskly into the arboretum and called Jade.

"I think Dr. Herman knows something's wrong," he said hurriedly, skipping past any sort of greeting.

"What? Camden, what's going on?"

"He told me he's taking Consurge now. I tried to sound happy for him, but I don't think I was very convincing. I think he's becoming suspicious. He's got this look in his eye like he knows what's going on. He thinks there's something wrong with me. Told me to take a vacation. Why would he bring it up otherwise?"

"Cam-!" Jade's voice muffled as she turned away from the phone to shout at someone. He heard her again, clearly, after a moment. "Listen. Let's not jump to conclusions, babe."

"I don't trust him. I think Dr. Herman–"

"*Camden.* You're not sounding rational. You've told me that he's a decent man who looks after his staff. He's probably just concerned about you."

Camden gave a deep sigh. "Maybe you're right."

"I am, babe. I'll see you soon. Keep texting me. It's nice to hear from you."

Click.

"Is there anyone with you?"

The following Monday afternoon, Jade had phoned Camden to say she was coming over that evening. She said it was 'time to talk', but hadn't offered any clarification.

"No," said Jade. "It's just me. Why would there be anyone with me?"

Camden poked his head out the door past Jade and surveyed the hallway. She stood there, tapping her feet, until he was satisfied. "Okay. Come in."

She stepped in, kicked off her boots, and cut to the chase. "We said we'd give it a fortnight, I know, but it's been a week, and there's been no improvement. I'm concerned."

So was Camden. He was still barely sleeping.

"So, what should we do?" asked Jade.

Camden rubbed his neck. "Pretend everything's okay and carry on?"

"I wish we could."

"What about all the extra tests we did last week?"

She shook her head. "Nothing. And not for want of trying. I've been fitting in research around everything else. It's been mad. I don't have the time I used to have now that I'm sleeping again." She flopped onto the sofa, massaging her temples. "It's absolutely bizarre. Every single test case started to get sleepy again within three days and slept fully again within six days. This is unmapped territory, medically speaking. It's been seven days now!"

Camden sat down next to her. "So that's it? You're stumped?"

"As I see it, there are two main reasons why you haven't started sleeping yet."

"I'm listening."

"First of all, no one has ever been on Consurge as long as you have. And because of that, your body just needs more time to return to normal sleep patterns. If so, continuing to stay off the drug is the natural solution. And it's something we need to document."

"What's the other reason?"

"Stress. I think the stress of this whole thing isn't helping you recover. Stress has a recognised measurable effect on the body. I think you need to rest, and I don't mean just physically."

"What *do* you have in mind?"

She smiled. It brightened the room and made Camden feel warm within. Jade reached for his hand. "I think we should get away. Go to a place where you can get your mind off everything for a while. Clear your head. Give your body some extra time in a peaceful setting to get Consurge out of the system. It'll help, I'm sure it will."

"Where were you thinking of going?"

There was a twinkle in her eye. "Do you remember our first date?"

"You want to go to an Irish pub?"

She laughed. "Not a pub, silly. Ireland!"

"Ireland?"

"Just for a week or so. I've cleared it with work already."

"What would we do in Ireland?"

"What would we *do*? We'd have fun! Unwind. *De-stress*. Be tourists. Remember I have family in West Cork who haven't seen me in years. They'll fall over themselves to see us. We can stay with them. They're crazy, I don't deny it, but you'll love them."

Camden remembered being "introduced" to Jade's aunt and uncle on their first date - Kells Irish Pub almost a year ago. In fact, since then, if Camden had a euro for every time Jade had reminisced about Ireland, he figured he could buy County Cork. But to see it in real life...

"Well – when would we go?" he asked.

"Let's go tomorrow!"

"Tomorrow?! Are you crazy? You can't just jet off at a moment's notice."

Jade pulled her laptop out of her bag. "Why not? September is a great time of year to see Ireland, and we're certainly not short of funds. We've been working so much, we deserve some sort of reward, don't you think? Come on, let's book a flight!"

Camden stared at Jade with a mixture of disbelief and surprise, but this wasn't an invitation he was inclined to turn down.

"Okay! Here's to spontaneity."

CHAPTER TWENTY-ONE

"Camden, over here! Car hire is this way."

"Hire? Don't you mean rental?"

"Hire," said Jade, firmly. She grinned at him. "You're on *my* side of the pond now."

Camden trailed Jade, who obviously knew her way around, through the heaving masses of Shannon Airport. He'd stuffed far too much in his backpack and was struggling to keep up. Jade, in contrast, whisked her way through the crowd, her bag slung comfortably over her shoulder and a small rolling suitcase at her side. In any case, having been stuck on two flights for a total of eleven hours, Camden was just grateful to stretch his long legs.

"You people just have to be different over here, don't you?" he said, catching up with her.

She stopped and narrowed her eyes at him. "What do you mean, *you people?* You do realise," said Jade, putting a flirtatious finger on his chest, "that you're speaking the language we invented?"

"Yes, but we perfected it."

"Oh!" Jade's eyes gleamed. "You cheeky thing. Just try and keep up, and maybe you'll graduate from American English to the real thing."

Camden huffed and puffed after her, as she skipped out of the terminal and into the bright sunshine of the late Irish summer.

"You even drive on the wrong side of the road!" he said.

"Keep it up and I'll make *you* drive!"

They collected their 'hire car' – a Fiat 500, which to Camden looked like it could be crushed into oblivion from a collision with a semi-truck. Jade, however, insisted it was precisely what they needed for the narrow roads in rural Ireland, and within twenty minutes they were heading south on the 'wrong' side of the road.

They passed a ruined castle and thatched cottages in the town of Adare, onward through oak forests, sparkling lakes and majestic mountains in Killarney, around colorful, quaint shops and pubs in

Kenmare, and over a rugged pass with commanding vistas of Bantry Bay and Glengarriff Woods below.

Camden didn't dare blink. As beautiful as the Cascades could be, or Lake Chelan in the summer, this was something else entirely. This place had an earthy fullness to it, the deep and fundamental solidness of history and a hundred generations who'd lived and died here, sinking their culture into the soil. He wound down the window and let the wind blow across his face; he breathed deeply and filled his lungs. It was the freshest, purest air he'd ever tasted, and he felt it clearing his mind and brightening his mood.

"It's amazing," he said.

Jade smiled, keeping her eyes on the road. "It's a place apart."

"It's awesome..."

"*Sew ahsowme*," she shot back in her best Valley Girl accent, mocking him. "You sound so American."

"Newsflash – I *am* American."

"Well, can you tone down the Americanness while you're here, please? You might infect the whole place."

"Who's cheeky now?"

She stuck out her tongue at him.

Eventually, Jade abandoned the main road near the town of Bantry and headed up a wild valley. A clearing in the woods revealed a shimmering lake with a lone fisherman on his boat.

"Here it is," she said, turning the car down a one-lane track.

The crumbling road, slowly being reclaimed by the grass, snaked around lush green fields with sheep grazing in the warm sun. The hedgerows were bursting with flowers and birdsong.

God himself would go for a vacation here.

"My family's looking forward to meeting you," said Jade, as she pulled their car up to an old white farmhouse with red trim. "I've told them nothing but good things."

"There are only good things to tell!" he quipped, eyeing the open doorway. Ever since he'd known her, Jade had spoken fondly of her Aunt and Uncle O'Donovan in West Cork, and he couldn't wait to meet them. But pleasant as the day had been thus far, he was still about to meet his girlfriend's family and that was never anything less than fraught with danger.

The farmhouse, up close, made Camden feel like he'd traveled back in time. It wasn't just the red geraniums in the windows or the pale lace curtains behind the small windows. He had the same feeling as when he'd looked down on the Black Valley near Moll's Gap: a deep feeling of appreciation for something he'd never known, a profound pastoral tranquility.

"This is where my dad was born," said Jade, softly.

"It's *perfect*."

As they stepped out of the car, a booming voice bellowed from behind them.

"What's the craic, Camden!"

A stout man in rubber boots hopped over the gate from the field, carrying an empty bucket in his hand. His bright blue eyes gleamed as he inspected them.

"Uncle!" Jade ran over and leaped into his arms. Taller than him though she was, he wrapped his arms around her waist and swung her around. Camden looked at the man's arms. They were thick and powerful, like the branches of a solid tree.

"Camden," said Jade, cheeks flushed pink, "I'd like you to meet my Uncle O'Donovan."

"It's a pleasure, sir," said Camden, shaking the farmer's calloused hand.

He winced.

Show no weakness...

"Oh no, none of this 'sir' business here, boy. We're not that formal 'round here." The farmer released his hand and slapped Camden on the shoulder, almost felling him.

"Gotcha." Camden tried, as surreptitiously as possible, to shake some life back into his mangled appendage.

"You're very welcome to our humble home. You must forgive my scruffiness. I've been in the fields all morning."

"No apology necessary. It's great to be here."

Uncle O'Donovan paused, looked Camden up and down, then winked at Jade. "Well, I'd say he'll do, Jade. A fine tall man. He'll make a grand husband."

Jade blushed. "Uncle!"

Her uncle next motioned to Camden. "C'mere to me," he said.

Camden turned to Jade for a clue.

"It means he's got something to tell you."

"Oh, okay.

O'Donovan leaned in closer. "Tell me, what do you think of the Institution of Marriage?"

"*Ah*... Well... I, uh..." Camden glanced quickly at Jade who seemed eager to hear his response. "Well, I've never been institutionalized before..."

The farmer let out a roar of laughter as Jade rolled her eyes and gave an exasperated chuckle.

"However," Camden cleared his throat, "I'm sure I'd enjoy the stay."

Uncle O'Donovan laughed again. "I'm sure your one'll be grand. She's a good girl."

Camden smiled and wrapped his arm around Jade's waist.

However, the smile abruptly vanished from O'Donovan's face and his eyes became distant. "They're not all like our Jade, though. In fact, the other night I was at the pub, and Paddy said to me that his wife was driving him to drink."

"That's terrible," said Camden. Jade tutted.

"Well, I told him he was lucky. My wife makes me *walk*!"

Jade shook her head. "You need some new jokes, uncle."

"Ah! Shpeak of the Divil," he said. "Here's me oul' doll now."

A smiling woman with a flour-covered apron emerged from the farmhouse, dusting off her hands. She was the same height as O'Donovan, her brown hair flecked with gray and tied into a tight bun behind her head. "You're early! I've just put the soda bread in the oven."

"Auntie!" Jade ran to embrace her with the same vigor as she'd done her uncle, almost knocking the poor woman to the ground.

"Oh dear," said the lady, once she'd been released. "Now you're covered in flour!"

"No matter. Camden, this is my dear Aunt O'Donovan."

He shook the woman's hand – a far gentler handshake than Uncle had given him, though an equally calloused hand.

"A pleasure to meet you, Camden. We've heard good things."

"It's lovely to meet you too. You have a beautiful farm."

Uncle O'Donovan chose this moment to object. "Now just a minute. How come she's 'dear' Auntie O'Donovan, but I'm just plain oul' Uncle O'Donovan?"

"Oh, uncle. You know you're dear as well."

He smiled and put his arm around his wife's shoulder. She batted him away with a laugh.

"Pay no attention to him," said Aunt O'Donovan. "Come inside for a cuppa tea, then I'll show you your rooms." She raised her hand and pointed at Camden. "I said *rooms*. In the plural. Just remember, no patty fingers."

"No, ma'am."

That evening, Camden and Jade strolled hand in hand up the hill to watch the sun set over Bantry Bay. A gentle breeze caressed them, and the painterly clouds shifted and evolved above the surface of the glistening water.

"You were right, babe," said Camden. "I feel better already. This is what I needed."

"I'm glad."

"It's been so confusing these past couple weeks," he continued. "First the false memories. Then, coming off Consurge made me freak out about my grades. And my career..."

Jade draped her arm around Camden's shoulder like one of the guys. "You know what you need?"

"I need to start sleeping is what I need."

"No babe, you need a pint!"

Camden nodded. "That *does* always help."

"C'mon. I'll take you to Ma Murphys."

"Sounds awesome."

"And I'm buying!"

A small smile crept onto Camden's face. "Even better."

The tiny pub was divided into two parts. At the front, an old shop sold everything from Corn Flakes to tinned beans. As they walked in, an old man behind the counter reached for a tub of powdered custard from the shelf and rang it up for an even older woman.

Through a set of double doors was the bar, only slightly bigger than the shop. The two ancient farmers propping up the bar and the couple at the table all turned in unison, casting their gaze at the newcomers. Jade beamed. Camden didn't know where to look, so tried his best to smile along.

"What can I get you?" The barman, now finished at the shop, leaned on the draft beer taps.

"I'll have a West Coast Cooler," said Jade, eyeing the selection.

"Murphy's," said Camden. *Drinking Murphy's – in Ireland. Sam and Johnny will be so jealous they'll explode.*

"Good choice," said the barman. He poured the pint nearly full and walked away, letting it settle. All the while, Camden could feel the eyes of the two men at the bar bearing down on him.

This is nothing like Kells!

"Enjoying your holidays?" asked one of the men.

Camden just about understood the man through his accent. "Yes, very much, thanks. We just arrived."

"Where you from yourself?"

"Seattle, Washington."

"Washington! Ohhh, you must say hi to the president for me!" the man joked.

"Oh, no, not that Washington. Washington State. The west coast."

"You ejit!" said the other man, welting his friend on the arm. "You never saw Frasier?"

"Oh, right. Good show."

Camden smiled. "Yeah."

"But your lady friend doesn't sound like a Yank, now."

"I'm from London," said Jade. "We're visiting my aunt and uncle, Teddy and Áine O'Donovan. Do you know them?"

The man's eyes lit up. "Then you must be... Denis Reilly's little girl!"

"That's me."

He reached out and shook her hand vigorously. "Pleased to make your acquaintance. I knew your father when he was just a boy. I've not seen him in donkey's years. Is he well?"

"He's fine. Still in London."

"Would you believe it, Denis Reilly's girl." He shouted to the barman. "Gavin! Next rounds on me!"

"Okay, Finbar!"

They passed the evening comfortably, listening to Finbar, a self-proclaimed local historian, expounding the history of the maritime paraphernalia adorning the walls of the pub. When Camden had questioned the veracity of one of the stories, the reply he received was: "Sure 'tis hard to know when I've drink taken, like." Pondering the grammatical construction of this sentence soon caused him to forget whether anything he'd heard that evening was actually true.

By eleven, Jade's eyelids were beginning to droop. "I need to gessome sleep, babe," she said, running her hand over his shoulder. "'S time to go home."

Camden, however, had already set out a few euros on the bar for another round of drinks.

"Don't you worry about our boy, Jade," said Finbar. "We'll bring the Yank home."

The bartender cackled, and Camden grinned apologetically at Jade. She gave him a sleepy smile and bade them good night.

Into the early hours, the small group traded stories, occasionally bursting into an Irish ballad. Camden could rarely remember feeling so happy, so swept up. Even the most raucous night at Kells couldn't compare to this. It didn't matter that he'd never set foot on this side of the Atlantic before – in one night, he'd gone from outsider to a local.

Back at the family home, Camden's power nap that morning was still only 15 minutes, but it felt more like a couple of hours.

Must have been that last poitín.

Slowly, he backed into Jade's bedroom holding a laden breakfast tray.

"Wakey, wakey. Rise and shine."

Jade let out a grunt and turned over.

He lowered the tray on the table and threw open the curtains. Light poured into the room, eliciting a fierce objection from Jade.

"Too bright," she grumbled into her pillow.

"I have something for you, me love," said Camden, attempting his best Irish accent.

By now she could smell it, and stirred herself. "Did you bring me a full Irish?"

"Complete with something called white pudding."

She propped herself against the headboard and rubbed her hands together.

"Eat up, me love," said Camden, "for I'm ready to hit the road. Your good auntie's told me it's a fine soft morning, but it'll clear up soon enough."

"Well, don't you sound just like a local," said Jade, her sarcasm unimpeded by the stout combination of bacon and potatoes in her mouth.

Exploring the wilds of the Beara Peninsula filled the remainder of their morning. As the car rounded the bend at Adrigole Bay, the rocky slopes of Hungry Hill loomed on the horizon. For the first time that day, the sun deigned to make an appearance between the clouds.

Jade pointed. "That's the highest waterfall in Ireland. At least that's what the locals will tell you. The internet says different, but you know – you can never trust the internet."

"Indeed..."

Leaving the main road at a small shop, they followed a snakelike ascent to a remote mountain pass. The wind began to swirl through the car's open windows. Camden breathed in deeply. He wanted to get enough of this air, this grassy, salty smell, to last him the rest of his life.

"Stop here," he said, halfway up the ascent. "I wanna get out and take a picture."

Camden stood, aiming his camera down the wild valley. Through the lens, seemingly out of nowhere, appeared a farmer and his sheepdog. Wild hair, a sweater riddled with holes, dirty jeans, rubber boots and brandishing a stick. The man was striding towards him with purpose.

Should I be worried?

The farmer reached out with soiled hands and grasped Camden's, shaking it firmly and launching a volley of words at him. There was only one problem: Camden couldn't catch one of them.

He leaned over to Jade who was still in the car. "Is he speaking in Irish?" he whispered out of the corner of his mouth.

Jade laughed. "No silly. West Cork English. He's asking you where you're from, if we're married, if we have kids, if we don't have kids why not, what we do for work, what we think of Ireland..."

"Oh. Is that all?"

"He's just being friendly."

Without warning the farmer took a swipe at his dog with the stick and shouted. "Go back! Go back!"

"Yeah, friendly," said Camden.

Carrying on, Camden and Jade eventually arrived at the village of Eyeries, where each house was painted a different color. Bright shades of yellow and blue seemed to be the favorites, though Camden spotted at least one purple, one a sort of mossy green, and one a vibrant, cheerful orange. Jade suggested the nearby sandy beach to enjoy their lunch, and this time it was her turn to treat Camden.

"Will you get the basket out of the boot for me please?" she asked.

"The boot..." Camden chuckled under his breath.

"What was that?"

"Nothing."

"Follow me, cheeky monkey."

At the water's edge, a voluptuous mattress of grass covered a rocky outcrop which jutted into the sea. Together, they spread a blanket in the soft salty breeze and laid out bread, wine, and olives along with local meats and cheeses. Conversation suspended, they sated themselves.

With a full belly, Camden lay heavily on the blanket, watching large white clouds drift and flow across the blue sky. Jade laid down beside him, her arm across his chest. A feeling of deep contentment welled up inside him. He felt so relaxed, so peaceful. He was almost a bit... drowsy.

CHAPTER TWENTY-TWO

"I fell asleep, didn't I?"

Camden opened his eyes to find Jade gazing down at him with a serene look in her eyes. Her contented smile gave him the answer. His mouth felt dry and his teeth a little unnatural when he probed them with his tongue. He tried to stir, but his head felt heavy as a cinder-block.

"How long was I out for?"

"Over an hour."

He managed to sit up, blinking a few times. The sun seemed remarkably bright compared to when he'd first laid down. "An hour?"

Jade nodded. "How do you feel?"

"Fine. A little light-headed, if I'm honest."

He slowly stood and took a deep breath. Jade leaned her head against his leg as the two of them gazed at their surroundings.

"It's this place," she said softly. "The salt air, the breeze, the sound of the ocean. And, well, in reality, maybe you just needed a couple of extra days. Either way, it's the result we wanted."

"I never thought I'd be so happy to *sleep*," said Camden. "I've spent years making like it's the enemy. Now, it feels like the best thing in the world!"

"I'm so relieved," said Jade. "It shouldn't have taken this long, but then again, no one's ever been on Consurge as long as you."

Camden's chest felt like it was filling with a big, warm balloon. He wanted to do something exciting, something explosive. He wanted to run, to leap, to embrace every one of his senses.

"I'm going swimming!"

"Swimming? It's freezing!"

Ignoring this statement of the obvious, he ran full tilt across the grass, launched himself off the outcrop and landed with a mighty splash in the ocean. He surfaced from the waters with a scream, his clothes stuck tightly to his body. "It's *freezing!*"

Jade laughed at him from her vantage point on the rock. "Imagine that."

Camden kicked hard, away from the shore. He could sense his muscles responding as he swam in a wide arc, his steady breaststroke kneading his shoulders. The currents snatched at his legs. He plunged below the surface, salt stinging his eyes, and kicked down several feet to the sea floor. He grasped a handful of sand and shook it, scattering grains through the dark water, cheering soundlessly, bubbles escaping from his mouth and traveling back towards the sunlight.

Finally, he dragged himself from the ocean and staggered up the beach, water pouring from his sodden clothes. Jade watched him as he approached, an amused look on her face. He gave her an apologetic smile, and she blew him a kiss.

"Come now," she said. "You're lucky I thought to bring towels. Let's get back for dinner."

Over the next two days, Camden and Jade explored the mountains, rivers, and lakes of West Cork. They stepped through tiny villages, perused local craft shops, and sampled whiskeys at pubs along the way. Camden had even managed to find an Aran sweater that fit his elongated frame. It was by far the most romantic series of events Camden had ever experienced, though the competition from his last relationship wasn't up to much – a bunch of flowers left on Samantha Mitchell's doorstep two years ago that wilted and died because her family had gone away for the weekend without him realizing. This holiday was something far more likely to induce envy: their friends in Seattle were already beginning to voice passive-aggressive complaints about the sheer number of kissing selfies being plastered over Instagram. Of course, this did nothing more than spur them on.

Beyond the glee of being in a gorgeous country, and spending so much time with Jade, Camden was sleeping a little more each day. The false memories also seemed to have ended – each day he and Jade would run through what they'd done for the previous few days, and their stories always matched.

On Saturday morning, Camden wandered downstairs to find Jade reading in the kitchen next to the wood stove. She looked up, anticipation in her eyes.

"Well?" she asked.

He beamed. "Six hours!"

"Brilliant! Your first full night of sleep. Well, close enough. There's plenty of fully-functioning people who would kill for a natural six hours. I think this deserves a celebration."

"Oh yeah? What do you have in mind?"

"It's sunny and warm," she said, snapping the book shut. "Eat your breakfast and get your hiking boots. I want to take you to one of my favourite places. I've been keeping it for a special occasion. Might as well be today."

"Sounds promising." Camden hastily shoveled a plateful of scrambled eggs and soda bread into his mouth, before stuffing his backpack for the hike.

While driving, Jade whistled to herself. Camden couldn't identify the tune, but it sounded somehow familiar, the kind of memory that was just on the edge of clarity. It gave him a tranquil, contented feeling.

As the hiking trail reached the brow of a hill, Camden understood why Jade had described this spot as one of her favorites. From where they stood, a grassy path meandered all the way down to the foot of a small castle, beaten with time, its battlements crumbling and holes in its walls, sitting beside a small, calm lake. The edges of the lake bristled with reeds, and he could see birds gadding about the water's edge. Just beyond the lake, a line of sheer cliffs dropped away to the Atlantic; the waves from the ocean tore into the rocks, sending white spray flying into the air.

"It's remarkable," said Camden, pulling out his camera. If there was anything he wanted to remember from this holiday, it was this view.

Jade had already started running down the hill. "Come on! You can't explore it from back there!"

He followed, bounding over rocks and grass until the two of them reached the castle. Washington State not being known for its castles, Camden thoroughly absorbed his surroundings. He tried to imagine what it would have looked like in its prime. Perhaps the walls would have been hung with marvelous tapestries; great braziers hanging from the ceilings to provide warmth and light; a huge table in the center of the great hall where the lord could entertain others and curry favor in his stead.

After exploring the castle ruins, they strolled around the lake and up to the clifftop. From here, the two could see for miles down the magnificent coastline, and as they soaked in the view, Camden felt a deep sense of certainty. He knew this was the place, and he knew this was the time.

He turned to Jade. "This is amazing."

"You've been saying that a lot lately."

"Well, I blame you for that."

She smiled.

"Thank you for bringing me here," he continued. "I mean, to Ireland. I mean thank you for fixing me."

"I'm glad it worked."

He took her by the hands and met her eyes.

"I have a lot to thank you for actually. You're an incredible woman. Smart, funny, kind, patient. *Ha.* Everything I wish I was. And the fact is, Jade, I can't imagine my life without you in it."

Jade scoffed. "Camden, if I didn't know you better, I'd assume this was a pro-"

In one swift movement, Camden reached into the pocket of his cargo pants, pulled out a small box, and dropped to one knee. He held up the box and eased it open. A tiny diamond ring sparkled in the midday sun.

Hardly daring to breathe, his eyes connected with Jade's. Her eyes were wide, and her mouth formed a perfect 'O'.

"Will you marry me, Jade?"

Come on come on come on!

After a moment of silence that felt like a lifetime, Jade's face slowly softened, moving away from outright shock. She stared at

Camden as though having never seen him before, with a look of hope and wonderment. Tears began to stream down her cheeks.

She drew a deep breath and finally smiled. "Yes, Camden. Of course I will."

Yeeeeeeeeeeeeeeeeeeeeees!

Gently, Camden slid the ring on her finger. He stood and caressed her face for a moment, wiping away her tears, his forehead touching hers. Nearly bursting with emotion, waves of hope and happiness and exultation began to crash within him. He gathered Jade up in his arms, swung her around and kissed her firmly on the lips. When he broke away, she grabbed the side of his head and pressed her mouth to his once more. There they stood, locked together, for what seemed like hours, until Camden remembered the other item he'd carried all this way.

"Wait, wait," he said, gently letting Jade down. "I brought something else."

He walked over to his backpack, which up until this point had sat forgotten several feet away, and pulled out a bottle of champagne.

Jade placed her hands on her hips and gave him a wide smile. "So. You knew I'd say yes, did you?"

"I had a reasonably good idea."

"Any glasses to go with that champagne?"

"Nope, sorry. Couldn't risk them breaking. Gonna have to do this wino style."

The two of them cackled with laughter and Camden popped open the bottle. The cork landed somewhere in the Atlantic and the foam flooded his hands, causing Jade to double over and laugh even harder. They both took a deep swig.

Then the questions began.

"Where will we live?" asked Jade.

Camden wiped his chin clean, handed the bottle back to her and smirked. "Well, you could move in with me and Jeremy. Or..."

"My place it is, then."

"What about Chetana?"

"She can move in with Jeremy."

"*Ha!*"

Jade's next question was the one he was waiting for. "When should we get married? I'm not sure about a winter wedding, not in Washington. Perhaps next spring? We could travel to-"

"Why wait?" said Camden, cutting across her.

"Well, we want to be happy with the day, don't we?"

"I agree. We want it to be a beautiful day in a beautiful place, one that we'll remember for the rest of our lives."

She stopped and looked up at him suspiciously.

"When are you thinking?"

"Well, I don't know. How does your schedule look for tomorrow?"

"Tomorrow?!"

"Yeah, why not? I've learned all about spontaneity from you."

She cocked her head as if to say *That's not what I meant!* "But... what about friends and family?"

"They'll understand. We're in Ireland! Besides, we can have one reception in London and one in Seattle."

She folded her arms. "And where do you propose we get married on such short notice? Here, on this hill? Is a preacher about to jump out from behind a rock?"

"Well," he said, looking sheepish. "I may have already reserved the Bantry House for tomorrow."

"No..."

"And a local judge."

She smacked his arm, looking both aghast and highly amused. "You didn't!"

"I did."

"You *did* know I'd say yes!"

"I had a reasonably good idea."

"May you both live as long as you want, and never want as long as you live!"

Back at the farmhouse, Aunt O'Donovan had shifted into high gear. Jade had phoned to tell her the good news and the intrepid aunt had wasted no time. Camden had no doubt that this woman considered it the highest of honors to be asked to put on an emergency wedding.

"Now, so," said Jade's aunt. "Teddy's gone into town to do the messages and I'm after ringing the florist. 'Tis all arranged."

"Wonderful!" exclaimed Jade.

"I've invited the rest of the family and told them to spread the word."

"Already? Great."

"And," said her aunt, looking very pleased with herself, "your parents are flying in from London in the morning."

Jade embraced her. "Brilliant! Thank you so much, auntie."

"'Tis no bother. But we've still more to do. You'll be needing clothes, food, and photos."

"Let's do it!" said Camden.

"But, first things first," Aunt O'Donovan smiled, slowing the conversation. "Come inside for a cuppa tea."

CHAPTER TWENTY-THREE

"'Tis a fine day for a wedding."

Aunt O'Donovan placed another chair for the wedding guests, turned to Jade and smiled. "I told your father he'd lose you to a Yank."

"It could be worse," interrupted Uncle O'Donovan, resplendent in a grey three-piece Donegal tweed suit. "She could be marrying a Kerryman."

Aunt O'Donovan whacked him on the arm. "Oh, shtop!"

He jumped in the air, clicked his heels and hurried off to find more chairs. *"There'll be rakes of fun tonight!"*

A grand mansion from the 18th-century, the Bantry House stood as a testament to the opulence of its former residents. Because the weather forecast for the day showed sun, they decided to be wed in the sprawling gardens behind the house, atop the famous hundred stone steps overlooking Bantry Bay and the mountains of Beara.

Camden had strapped himself into a borrowed suit, the largest in the town shop. It fit his height but had clearly been designed for someone a great deal broader than he was. He would have to hope he didn't look too ridiculous in his photos, but he wasn't unduly worried. Everyone would be looking at Jade, who looked ravishing in a white dress and billowing ruffled petticoat, the edges laced with a design of ivy and wild marigolds. Jade and her second cousin had left early in the morning and driven an hour and a half each way into Cork City to pick out a dress. Jade had returned beaming.

By now, the sun had risen high in the sky – Aunt O'Donovan had referred to it as "fierce good weather", whatever that meant, and guests were beginning to arrive. Jade's cousins, Tadhg and Diarmuid, wandered over to introduce themselves to Camden. She had described them as even more "colourful" than her aunt and uncle, and he was anxious to make their acquaintance. Frankly, he thought they looked identical: slightly taller than their parents, but far leaner, with ginger hair and hazel eyes, and wearing matching blazers of blue velvet.

"How's the form?" Tadgh asked Camden.

Camden's brow furrowed. "Form? What, form?"

Diarmuid burst out laughing. "Oh, I like this one Jade. You've a joker here."

Camden simply nodded in agreement. "How are you guys?"

"Happy out," said Diarmuid.

"Now, so – let's get a picture of the happy couple," said Tadgh. The young man held up his phone. "Say, 'ball and chain'!"

He snapped several photographs, as more people decided to wander up and join the frame.

"Thank you," said Camden, after Tadgh had finished. "Actually, you know what; we couldn't find a photographer in time for the wedding. Would you mind emailing those pictures to me?"

"I will, yeah."

"Great, thank you."

As Tadgh walked away, Jade leaned in and whispered to Camden. "Don't expect to see the pictures, babe."

"But he said–"

"Over here, 'I will, yeah' usually means, 'No, I won't'."

Camden squinted. "Curious."

"Ah, never you mind," said Diarmuid. "Tadgh's about as useful as a Kerryman with a hurley. I'll send you the photos, don't you worry."

"Thanks," said Camden scratching his head. "What's a hurley?"

"Jade, have you not educated the Yank?"

"Go on," she said, "you're the expert."

He obliged. "It's a stick used in hurling, the greatest game in the world. Made from the wood of an ash tree."

She rolled her eyes. "Hurling's like a cross between hockey and baseball."

"A crude comparison," said Diarmuid.

Jade passed over his comment. "Diarmuid makes hurley's in his workshop."

Camden nodded. "Oh, cool."

"Sure, 'tis grand, but..." Diarmuid's voice trailed off. "'Tis all change. Most of the ash now is from the continent. And the quality of the wood is after seriously disimproving."

Camden turned his bulging eyes toward Jade who was grinning at him.

"See," she said, "I told you it's a real word."

Over the next two hours, Jade's family poured in. Actually, more people had responded to the last minute invitation than Camden ever imagined. He remembered Jade's words about her aunt and uncle last night: "They know half of West Cork and are related to the other half." He soon felt like he could have simply hired a camcorder, shot indiscriminately and titled the result *My Big Fat Irish Wedding*.

By four in the afternoon, Camden and the judge stood beneath a simple trellis, waiting patiently. Camden's heart was thudding in his chest, but he felt strangely calm. He'd rarely been so sure, so certain of what he wanted. Turning your wedding into a day of actual happiness, rather than one full of stress and tantrums, was a billion-dollar industry, and yet Camden and Jade had managed it at a moment's notice with the aid of just a few Irishman and a fortunate sunny late summer afternoon.

Finally, out from the grand woods of the Bantry House Estate appeared his glorious bride. She had added a veil and an ethereal wedding train, which flowed behind her on the lawn. Jade's father, a portly, shy man whom Camden had liked very much, proudly extended his arm to walk her down the aisle.

"Céad míle fáilte," began the judge, addressing the seated crowd. "One hundred thousand welcomes. We're happy to be here this day to witness the union of Camden Walker and Jade Reilly..."

Although Camden was conscious that sound was coming from the judge's mouth, at that moment, he could focus on one thing only: Jade's eyes.

Is it me, or are they greener today...

How is it even possible that this vision in a lab coat has become a vision in a wedding dress, standing in front of me today, wanting to be my wife? That beautiful mind, that strength of character, that generous nature. That hair, that smile, those lips, those-

"Camden... Camden!"

He turned to the judge, awoken from his daydream.

"Yes?"

"You may kiss the bride."

"*Should you so choose,*" whispered Jade, grinning behind her veil.

He smiled. "Thank you."

Lifting her veil, he kissed Jade with all tenderness, trying to communicate through only the touch of his lips how much he loved her, how happy he was that they were there, surrounded by so much beauty. The audience cheered, and even louder when Jade threw an arm across Camden's shoulders and returned his kiss with far greater force.

Arm in arm, the newlyweds descended the grand steps of Bantry House Gardens. Reaching the formal garden below, they rounded the fountain under a trellis of blooming wisteria. From there, a wrought iron staircase led up to the glass double doors of the majestic library, a room adorned with marble columns, a chandelier, and a grand piano. Seeing them coming, the elderly pianist rubbed her hands and began a vigorous recital of Mendelssohn's "Wedding March".

"Look!" said Jade, pointing through an open doorway into the next room.

A feast had been spread on a long elegant table, a veritable cornucopia of the best local produce: salmon, mussels, smoked meat, cheeses, preserves – and, of course, an entire keg of Murphy's stout.

An hour later back in the library, with full bellies, a first dance to The Cranberries' "Dreaming My Dreams" was impatiently observed by an audience desperate to involve themselves. Camden thought it was an unusual choice of a song considering the circumstances, but Jade insisted it was one of her favorites so Camden acquiesced.

By ten in the evening, the wedding party had migrated to the Bantry House loggia to enjoy their champagne in the night air.

"I can still remember the romance of our wedding night," said Uncle O'Donovan, wistfully. "My bride said the sexiest things to me."

Jade shifted uncomfortably. "Hmmm."

"She said, 'Did you know the ceiling needs painting?'"

Aunt O'Donovan repaid this anecdote with a well-deserved smack, failing to contain her laughter in the process. It was clear that even the most mature members of the party had indulged themselves a little.

"On that note," smiled Camden, lifting himself from his seat and draining the last of his whiskey, "we bid you all goodnight."

Leaving the cheers of family and friends behind, the happy couple reached the door to their honeymoon suite. Jade turned to Camden with a twinkle in her eye.

"Are you ready?"

Camden took a breath. "I'm not sure, Jade. This will require a serious performance."

"Don't worry, I have faith in you."

With that, Jade stormed into the bedroom, slammed the door and pretended to lock herself in. Camden kicked open the door, walked over to the bed, tore the covers off, grabbed his bride, and spun her around.

In his best John Wayne impression, Camden roared: "There'll be no locks or bolts between us, Jade Walker, except those in your mercenary little heart!"

Forcefully, he kissed his bride as she acquiesced to his embrace. Picking her up, he launched her onto the bed – which fortunately remained intact. He marched back to the door and turned to Jade, the furious intensity of his performance softening.

"I think," he said lightly, slowly easing the door shut, "I'll close it from the inside."

She nodded, beckoning him with a come-hither smile. "Good choice."

CHAPTER TWENTY-FOUR

Is there anything more peaceful than watching her sleep?

Just seeing Jade lying there, no cares, no worries, contented Camden beyond words; seeing her chest rise and fall, her lips parted just a fraction. He leaned over and brushed a strand of hair away from her face, tenderly kissing her cheek. The morning light was flooding into their suite, and he could hear the birds outside performing an early aria.

Jade slowly opened her eyes and looked around, slightly bleary. He waited for her to focus on him.

"Morning," she said.

"Good morning lassie."

He reached out and held her hand, gently playing with her wedding ring. "It looks good on you."

More awake now, she grinned, and shifted herself toward him, nestling her head into the crook of his neck. "It feels good on me."

"I'm most glad, so I am."

She sat up, resting on her elbows on the plush bed. "So, what shall we do today, husband of mine?"

"What would you like to do, wife?"

She giggled. "Husband," she said, testing out the word again. "I like the sound of that. You are my husband."

"I certainly am."

"Wife. I'm your wife."

"You certainly are. And don't you forget it."

She held up her ring finger. "A constant reminder of how lucky I am."

An hour later, they emerged from their bedroom, fully dressed and ready for breakfast. Jade had expressed a desire to see the market in town, and Camden had no objection to this, but did demand his right as husband to eat his body weight in bacon before they set out.

After successfully accomplishing this mission, the bustling market in Bantry Square was their initial destination, where Jade's first nuptial veto was used to prevent Camden from buying a donkey tethered to a lamppost. Heading deeper into town, they passed by quaint shops, old women catching up on the latest gossip, and their husbands slipping into the pub for an early drink. Camden was simply happy to follow along. Eventually, on the outskirts of town, they came to a sign that read: 'Bantry Hospital'.

"Ah!" said Jade, stopping. "There's a friend of mine who works here. He's a really good doctor. I haven't seen him in years."

"Oh. That's cool."

Jade looked up at Camden like a school girl asking her dad for ice cream money. "Do you mind if we say a quick hello? Show off my wedding ring?"

Not the first thing I wanna do on my honeymoon.

"Sure."

"Jade Reilly!"

The doctor rose to embrace her as they met him outside his office.

Dr. McDevitt was, as hard as Camden tried to avoid making the comparison, basically an Irish brother to Dr. Herman. With his full beard and long hair, he would've fit in selling hand-woven wicker baskets at the market.

The two broke apart, and Jade held up her left hand.

"Formerly Reilly, Aidan," she said.

"*Janey Mack*! I'm so happy for you. This is the lucky man, is it?"

"Yes. This is Camden."

"It's a pleasure to meet you, Camden, particularly under such favourable circumstances."

"Likewise."

"Come in, please. Sit down, make yourself comfortable."

Camden expected to be sitting in the doctor's private office, but this was an examination room on the ground floor.

"How are you finding Ireland, Camden?"

"I love it."

"Good, good."

With that, it seemed the doctor ran out of things to talk about. His eyes, which were starting to blink at a peculiar rate, shifted between the floor and Jade. His lips were pressed together so tightly as if drawn on his face with a pencil. He began contorting his hands, interlacing his fingers and squeezing them together.

This guy's got issues...

Jade reached out and grasped Camden's hand, making him jump. "Dear, listen to me. I had an ulterior motive for bringing you here."

"Hmm?" He turned toward her.

Finally, the doctor spoke. "Camden, Jade has been telling me about your condition."

"My condition?"

"Your false memories. Your not being able to sleep."

"What?" Camden turned back to Jade. "You mean you arranged this? When did you tell him all that?"

"It doesn't matter Camden," said the doctor. "It's a fascinating case. Jade would like me to perform a few tests on you, with your permission of course."

Camden stiffened. "Tests?"

"Just a couple."

Camden let out half a laugh. "What *is* this?! No. I'm on my honeymoon. Besides, I've had enough tests."

"I understand, but it won't take long."

Jade reached out and tenderly touched Camden's arm. "Dear, please. I just want you to have a checkup. You seem to have stabilised but I just want to make sure everything's okay. I didn't tell you because, well, I didn't think you'd come."

"You got that part right."

"But this is a good opportunity. Dr. McDevitt is very experienced. You have nothing to worry about."

Camden began to sweat. "You know I don't like tests, Jade. It's one thing if it's with you, but-"

"I know love, but it's for your own good, believe me."

He shuddered, but could see her logic. "How long would it take?"

"Not long," said the doctor, brightly. "Just hop up on the bed there and lie down. You're a medical man, so I've been told. I'll talk you through everything."

As Camden lay back on the bed, an older female nurse entered the room.

"Nurse O'Sullivan is here to assist," said the doctor.

She moved around to his left and opened a drawer. "Hello. It's Camden, isn't it?"

He nodded uncomfortably.

The doctor, on Camden's other side, pulled out a small flashlight. "Okay, Camden, I'd like you to turn this way, please. I'm going to examine your eyes."

As he shone the light in his eyes, Camden felt a sharp sting in his left arm and he jerked. "What was that?!"

"Just a little something to make you more comfortable," said the nurse.

Camden sat up and raised his voice. "Needles don't make me comfortable!"

The nurse smiled serenely at him. It would have been less disturbing if she'd cackled. "Don't you trust us, Camden?"

He felt his body begin to weaken. His eyelids were fighting gravity and his limbs were refusing to obey. "You... you drugged... *meee...*"

In an attempt to escape, he sluffed off the bed, but his legs merely gave way underneath him. As he collapsed on the floor, the room began to grow darker, black shadows creeping in from the corners of his vision.

"*Jaaade...*" he murmured, now barely audible, "*pleeease...*"

There was a voice, just on the edge of his hearing: "I'm sorry, Camden. I didn't have a choice."

CHAPTER TWENTY-FIVE

How long was I out for?

Camden woke with a start. His breath came in harsh, staccato bursts. His eyes darted around the room – a different hospital room to the one he'd been drugged in – and he was lying, unrestrained, at an angle in bed. A blue gown covered his flesh. In the corner of the ceiling, a television was playing some kind of American daytime talk show. The window curtains were closed, but the door was open, and feeling was beginning to return to his limbs. As he swung his legs around to the edge of the bed, however, his neck stiffened, and a searing pain stretched across the back and side of his head.

What the...

He reached to massage his neck, and with his other hand he gently felt his scalp. His fingers came across something rough and fibrous – a gauze pad. He stood up, the throbbing in his head reaching such a level he almost collapsed forward, and picked up a small mirror lying on a table at the foot of the bed. He inspected himself. An oval gauze patch, its center dotted with a small maroon stain, clung to the side of his head. The area around the patch had been shaved, and the skin looked a sickly, sallow white.

Gingerly, he peeled away the gauze. Beneath it was a thin line, a surgical incision into the side of his head that had been neatly stitched.

Brain surgery?! I come here for a holiday, stay for a honeymoon, and end up having my skull cut open?

His pulse was beginning to race, which only made the pain in his head worse. He wasn't being observed, as far as he could tell – no cameras, no guard at the door. It was time to make a break for it. Maybe he could jump out the window and sneak back to the road; run to the police station. He remembered passing it in Bantry and asking Jade what 'Garda' meant.

He ran to the window and threw open the curtains; daylight flooded into the room. However, instead of unlatching the window, climbing out onto the street, and running for help, all he could do was stare, his eyes gradually widening to maximum diameter.

Spread out far below him were pine trees, a lake, a sports stadium, a wide street dotted with large cars; people driving on the right side of the road! He knew this view well: the eighth floor of the University of Seattle Hospital – the neurology wing!

I work here! Why would they drug me and ship me back to Seattle?

A hideous thought wrapped around his brain:

Drax found out that Consurge has gone wrong. Now they're dissecting the evidence. Walter's using Jade to protect his empire. Or is she an accessory to a crime? What about Dr. Herman? Williams?

"Camden, what are you doing?"

The sudden voice caused him to almost jump out of his skin.

Camden turned. An older woman was standing in the doorway. Her voice was firm. "You need to leave your dressings on! You'll risk infection."

Camden pointed. "You! You're the nurse that drugged me."

She cocked her head. "Drugged you? I'm Nurse Sullivan... You seem disoriented, Camden." Slowly, she began walking towards him. "Why don't you lay back down and I'll bring you a fresh bandage, okay?"

Camden took a step back and raised a shaky hand at her. "You stay away from me!"

She stopped. "I don't understand. What's wrong?"

Camden nearly laughed. "You don't *understand*!? You drug me, cut me open, and you have the nerve to ask me what's wrong?"

"You seem very confused, dear."

"Where's my wife?"

"Your wife?"

"My wife!" he shouted.

"Maybe we need to change your painkillers. Perhaps you've had a reaction..." Slowly, she reached for a button around her neck. "Why don't we get the doctor to check you?"

"Don't touch that thing!" he screamed, but he was too late. The nurse had activated her alarm, and within minutes the hospital orderlies would arrive. She hurried out the door and turned left down a hallway. He needed to think fast, or he'd end up drugged again.

Rooting around in the closet, Camden found his clothes, shoes, and phone. As he tore off his hospital gown, he glanced in the mirror and felt his ribs.

I've lost twenty pounds! What have they done to me?

After dressing at breakneck speed, he slowly poked his head out the door, eyeing a medical trolley to the side of the hallway straight ahead of him. He ran as fast as he could to it, the side of his head ready to explode, and grabbed one of the shelves. Scrambling, he located a pack of what he wanted and tore it open. Thin steel scalpels rained to the floor with a high-pitched clattering as they made impact. He snatched one of them.

Passing a dozen people staring in the waiting room and clearing the doors of the clinic, he bolted down the hallway and into the fire escape stairwell, hoping that the orderlies would take either the elevator or the main staircase. He collapsed against the wall of the narrow passage, the pain in his head threatening to overwhelm him, but he knew he needed to keep moving. The orderlies weren't stupid. They would search anywhere, and nature hadn't given him an inconspicuous frame.

Right at that moment, the door behind him burst open. Camden yelled, and jumped halfway down the staircase. Spinning around, scalpel aimed at the door, he saw someone he recognized from far closer to home.

"Dr. Herman!"

"Camden." The doctor was followed into the small staircase by a heavily-built orderly who looked stern. By contrast, however, the doctor's face was serene, and he gently reached out a hand toward Camden, beckoning him. "You should rest. It's not good for your recovery, all this activity."

Camden kept the scalpel raised in the air. "You're in on this too?"

"What am I meant to be in on, Camden?" asked the doctor in the same calm tone.

Camden began backing further away down the staircase. "I don't understand."

"That's why I'm here, Camden. We're treating you."

Nurse Sullivan appeared behind the doctor with a syringe in her hand.

Camden took another step back. "What's going on? Who is she?"

He heard the doctor mutter under his breath, "I was afraid this would happen... That's Nurse Sullivan, Camden. Don't you remember? She was hired the day you arrived. She's been looking after you since you've been here."

"What's in the needle?"

"Just something to make you more comfortable."

"I told her before, I don't need to be more comfortable!"

Another orderly pushed open the door below him, waiting at the base of the stairs. He was trapped.

Camden tried to block out the pain, but could only close his eyes against it. His legs shuddered.

"I think," said Herman, taking a few tentative steps towards him, "that we should go back to your room, and you can just lie down for a bit. I can answer all your questions there."

Camden felt a line of fury whip through him. "Oh, I don't think so. Fool me once..."

He raised the scalpel up and pressed it against his neck. The three men in the stairwell with him all stopped dead. An eerie stillness settled on the scene.

Herman kept the peaceful look on his face, but his eyes betrayed his sudden panic. "Camden, are you sure you know what you want to do?"

Turning away, Camden ran towards the lower door, blade still pressed flat against his neck. He heard Herman shout for the orderly to let him past, and the burly man pressed himself against the wall as Camden shouldered through the door and into the corridor beyond.

Thirty feet separated him from the elevator. Two security guards stood between it and him.

"Get out of my way!" he screamed at the two men. "Get out of my way, or I'll slice my jugular right here and I'll die before you can touch me."

"Let him past! Let him past!" Herman and the two orderlies had followed him into the corridor. "He's not a risk to anyone but himself!"

Camden sprinted past the two guards, who recoiled from him as though he were infectious. Barreling into the elevator, he slammed the lobby button repeatedly, the doors closing on the concerned face of Herman.

The elevator made Camden feel sick, trapped in an airless aluminum box, watching the numbers tick down.

What did I do to deserve this?

Arriving at the first floor, he strode through the doors and walked as quickly as possible for the exit.

A voice again shouted from behind him. "Camden, stop running! You'll hurt yourself!"

As he'd expected, Herman and the guards had taken another elevator and were right behind him. He tucked the scalpel into his back pocket and accelerated to a run, bursting through the front door of the hospital and knocking a number of visitors aside. The fresh air caused a spike of adrenalin, and Camden hurdled over a fence and into the busy road, dodging cars and bicycles. His head was screaming like an air-raid siren. He desperately needed to find somewhere to take shelter and, if necessary, pass out until the pain stopped.

Making it safely to the other side of the road, he chanced a glance over his shoulder. Undeterred, the orderlies were likewise weaving between the traffic in pursuit. Camden, still running, took a moment to assess his options. The arboretum would provide good cover, he knew, so he veered into it, feet crunching on the gravel path, and located a good tree. The last of his adrenaline gave him the boost he needed to grasp the first branch and haul himself up, and he was soon concealed by the evergreen's boughs.

Moments later, while still attempting to catch his breath, Camden noticed movement through the branches below.

"He could've gone anywhere," said one of the orderlies.

"We'll probably get a call in ten minutes, saying he's collapsed in the street and we need to send an ambulance," was the response from the other.

That bad, huh?

Approaching Camden's tree, one of the orderlies slowed his pace while the other carried on. Camden held his breath. Every muscle in his body was frozen except for his heart, which was beating on overdrive. The man stopped, thoroughly surveying his surroundings. Camden was sure the man was about to look up and that would be it. He'd be exposed; dragged back to the hospital to be prodded and tested and who knows what.

Just then, the other orderly called to him. "Let's try over here."

Camden breathed out.

He decided to stay in the tree until he was confident the orderlies were gone. He turned on his cell phone and checked the time – 8:18 a.m., Wednesday, September 22.

Abducted from Bantry Hospital on Sunday, which means... They've been carrying out tests on me for at least three days!

As he waited in the tree, Camden realized his clothes were completely drenched. Sweat was dripping into his eyes. By now, it had been ten minutes, but his heart rate told him he was still running from the orderlies.

That can't be good.

He needed answers, and he knew where to begin.

CHAPTER TWENTY-SIX

"Camden!"

Jade nearly screamed as she opened her apartment door. Her appearance caught Camden off guard: red eyes, mascara running down her cheeks, a tissue in her hand. For a moment, he hesitated, then forced his way in and slammed the door behind him.

He raised his stolen scalpel to her face. "You scream or make one wrong move and I swear you'll have a scar to show your grandkids. Understand?"

Jade froze. "Camden, what are you doing?"

"Go on," he motioned with the blade, "sit down."

She obeyed.

"I didn't wanna have to do this," said Camden, "but I don't know which side you're on."

"Side? What do you mean?"

"Where's your phone? Gimme your phone!"

"It's on the counter," she said, pointing.

He turned, blade still pointed her direction and put the phone in his pocket.

Jade wiped the tears from her eyes. "Camden – I just got off the phone with the hospital. They told me you went berserk and ran out."

"I *bet* they did."

"What's that supposed to mean?"

"It's time to level with me, Jade. This has gone too far."

"What's gone too far?"

"Stop it! *Stop it!* Just tell me why you did it. Why would you let them drug me? Did Walter promise you a raise?"

"What are you talking about?"

He leaned over and pointed at the scar on the side of his head. It was still throbbing, like he'd been struck with an iron bar. "Look at this! I suppose you don't know anything about this, either."

"That was part of the tests, love."

His eyes widened. "When I agreed to tests, I thought it would be a blood sample or something. Not drilling into my skull! What kind of tests are they? And why couldn't they wait until we got back from Ireland?"

"Ireland? Oh no..."

He waved the scalpel in the air. "Now is the time," he continued, getting angrier by the moment, "for you to explain *exactly* what's going on. Who's orchestrating this? Did Drax find out there's a glitch with Consurge? Did you ever consider that maybe I would've come back of my own free will and *agree* to be tested?"

"Ca-Camden," said Jade, her lip quivering, "please calm down. You're scaring me."

"How long have we been back anyways?"

"Back?"

"From Ireland!"

"You think... You think we went to Ireland?"

A cold silence descended. He stepped back. Confusion, pain, exhaustion; all of them were fighting for dominance. His legs began to shake.

"Wait a minute." His eyes darted around the room. "You're telling me that..."

Camden reached out and grabbed her hand.

"Where's your ring?"

"My ring? What ring?"

Camden's breathing became heavy. He shook his head. "No. No, don't tell me that."

"Camden, please sit down."

"I don't want to sit down."

"You're going to hyperventilate."

"We never went to Ireland?"

"No."

"We're not married?"

"Married?" Jade's face was a picture of tear-strewn bewilderment. "No, love."

"I'm still not sleeping?"

She shook her head.

Nausea gripped his abdomen, and he sunk to his knees, dropping the scalpel to the floor. He grabbed his head with both hands; it felt as though it was about to explode.

"The entire *trip* was a false memory?"

"And you were never drugged against your will, believe me."

He raised his head. "But how did I end up in the hospital?"

"Just sit down, babe. I'll get you something to drink. And some painkillers. Your head must be killing you by now. I'll get you a gauze pad as well."

He slowly heaved his bulk onto the couch and Jade swiftly confiscated the scalpel. She handed him some ibuprofen and a glass of water, waited for him to drink it, and slid her arms around him, hugging him tightly.

After a moment, she pulled away and gently tended to his wound.

"I know this must be a terrible realisation," she said, "but we need to approach this in a methodical manner." She pulled a tissue from her pocket and blew her nose loudly. "What's the last thing you remember?"

He raised his eyebrows at her and gave an exhausted look. She put her forehead to his shoulder. She clarified. "I mean, the last thing here – here in Seattle."

"Well, the airport, I suppose."

"Right, of course. Okay, well let's work back from there. When was that?"

"Tuesday, September... fourteenth."

"Okay, just over a week ago. Keep going. Before that?"

"We drove to the airport. Before that, we packed our bags. Before that..." He shook his head. How could it be that his memory was becoming fuzzy at this point? "I think we booked our tickets the night before. We got a decent price, I remember that. Before that, you came over to my apartment and suggested we go to Ireland. Before that-"

"Wait." Jade cut him off. "I did come over to your apartment that night. I said something about you being stressed out and that you needed to rest. Do you remember that?"

"Yeah. I asked you what you had in mind and you said let's go to Ireland."

The look in her eyes said it all.

He sighed. "But, you probably never said that... did you?"

She shook her head. "When you first told me about your false memories, we agreed to give it a fortnight, didn't we?"

"I remember."

"Love, when things hadn't improved after a week, I suggested we go to the *hospital* together to figure out what was going on."

He lowered his eyes. "I see."

"Camden. They've been running tests on you for a week. They've looked after you very well. Dr. Herman insisted on caring for you himself. I mean, I visited you of course. We talked about what we would do once you recovered from the surgery. You seemed... pretty positive."

"Surgery? You mean this hole in my head?"

"It was one of the tests."

"What did they find out? Why am I not sleeping?"

Jade hesitated. Tears started rolling down her cheeks again.

"You're making me nervous, Jade."

"They only found out last night..."

"Found out what? *Tell me.*"

"They say you have some form of sFI..."

Camden closed his eyes, racking his memory. But there was nothing. "I don't know sFI. I can't remember ever reading about it."

Jade was now shuddering as she tried to control her sobs. It shocked Camden to his core. Jade was the strongest, most confident, most in-control person he'd ever met. She had an answer to every question, a solution to every problem, and would trust only herself to implement them. To see her now, racked with misery, hopelessly tripping over her words, trying to piece together the most basic sentences, gave him a deep, pitiless feeling of dread.

"It stands for... sporadic fatal insomnia."

"Did you say fatal?"

"Yes. It's rare. Extremely rare. I'm not surprised you've never come across it." Jade walked slowly to the kitchen and refilled his glass. "Even Dr. Herman had never dealt with it directly. He had to call a friend of his in Austria who had a patient with it a few years ago. It's a prion disease of the brain."

She emerged from the kitchen and handed him the glass. He drained it, but the water did nothing for the bruised feeling in his throat.

"Prion disease," he said. "We touched on those once or twice."

She dabbed at her eyes with a tissue. "Let me explain. Sporadic fatal insomnia is related to fatal familial insomnia – FFI. Only a few families in the *world* have recognised cases. It's been around for hundreds of years, but it was only identified in the mid-seventies. Before that, people with FFI were thought to be insane."

"Wonderful."

"It's inherited from one or both parents. But *sporadic* fatal insomnia is just that: a sporadic, random mutation leading to the same outcome."

Camden forced the next question from his mouth. "Which is?"

Jade looked to be having just as much trouble getting the words out as he did. "I-increasingly severe insomnia until... well, it leads to a complete inability to sleep. The brain can't relax at all while the patient is awake. They'll go for months without sleeping. There are only a few recorded cases in the world. And Dr. Herman said your case appears different than any of them."

"Different? How?"

"Well, for one thing, you're still sleeping fifteen minutes every day. People with FFI don't sleep at all."

Camden gave an almighty groan and buried his head in his hands. "Consurge."

She paused. "I bet you wish you'd never met me."

"But you did an MRI on me. Everything was fine!"

"It's a disease that's difficult to identify on a brain scan. That's why your MRI appeared normal. It was only when they did the brain biopsy that it turned up."

"How can they tell from the brain tissue that it's sFI?"

"There's, um..." Jade tried to get herself under control. She was breathing quickly and looked even more distressed than he did. "I need to talk you through it. Basically, there are certain proteins in the brain called cellular prion proteins. What they do exactly is... is unclear, but they're thought to play a protective role in cells. Anyway" – she stood up and began pacing around the room, not looking at him – "there's a gene that's responsible for providing the instructions for making that protein. It's called the PRNP gene, and it... Well, when you have either FFI or sFI, the gene mutates. It causes the protein to mis-fold. Once they mis-fold, the healthy proteins convert to an abnormal prion form. The- the process happens exponentially and the result is..." She took a deep breath. "Countless microscopic holes in the brain."

The two of them stared at each other for a moment: Jade's face a frenzy of panicked emotions; Camden's blank and hopeless.

"So my brain's full of holes?"

Jade nodded, her arms crossed and her chin tucked into her chest.

"Does this explain the false memories?" he asked.

"I think so. Do you remember I told you about the stimulation of the dopaminergic pathways in the brain during the stage two trials?"

"Yes."

"When those pathways are stimulated, the frequency and vividness of dreams increases. It's my guess that for someone on Consurge, dreams are still being produced by the brain – while you're *awake*. But those dreams never manifest themselves because you're only asleep for fifteen minutes of the day, not long enough to reach REM sleep.

"Now – Dr. Herman said there's extensive damage, not only to your thalamus but to your PTO – the Parieto-Occipito-Temporal junction."

Camden muttered to himself: "An area at the back of the brain thought to be involved in the generation of dreams." He could recite the definition as easily as throwing a ball into the air and catching it again.

"Good, good." Jade continued awkwardly, not expecting to have been interrupted: "It's where perceptions are converted into abstract thoughts and memories. If it's damaged, then... the result can be an inability to distinguish dreams from reality while you're awake. When the damage to your PTO became severe enough, I think the dreams produced by your brain found an outlet: your consciousness."

She sighed deeply. "Some dreams can be pleasant, of course, but others, like in your case, seem to be bringing your fears to life."

Camden swallowed. "You mean nightmares."

He took a moment to chew this over. "But how come I never remember 'waking up' from those dreams?"

"I don't know. Maybe your actual memories are only replaced during a Drax Power Nap."

He sighed, unsatisfied with the answer. "Are there other symptoms with sFI, other than not sleeping?"

Jade sat down and reached for the medical reference book that was open on the coffee table. "I was reviewing it last night after I got the phone call from the hospital. The symptoms are varied, it's true, but they include panic attacks, paranoia, phobias, rapid loss of weight, profuse sweating, neck stiffness, loss of power to distinguish between reality and dreams, and elevation of blood pressure and heart rate. Sound familiar?"

"Explains why I can see every one of my ribs now."

Jade hurried on. "Normally the symptoms would occur over a space of several months, but yours are advancing faster. Everything's been over the past few weeks. At this kind of accelerated rate..."

She fell silent. Camden groaned inwardly.

I won't ask 'if' there's a cure...

"How is it cured?" he eventually said.

Jade looked around wildly, as though the answer would be painted on the walls. But she didn't need to reply. Camden could see the answer in her eyes, her body language, the sharpness of her breathing.

He returned his gaze to the floor. "How long do I have?"

"It's... it's hard to know. It's different for everyone. People can live for seven to eighteen months after the onset of the disease. But... your situation is different. Doctors say you have a *form* of sFI. Everything's happening faster for you."

"So I could be dead in a few days?"

Jade was silent.

Camden stood up and began to pace back and forth, clenching and unclenching his fists. After a few seconds, he rounded on Jade, pointing his finger in her face.

"Did you know this could happen? Did you *suppress* it?"

She looked up at him, eyes wide with shock. "No! No, of course not. I had no idea-"

"But you did make sure that your *revolutionary* drug was rushed through testing and flung out into the world!" He felt the anger in himself building with every word, railing against his own hopeless situation.

"Believe me, I'm sorry, Camden. But please understand: this is the last two years of my *life* we're talking about. All that work – all in good faith! – to find out I've helped create something that could kill people..."

He slumped on the couch. The two of them sat there for what seemed like hours. Despite the pain and the fear, he could feel himself softening, piece by tiny piece. He believed her.

"Well," he said, eventually, "we all want to believe we're doing the right thing."

Jade nodded, a hopeful smile breaking through the layer of tears on her face.

"Did Herman say anything else?" he asked.

"Yes, actually." She sat up straight. "They said that based on the rate of decay of your brain tissue, they estimate that the onset of the disease occurred at the beginning of January. You'd been on Consurge for about two months by then. My guess is that at that point, Consurge must have triggered the sFI somehow. The microscopic holes in your brain increased during the eight months after that and became so bad that by the end of August you began having false memories."

"But why two months? What triggered it then?"

"I don't know. Maybe Consurge has a cumulative effect in the system."

A sickening realization suddenly struck Camden. "How many people are on Consurge now?"

"Over thirteen million."

"It went on sale July twenty-ninth, right?"

"Right."

"That means that if Consurge causes sFI after two months, it'll be triggered in other people by..."

"I know," she said. "The end of the month."

"That's days from now!"

Jade nodded.

"We've gotta get people off Consurge!" he exclaimed.

"Our problem," she began, "is that our only other case studies will be when the early adopters, the people who've been taking it since the July twenty-ninth, start showing your kind of symptoms. That won't be for months, and it'll be hundreds of thousands of people. By that point, it'll be too late. All of those people will die."

"Look, there's got to be something we can do. What did Herman, or any of his colleagues, say about the role of Consurge in my diagnosis?"

Jade sighed and shook her head. "The night we went into hospital, you made me swear that I wouldn't tell the doctors you'd been on Consurge until a diagnosis was made. You didn't want me to lose my job. I thought it was noble, at the time... I was coming to the hospital today to talk to you about it."

What a time to be chivalrous...

"Then we need to tell Walter," he said.

"I know. But I can hear him now: he'll want more proof. He'll say that sFI is a *random* mutation, maybe you were just really unlucky. He'll say, 'You present one problematic case to me and you expect me to recall millions of dollars' worth of Consurge?' And then he'll fire me. And his lawyers will crucify me."

Camden gritted his teeth hard. It was one thing to not be able to motivate himself to remember lectures without medical help, or to join the basketball team because of the wearying practice sessions, but the lives of literally millions of people were suddenly depending on him. If this wasn't a time to dig deep and come up with an idea, when was?

"What if there *was* more proof?" he blurted.

"What proof?"

"What if there wasn't just one problematic case – me?"

"What do you mean? You're the only one who's been on Consurge this long."

Camden shook his head, a glint of newfound conviction in his eyes. "Maybe I'm *not* the only one..."

CHAPTER TWENTY-SEVEN

"How much Consurge did these guys steal?"

Jade stared at the floor, rubbing her temples. Camden had related his less than pleasant experiences with the two rough-looking types at the Drax orientation; in particular, how they'd stuffed their backpacks with enough Consurge to start a chain of pharmacies.

He shook his head. "I don't know. But enough to last them for months, that's for sure. I wanted to stop them, but, well, they threatened me and I chickened out."

"Stupid, stupid, stupid..." Jade slapped the arm of the couch in deep frustration, stood up and began pacing around the room.

"I'm sorry, Jade. They were big guys!"

"No, no, I don't mean you. I *told* Walter the tours were a bad idea..."

She shuddered with irritation, but then calmed. She took a hair clip from her pocket and pinned her hair back; she massaged the back of her neck for a moment and looked him in the eyes. "So in theory, they could still be on Consurge."

"Right."

"And they could be having the same symptoms as you."

"Exactly."

Jade paused and rested a finger on his chest. "Wait a minute. Camden, are you sure this really happened? Are you *sure* this isn't another false memory?"

Camden sighed. "No. I can't be sure. At this point, I'm questioning everything... But I think there's a way to find out."

Jade was clearly following his train of thought. "Pictures from the drug trial orientation."

"Exactly. If I saw their faces, I'm sure I'd recognize them... if in fact it actually happened."

Without another word, Jade rushed to her desk, opened her laptop and began furiously typing.

"You were the ten a.m. slot on the Saturday, right?"

"Right."

She turned her head slightly his direction, a small smile creeping through the sadness in her face. "I remember it well..."

Camden pulled up a chair and looked on as she began scrolling through pictures of the fifty test subjects from that slot.

James Anderson, no... Gene Mackay, no... Ed Park, no... Steven Trimble, no...

He could feel the sweat building. Maybe he *had* imagined it.

Maybe none of this is even happening right now. Maybe at this exact moment, a false memory is shredding my consciousness. Maybe I'm in a medically-induced coma, dreaming wildly while my body is strapped to a hospital bed, and this is how it'll be until they pull the plug...

"Stop!" he said, pointing at the screen.

"Tony Underwood?"

Camden looked closer. *Unkempt stubble, nose ring.* "That's one of them. I'm positive."

"Thirty-two years old, unmarried, works at a paper factory. Fine. Let's give him a ring."

She stabbed the number into her phone, placing it on speaker. Finally, a shaky voice answered. "H-hello?"

"Hello, is this Tony Underwood?" said Jade, shifting to her clientele voice.

"*Who is it?*" the voice shot back.

"Hi there. This is Drax Pharmaceuticals. Thank you for answering the call. Umm, we're a conducting follow-up for those who were involved with the stage three clinical trial for Consurge earlier this year."

"I didn't steal any Consurge!"

Jade paused, blinked, and continued. "Ah, I didn't say anything about stealing anything, Mr. Underwood."

"Good, 'cause I didn't."

"We're calling to see how you've been since the trial."

They heard the sound of loud, labored breathing. "Umm, uh, fine. Yeah, just f-fine."

"May I ask, sir, did you resume taking Consurge after it became available by prescription?"

"Look, lady, you can't proove *anything*!" The voice became increasingly agitated. "I know you got my address, but if you even think about coming oover here – even with a SWAT team – it'll be the laast thing you ever do. The whole place is secuured. Guns, grenades, booby traps-"

"Mr. Underwood!" said Jade, trying to rescue the conversation. "Believe me, sir, we have no intention of coming to your house."

"Very wise, very wise, very wise..."

"Sir, our records show that you work in a paper factory. Would you say that your time on Consurge had a positive effect on your job?"

"My job?" A burst of laughter came squawking from the phone, sounding like the harsh buzz of static. "Those jerks! They f-fired me a week ago. They *never* appreeciated me."

"Why were you fired, if you don't mind me asking?" continued Jade, her voice smooth.

"*Hmph.* They told me I was 'unsstable'. I tried to warn them. But did they listen? Oooh, no."

"Warn them of what?"

The voice sped up. "I saw it with my own eyes! Creatures – they slithered into the faactory. They didn't see me 'cause I hid. They implaanted their eggs into the *toilet paper*!"

"Is that right?"

"Consider yourself waarned, lady. Unless you want aliens growing inside you where the sun don't shine, *stop using toilet paper*!"

Jade blew out through her cheeks. "I see... Well, thank you for the warning. Umm, Mr. Underwood, how are your sleep patterns now?"

"Sleep?" His laughter grew until it changed to a loud, guttural cough, and the call went dead.

Jade rolled her eyes and turned to Camden. "Well, I think we can safely say he never stopped taking Consurge."

"I'd take that bet."

"I think it's also safe to say he's a sci-fi enthusiast. From the sounds of it, he hasn't figured out he's having false memories yet. And his paranoia sounds even worse than yours."

"Thanks…"

"Come on, let's look for the other guy."

Camden refocused on the screen.

Peter Vaughan, no… Jacob Wilson, no… Michael Yang…

"That's him!"

"Thirty-six years old, also unmarried, works at a grocery store."

Again, Jade dialed the number, and again, they waited. After nearly a minute of fruitless ringing, Jade was about the cancel the call when an older-sounding woman answered the phone.

"Hello?"

"Ah, hello, ma'am," said Jade, putting on a clear, upbeat voice. "I'm looking to speak with Michael Yang. I'm, uh, I'm an old friend."

They heard the sound of sobs from the other end of the line. Jade and Camden exchanged a worried glance.

"Are you okay, ma'am?"

"I'm sorry" – the sound came of someone blowing their nose – "but Michael passed away two days ago."

Jade's eyes widened. "He passed away? Oh, I… To whom am I speaking, please?"

"This is his mother."

Jade paused for a second to gather her wits. "I'm so sorry, ma'am. That's terrible. My name's Amy, I- I knew your son. Do you mind if I ask what happened?"

"I don't really know. The last time I saw him was about two weeks ago. He seemed different."

"Okay, I see. In what way, different?"

"Like he was under pressure." The voice was heavy with misery, and Jade looked pained at having to pursue her questions. "His friends told me he'd been acting strange for a while – anxious, paranoid even. They said he'd been full of weird stories."

"Stories? Stories about what?"

"They didn't say. One of his friends couldn't get in contact with him so he broke down the door of his apartment and found him on the kitchen floor. There was a bottle of pills in his hand and he looked like he hadn't eaten in days."

Jade glanced at Camden. "Ma'am, do you know what the pills were?"

"Oh, it wasn't drugs if that's what you're thinking. My Michael was a good boy. It was just those anti-sleep pills everyone's on nowadays."

Camden made a cutting motion to Jade: *call it quits.*

"I'm very sorry for your loss. I truly am."

"You're very kind. Thank you."

"Goodbye."

"Goodbye."

Jade lowered the phone and placed her forehead on the desk. "I killed that man, Camden," she said, her voice muffled. "He's dead because of me."

Camden rested his hand on her shoulder. "You didn't know this would happen."

"Maybe not," Jade pulled her head up and took a deep breath, "but I've got to fix this before it turns into the worst medical disaster in history. We need to talk to Walter right now."

"At least we've got something resembling evidence."

"I just hope it's enough. Walter's a proud man."

Camden's eyes dropped to the floor. "He'll fire you, won't he?"

She nodded her head while her eyes shifted back to the laptop. "And that's why I need to do this." She opened the desk drawer and pulled out a portable hard drive.

"Do what?"

She plugged it into her laptop. "Copy the entire Drax database. After I'm fired I won't have online access to it. You never know, we might be able to use something in it to our advantage. Even if it's just sticking it on the internet and seeing what happens."

"Good thinking."

Jade stood up, walked into her bedroom and came back holding a baseball cap. She tossed it into his hands.

"Put this on," she said, pointing at the wound on his head. "We can't have you wandering around Seattle looking like you just escaped from hospital."

"Mariners?" he said, looking at the cap.

She smiled. "When in Rome."

When the files finished transferring, Jade closed the laptop and pulled her raincoat from the rack.

"What time is it?" she asked.

"Almost noon."

She grabbed her purse. "Come on. We don't have much time."

CHAPTER TWENTY-EIGHT

"Jade! I thought you were taking the week off."

Camden and Jade had barely spoken to each other in the cab to Drax headquarters. Jade's mouth was set to a firm line, and her brow was knitted tight. They had stepped into the elevator bound for the top floor when Jade reached out and, without looking at him, squeezed Camden's hand tightly. The briefest of moments passed. She then let go and continued to look unblinkingly at the flashing lights, ticking off each floor as they went. Finally, the elevator had pushed them out into the Drax atrium.

"Hello Chetana. Camden and I have come to speak to Walter."

Chetana stood up. "Is everything alright? You look like you've seen a ghost."

Jade gave a mirthless chuckle. "Well, perhaps. Listen, Chetta," Jade leaned over the desk, lowering her voice. "Do you trust me?"

She returned a look of wide-eyed surprise. "Of course. Completely."

"Our conversation with Walter isn't likely to go well. I may need you to be my eyes and ears in the office for a while."

"You don't mean..."

Jade gave a sharp nod. "Would you do that for us?"

Chetana looked around uneasily, clearly uncomfortable at this turn of events. "I mean, yes, sure. I'll do what I can. Do you mind telling me-"

"Thank you," said Jade swiftly, speaking over Chetana's attempted curiosity. "I'll fill you in later, okay?" Chetana nodded as Jade touched her arm.

"Is Walter with anyone now?" asked Jade.

"No, you can go right in."

They left behind a clearly alarmed Chetana and marched through the double doors leading into Walter's office. In spite of everything, Camden had to take a moment to admire it. The office was almost as impressive as the Drax auditorium. A vaulted glass ceiling curved over their heads, and a grand arched window framed a sprawling view of the city behind his desk. The imposing wooden furniture looked exotic: heavy carved pieces from Asia sporting intricate patterns in bright threads on the upholstery; antique statues and artifacts from Africa and the Middle East displayed by the walls. Camden wasn't sure if the office was meant to be inspiring or imposing.

The man himself was sitting at his desk, rattling away in fluent Japanese to someone on his laptop, and drumming his fingers on the desktop. When he noticed Jade, he briefly looked up and motioned them forward.

The pair seated themselves on a long sofa, its arms of dark wood carved with animal shapes. Jade tapped her foot, displaying her nerves.

When the call ended, Walter laughed, sighed, and turned his attention to them. He gave Jade a tired look. "Jade, my love. It's good to see you. Maybe you could make more headway than I've managed. I tell them that the price of Consurge is not negotiable. This isn't a fish market in Tokyo. *We're* the sole supplier, *we* set the price."

Camden, looking around the vast room, noticed a picture on the wall next to him. It was a college graduation photo from the Class of 1982, University of Seattle. He squinted, sure that he recognized one of the faces in the front row.

Walter rose, walked from his desk, and took a seat in a large armchair across from them. He placed his elbows on the armrests and interlocked his fingers. "What do you think, Jade?"

He wore a wide smile and was even better-looking in the flesh than on television. Despite his age, his hair was still thick and dark, the skin around his eyes taut, his jawline well-defined. Camden knew the work of a good plastic surgeon when he saw it.

"I think," said Jade, "that you warn them about the risks of falling behind in a competitive global marketplace." Her tone was formal, her words precise. Camden could see what she was trying to do: put Walter in the frame of mind to make tough decisions, and think about the future. "Remind them that they're where they are now because of shrewd investment. And then, withhold the supply. Take a small loss now for a guaranteed gain in the future."

Walter raised his eyebrows and smiled. "That's certainly a sound option. It's always best to put the future first. I'll bear it in mind for when I call them again. Now," he leaned forward in his seat, "is this the Camden I've heard so much about?"

Camden leaned forward to shake his hand awkwardly. Walter gave him an appraising look, before turning back to Jade.

"What brings you into the office on your week off?"

"I was hoping the two of us" – Jade motioned to herself and Camden – "could talk to you."

Walter chuckled. "Oh? Sounds serious. Well, I'm all ears. What's on your mind, Jade?"

"Walter," said Jade, her face not betraying an iota of emotion, "there's a problem with Consurge."

A pause.

"A problem? What problem?" asked Walter, tilting his head, curious.

She started at the beginning. The two men who stole Consurge. The extra Consurge she gave to Camden. The false memories and ensuing psychiatric damage. Camden's inability to sleep after discontinuing the drug. The sFI diagnosis from the hospital. The two other men: one psychotic, one dead.

Walter began to tap his finger on the armrest and fidget with his goatee as Jade talked. The more she enumerated the complications, the more Camden could see the smugness receding from his face. In a moment of surreal humor, Camden noticed the motivational poster behind Walter's desk: 'Be like a duck. Calm on the surface, but always paddling like the dickens underneath.' Walter appeared to be putting this into practice – his face was still a study in surprised curiosity – but Camden could see the panic building in his eyes, and the minute evidence of moisture collecting on his temple.

Finally, Jade arrived at her conclusion. "There's no other choice, Walter. There's only one option ahead of us: we need to alert the public, we need to stop production of Consurge and recall everything that's already been shipped. If we do this, perhaps the company will survive. If we don't, we'll be held responsible for one of the greatest acts of medical malpractice in history."

Walter sat back in his chair, shifting his position a few times. He inspected his fingernails for a moment. Finally, he spoke.

"No. No." He shook his head brusquely, as though all Jade had done was ask him for a raise. "A recall?" He chuckled. "You must be joking."

Jade kept her face icily calm. "I don't think this is something about which to joke. None of us want a Vioxx scandal on our hands."

"Whoa, whoa!" Walter pointed a stern finger at Jade; Camden had a sudden overwhelming urge to grab the offending digit and break it. "Let's not get carried away. Vioxx – that's a dirty word in these circles."

"Vioxx led to *thousands* dead," Jade continued, determined to say her piece. "You, and everything you've built would be responsible for the deaths of *millions*. Could you live with that?"

Walter stretched his neck, rolling his head from side to side.

"Jade," he said, his head lolling awkwardly to the side, "we need to think about this carefully. Calmly. Rationally."

She took a deep breath. "I would maintain that is precisely what we are currently doing. I understand it's a lot for you to take in all at once-"

"First of all," said Walter loudly, cutting her off, "I'm sorry your boyfriend here has sFI. I really am. But you can't prove it was triggered by *Consurge*. sFI is a random mutation. I don't need to define *random* to you."

"Walter, you're in denia-"

"*Secondly*, I think your methodology is highly questionable. Do you have anything concrete, any specific link between this company's product and any of the medical claims you're making?"

Jade raised her volume to match his, leaning forward, her anger beginning to escape. "The two men who stole Consurge experienced the same symptoms as Camden! One of them is dead! What are the chances of that?"

"A tenuous connection!" Walter shot back, his chest rising and falling with fury and tension. "Can you prove they were taking Consurge until now? Two drug dealers, by the description of them. I'm sure they ingested any number of substances that could have led to psychosis, or death. I'll put money on them just being another overdose. A *statistic*."

The three of them all stood at the same time. Camden stepped forward; he towered over Walter, though this didn't seem to bother the older man in the slightest.

"It's true," said Jade. "This is a one-week investigation by two people on a single case subject. But Walter, where does the *evidence* point you? What is the *reasonable* conclusion?"

"You want to talk about reasonable? How about illegally giving a trial drug to your boyfriend?"

Camden swiftly interrupted. "That was my fault. I pressured her."

"And completely irrelevant," said Jade harshly, stepping nose-to-nose with Walter. "You should praise me for doing that, Walter. It might be the only thing keeping you from spending the rest of your life in custody – following bankruptcy, of course!"

"*I don't care for your opinions,*" Walter spat. He marched to his desk and pressed a small button. "You're a thief. And you're disloyal. I don't want to see your face in this building again."

"*Yes, sir?*" Chetana's voice emanated from a grille next to Walter's hand.

"Chetana, please ask Bruno and Zane to come to my office."

"*Right away, sir.*"

The doors opened and two large security guards entered the room. One look told Camden that they'd clearly been recruited from the ranks of failed professional wrestlers. Both could look Camden dead in the eye but were three times his width.

"Clean out your desk, Jade. The boys will make sure you don't steal anything else from my company."

Jade made a final attempt. "What are you going to do, Walter? What's your plan? You're sitting on a time bomb. You can't claim you weren't forewarned."

Walter didn't look at her. "There's nothing in what you say. You're emotionally devastated because of your boyfriend's diagnosis and you're lashing out. It's familiar behavior to anyone who knows the human mind."

"That's rubbish, and you know it!" snarled Jade, as she was pulled toward the door.

The security guards dragged them out the office and into the lobby. Chetana clearly looked uncomfortable. One of the guards maintained a firm grip on Camden's arm while the other followed Jade to her desk. A few minutes later, she returned with a box full of her possessions. The guards escorted them down the elevator and out of the building.

Across the street in Westlake Plaza, Jade tossed her box on the bench and settled herself next to it, burying her head in her hands. "Walter's hubris is off the scale!"

"You did what you could," said Camden.

Jade pulled out her phone and dialed.

"Chetta," she said, quickly. "Listen – *listen* – I need you to keep me informed of every move Walter makes. His phone calls, emails, visitors, updates to his schedule. *Anything.* Can you do that for me...? Great, thanks. Don't worry, I know I owe you an explanation. Can you come by Camden's apartment tonight, say around six o'clock? Perfect. See you then."

Camden slowly sat down next to her. "What do we do now?"

He could see the determination building in her eyes. "Now we formulate a game plan. This is a race now. We have to sound the alarm."

"How do we do that?"

"We can't go through the proper channels, that's for sure. An FDA recall would take months."

"We've got days, not months."

"I know. But Walter wasn't wrong – right now, the only medical evidence we have is you, and Drax's lawyers will make the same arguments as Walter did in there. They'll throw in every roadblock they can. Until people start dying. We have to think outside the box."

An idea flashed in Camden's mind. Perhaps there was someone who might be able to help them. Someone with a little extra insight. With, perhaps, a back door.

"Professor Williams," he said, calmly.

"What?" replied Jade. "What's your lecturer got to do with anything?"

"He was the one who introduced me to Consurge in the first place," said Camden quickly. He knew Jade would have questions, but he didn't have time right now to answer all of them. "He's experienced and super-connected."

Jade sighed. "Fine. You go see the professor. Tell me what he says. I'll go back to my apartment and see what I can dig out of the Drax database. Maybe there's something there we can use. Let's meet at your place at six."

CHAPTER TWENTY-NINE

'This door is alarmed. What startled it?'

Camden gave a rueful smile, seeing the familiar sign on Professor Williams' office door. The door was open as usual; Williams, provided he'd smoked the required thirty cigarettes by midday, was always willing to sit, chat and encourage any students who poked their heads in. His name on the office door was a reassuring sight, no matter the hurricane of emotions whirling through him. Hopefully, the professor, who had always done his best to help him, could, this final time, help him once more.

Deep in his studies, accompanied by classical music playing in the background, Professor Williams raised his eyes above his glasses and noticed his visitor. "Camden, come in! What a pleasant surprise. You do know that the first day of class doesn't start until *tomorrow*, right?"

Williams reached out to shake Camden's hand. Camden grasped it firmly and took a seat in front of the desk.

"Hello, professor. Yes, I know."

Williams turned down the music. "Intermezzo from Cavalleria Rusticana. Do you know it?"

Camden shook his head.

"Sometimes I turn this piece up to full volume, sit here and just cry. It's so moving."

Camden didn't know what to make of this so he just nodded.

"But of course, you didn't come here to discuss opera, did you," continued the professor. "I'm glad to see you, Camden. It's been a while. I've been looking forward to seeing my star pupil in class again this year."

"Yeah, about that..."

"Is something wrong?"

"I'm afraid I won't be going to school this year."

The professor took off his glasses, putting them to one side. "But *why*? You were making such good progress!" He stared at Camden intently.

Camden felt a faint nausea. He didn't want to cause the professor anxiety or pain, but there was no way around it.

"Are you unwell?" asked Williams.

"I've had better days," Camden said, managing a tiny grin.

"Can I help?"

"I sure hope so. That's why I'm here. We need your advice."

Camden brought him up to speed, trying to speak as quickly as possible while also sparing no details. The professor listened politely at first, his mouth and eyes growing ever wider. When Camden finished, Williams leaned back in his chair with a deep sigh, staring at the ceiling.

"So as you can see," said Camden, "we're not sure what to do. Walter's clearly refused to help us, even though we've explained what's at stake."

The professor's eyes shifted around the room. He looked haggard, and his voice was quiet. "What to do..."

"And our options are so *thin!*" Camden plowed on. "Jade said we'd need to apply to the FDA for a Class One drug recall – which would take months, considering how hard Walter will fight it. Literally m-millions of people could be dead before the truth is out. We need to somehow alert people – blow this wide open on the news – but with proof, not just with two sick guys and a dead druug addict."

Professor Williams was nodding slowly. "Indeed... This is a difficult situation... for many reasons..."

"What can we do, professor? What are our options?"

Williams leaned forward with his elbows on the desk, staring straight at the handwritten pages in front of him. "Well, Camden, I... First of all, I would definitely suggest–"

At that precise moment, the professor's phone rang, cutting him off in mid-sentence. Williams looked at the number. "Sorry, I need to take this. One second."

As the professor yammered on about impractical curriculum schedules, Camden's eyes drifted around the office. His attention was caught by a picture on the wall he hadn't noticed before: a college graduation photo from the University of Seattle.

The caption below read: Class of 1982.

He cocked his head. *Wait a minute...*

Just then, his phone vibrated in his pocket. It was a text message from Jade.

'Drax records list a Carl Williams as an adviser to the company. Could this be your professor?'

Camden felt the strength drain from his body. He sat there, his eyes shifting between the phone, the professor, and the photograph, desperate not to believe what the logical part of his brain was screaming at him.

Williams finally finished his call and met Camden's gaze, looking just as uncomfortable as Camden felt.

"Is everything okay, Camden?" said the professor, looking terrified at his own question.

"Uh... Yeah, proofessor, yeah. Everything's fine. Sorry, something's just come up with my... I have to go."

As Camden stood up to leave, the professor's arm shot across the desk, locking onto Camden's wrist. A surge of rage flashed through Camden's brain then subsided.

"What are you going to do, Camden?"

Camden looked down at the professor's hand, then slowly looked up at him, burning a hole in his eyes. The professor released his grip.

"I'm sorry, Camden."

"I have to go."

CHAPTER THIRTY

I will cease to exist. Nothing will be left of me. The second Consurge death, a single line in a Wikipedia entry on the greatest medical catastrophe in history. My legacy will be a warning no one heeded.

Camden's mind blurred as he walked home through the university. He was weak. He was jittery. Panic threatened to overwhelm him. The gravity of the situation, held at bay until this point, was beginning to crash down upon him. Williams' betrayal had broken something; had cut cleanly through the last remaining strand of hope.

He sent a reply to Jade's earlier text: *'Williams is in on it. Looks bad. Coming back now.'*

He was going to die. Nothing could stop that now. But what about everyone else? Johnny and Sam: so motivated and passionate about life, so loyal to him? Dr. Herman: desperate to ensure that every patient beneath his hands had the privilege of his full attention and the full extent of his skills? His mom: the light in her eyes that shined when she spoke of defeating her illness and living a real life once more? What about the night worker juggling three jobs to pay off medical bills; the caregiver looking after her terminally ill father? What about the literally *millions* of unsuspecting, innocent lemmings who had no idea that they were on a sprint to the cliff edge?

His pace slackened as he approached a newsstand opposite the corner of his apartment. He passed an eye over the magazines on display.

National Geographic: *'The Science of Sleep – Overcoming Evolution.'*

People Magazine: *'Walter Johnson – The Man Who Revolutionized Society.'*

Time Magazine: *'Sleepless in Seattle: How to Create a Pharmaceutical Giant Overnight.'*

His fists tightened. Now was definitely not the time for self-pity or defeatism. Now was the time to move fast and break things.

As he crossed the street to his apartment, a taxi pulled up alongside him. "I got your text," said Jade, getting out of the car.

Camden could only nod his head.

"So the professor knows everything."

"Every deetail."

Camden slapped himself on the jaw. His tongue felt funny, like it was coated with oil.

Jade didn't seem to have noticed. "Do you think he's called Walter by now?"

"Is the Pope Caatholic?"

This time it was impossible to ignore. "Camden, what's wrong with your voice? You're slurring your words."

"I don't know. It's like my mouth isn't listening to my braain."

She took him by the hand. "You're shaking."

"It's been a loong day."

"Come on, I'll make you a cup of tea."

Inside the apartment, Jeremy was lounging on the couch playing video games. He looked up and smiled. "Camden! Good to see you, bro. How you doing?"

"Had beetter days," Camden mumbled. He collapsed onto the couch next to Jeremy.

"Hey, man." Jeremy paused his game and thumped Camden on the leg. "I thought you'd be in good spirits. Looks like Ireland didn't agree with you. And since when did you start wearing a baseball cap?"

Camden squinted at Jeremy, then turned to Jade. Her eyes were wide.

"What are you taalking about?" asked Camden.

Jeremy gave him a bewildered look. "What do you mean, what I am talking about?" He pointed at Jade and winked. "Your trip to Ireland – with her! How did it *go*?"

"What makes you think we went to Ireland?" asked Jade.

Jeremy's brow furrowed. "You guys are tripping me out... You telling me you didn't go? Where've you been all week? Camden called me a week ago and said you'd decided to be impulsive; get away to the 'home' country."

Jade turned to Camden. "Did he, now?"

Camden shrugged his shoulders. "Did I?"

Jeremy carried on. "Yeah. And I was like, 'Sounds great. Nice to have a vacation – even if it is with Victoria Frankenstein here.' No offense."

Jade ignored the comment and sat on the armchair next to the sofa, chin resting on her palm. "I remember now: on the drive to the hospital, you said, 'What'll I tell Jeremy?', and I replied with something like, 'Tell him the truth.' I believe the response you gave was a grunt of some description."

"I can honestly ssay I don't remember that."

Jade gave a sad smile and shook her head. "Hmm. Well, that no doubt contributed to the false memories."

Jeremy by now was looking completely nonplussed. He butted in. "False memories? What are you guys talking about?"

"Wee've got some things to tell you, Jereemy."

"I'll say you do! And why are you talking like that?"

A knock at the door interrupted their conversation. Jeremy answered to find a fidgeting Chetana.

"Hello-o-o Nurse!" he said.

Chetana raised an eyebrow. "Excuse me?"

Jade quickly intervened. "Don't pay any attention to him. Please, come in."

"Yes please, do come in," said Jeremy, extending his arm into the apartment.

Jade rolled her eyes. "Jeremy, this is Chetana, the receptionist where I... where I *used* to work. Chetana, this is Camden's roommate."

"Pleased to meet you," said Chetana.

Jeremy gently shook her hand. "The pleasure is *all* mine."

Jade quickly ushered Chetana past Jeremy. "Okay, okay, enough of that."

Chetana turned to Jade, wild-eyed. "Jade, you've got to level with me! Walter said he fired you for stealing from the company! Is that true? He said that if I knew what was good for me I wouldn't listen to your 'irrational gibberish'."

"Have a seat, Chetta. I'll put the kettle on and Camden and I will explain everything."

For the next half an hour, a confab ensued around the kitchen table, sipping tea while Jade explained, for what felt like the hundredth time that day, the events leading up to their current predicament. Much of the time, Jeremy and Chetana were quiet, absorbing every word. Camden simply sat and enjoyed his drink. Each sip temporarily warmed and loosened his tongue.

Jeremy's eyes grew as he began to put the pieces together. Finally, he turned to Camden. "I *knew* I saw your light on! Try and tell me I dreamed it!"

"I'm sssorry I lied to you," said Camden.

Jeremy slammed his fists on the table, standing up from his chair so quickly he knocked it to the floor. He paced from one end of the kitchen to the other a few times, before rounding on Jade.

"*You people*," he said furiously, "are *all the same.* You think you know better. You mess with... with biological realities and look what happens! Didn't I tell you? Didn't I tell you from the *start* it was a bad idea?" He raised his hands. "You didn't even know what you were messing with! You thought you did, but you had no idea."

Camden put up his hands. "Jeremy, it wasn't intentional."

"No. He's right." Jade gave a weary shrug. "We gave the impression we knew everything about sleep. But the truth is... well, it's not that simple. We know plenty about *what* happens, I suppose, but not enough about *why* it happens."

"We don't need a lecture from you right now," said Jeremy, harshly. "You're no better than medieval surgeons, cutting into someone's head while they're still alive to find out how the brain works. Oh, sure, 'We've made some sort of breakthrough'. Great! Just ignore the corpses!"

Jade didn't reply. She looked exhausted, and despite everything, Camden felt sorry for her. He was eager to keep the peace, but couldn't think of what next to say.

In the end, it was Chetana who spoke up. "We don't have time to argue. Surely with something like this, we need to work together. It doesn't seem like anyone else is on our side."

Jeremy sat back down. Having let go of the triumphant anger he'd bottled up, the seriousness of the situation was beginning to show on his face. He turned to Camden, a miserable look in his eyes. "Are you really dying, man?"

"Seeems I don't have much time left."

"In fact, a lot of people don't have much time left," said Jade. "The right or wrongs, where blame needs to be attached, that can wait. Right now, we need to get Consurge off the shelves, and Walter seems like he's going to do his level best to stop us."

"I might be able to help," said Chetana. She pulled out her phone and brought up a calendar. The other three all leaned in.

"Just before I left the office," she said, scrolling, "I checked Walter's schedule again – like you asked me to. He's cleared a two-hour time block tomorrow from nine 'til eleven to meet with a 'Katsu Yamamoto-san'."

"Who is he?" asked Camden.

"I looked him up. He's the CEO of Hīringu Pharmaceuticals in Tokyo, one of the biggest corporations in Japan."

"Why is Waalter meeting with the competiition?"

"I don't know. But I do know how Walter operates. The second he sets up a meeting, he enters it in his diary."

"Meaning?"

Jade interjected. "Meaning he only set up the meeting after we told him about the problems with Consurge."

"Yamamoto must be on a plane right now," said Chetana.

Camden placed his head in his hands, gripping his hair with his fingers. "Whaat's he *planning*?"

"We need to find out," said Jade. "We need to know exactly what happens at that meeting tomorrow. Chetana, can you get us into Walter's office tonight?"

"Yes, but believe me, if we're caught, I'm fired just the same as you, and then probably arrested. We'll only have one go at it. What do you have in mind?"

Jade drummed her fingers on the tabletop. "We need eyes and ears in that room. We need cameras. Jeremy, you've got the gear. Can you help us?"

"A chance to take down Big Pharma?" Jeremy thumped the table, psyching himself up. "Count me in."

"Thank you. Where can we watch the meeting from tomorrow?"

"Timbuktu if you want." Jeremy jumped up from the table.

"Good," said Jade. "Jeremy, get the equipment ready and then go with Chetana. By the time you get there, everyone in the office and the lab should be gone."

"Wait," said Chetana, "what about the security camera in the office?"

Jeremy smirked. "Leave that to me."

"And Chetta," continued Jade, "don't let the security guard get suspicious. Just tell him Jeremy is your boyfriend and you want to show him where you work."

Jeremy winked at Chetana for which he received a raised eyebrow in return.

"Focus, Jeremy," said Jade sharply.

"Yes, ma'am."

"If all goes according to plan, you, me, and Camden will meet at Westlake Plaza in the morning and watch the meeting. Chetana will keep watch in the office."

Jeremy rubbed his hands together. "Let's do this."

CHAPTER THIRTY-ONE

"Your first false memory was here?"

After Jeremy and Chetana left for Drax Pharmaceuticals, Camden had convinced Jade to catch the sunset at Gas Works Park. Camden had felt mildly sorry for Chetana, given Jeremy's unabashed interest in her, but as his experience taught him, she could take care of herself.

Jade had looked ragged; she'd fixed her make up before going to see Walter, but Camden could tell from the look in her eyes and the errant strands of hair, she was nearing the end of her rope. She'd tried to convince him to stay in and rest, but he still remembered Ireland; the peace and purity of walking through the fields with Jade. Maybe he could capture just a fraction of that.

"Yep," said Camden. "This is wheere I saw you and Walter. I mean – where I thought I saaaw you." Camden pointed down to the water's edge from their bench on Kite Hill. "You guys were going at it right there." Camden didn't know whether to laugh or feel sick. In a strange way, it was almost funny now.

Jade shuddered. "Ugh. Perish the thought. *Especially* now." She reached out and touched his face with a smile. "There's only one person I want to lock lips with." She leaned in and gifted him a kiss so tender and passionate as to almost replace the memory of her making out with Walter.

Jade settled her head on Camden's chest, his arm around her shoulder and his hand resting on her hip. The clouds above the lake were exploding and re-forming in slow motion, a symphony of wondrous colors. Several kayakers were paddling along the shore and a crowd of boaters were enjoying a late-night barbecue on the water. A seaplane roared as it touched down on the glistening pink waters. It was a soothing, romantic reprieve, and it almost took Camden's mind away from his growing physical discomfort.

Camden grinned and was ready to lean in again to meet Jade's lips when there came a faint, whining hum in the distance.

Jade pulled away slightly. "Do you hear that?"

He nodded. "It souunds like an engine... It's getting louuuder."

They turned around in unison.

"*What...?*" Camden couldn't believe his eyes, but of course, that was nothing new. A black SUV with a bumper guard was speeding along one of the pedestrian paths forcing people onto the grass.

Has somebody lost their mind?

Without warning, the vehicle veered left and abandoned the path, its tires chewing up the grass. As it accelerated up Kite Hill, its trajectory soon became clear.

In his mind, Camden had already jumped out of the way, but in reality, paralysis was in command.

"Look out!" Jade screamed, pulling him from the bench and throwing him away from her.

She had only time to take two steps. He rolled along the grass as the SUV launched into the air behind him. The bench exploded in a cloud of wooden shrapnel, raining down splinters on their heads. The vehicle skidded down the hill towards a concrete barrier on the lakeshore and spun around, the back end crashing into the wall, cracking the concrete and shattering the rear window of the SUV, sending shards of glass into the lake.

"*Jade! Jaaaaaaade!*" yelled Camden, struggling to lift himself. He felt two hands under his arms, dragging him to his feet. He spun around and almost collapsed with relief at seeing Jade. She had a large cut above her right eye and blood was running down her cheek.

"Follow me!" she shrieked, racing in the opposite direction of the SUV.

He ran after her, looking over his shoulder to see the vehicle starting towards them again. Camden scanned his surroundings; open grassland.

No trees to climb this time.

Jade appeared to be heading for the next best thing; the old gasification plant rising up from the center of the park.

Unbeknownst to her, however, the entire factory was encircled by a tall barbed wire fence.

"Jade!" he shouted. "Split up! Go left. Run to the road!"

She didn't reply, but took a swift left turn. Camden continued straight ahead, still sprinting towards the fence, his mind trying to catch up to his legs. He desperately hoped the SUV wouldn't follow Jade, or at least that she'd make it close enough to the main road that she'd be safe.

He glanced over his shoulder.

Well, that's one problem solved...

As the vehicle gained on him, Camden focused on the chain-link fence ahead, now fewer than fifty feet away. A large, rusty gas pipe ran horizontally above his head, just clearing the top of the barbed wire and entering the factory.

What if I could...

The SUV was almost at his heels. In one swift motion, he jumped, grabbed the top rail of the fence and wrapped his legs around the barbed wire. The vehicle plowed through the chain-link beneath him and crashed into the rusty pipework of the building. Camden writhed in pain, trying to stabilize himself on the top of the barbed wire. The sharp metal was ripping at his jeans, threatening to tear straight through his skin. He couldn't drop to the ground for fear of being run down – he could hear the engine of the vehicle bellowing as the driver tried to reverse it away from the building.

He reached up, managing to grab hold of the thick pipe above his head. As he pulled himself to a standing position, great patches of material tore away from his jeans. He could feel the blood running down his legs, but the pain hadn't yet arrived. Awkwardly, he heaved himself on top of the pipeline, gripping it with both arms and legs. He looked down to the SUV. The driver's front window was down, and he saw two cold eyes staring up at him from within. The man's gaze slowly shifted down and a sadistic smile spread across his face. Camden followed the man's line of sight to a thin post holding up the pipeline on which he was balancing.

Get up!

Camden placed both feet on the pipeline, which was just wide enough to stand on. He raised himself slowly, though every nerve in his body wanted him to rush, and began to inch his way along the top of the pipe, toward the old wreck of a building. As he did, the SUV roared to life again and reversed from the mangled steel and blackberry bushes draped across its hood and windshield. Camden jolted and wobbled at the sound, but managed to steady himself and then speed up, sheer adrenaline maintaining his balance.

This is going to be close!

When the vehicle obtained sufficient runway, it stopped. Camden looked up; ahead to his right were two rusty towers, one with a rickety old ladder. He could hear the tires of the SUV behind him spinning on the grass. Camden took three final steps and launched himself into the air as the pipe beneath his feet collapsed onto the ground, a length of it flattening the roof of the SUV. Catching a rung of the ladder with both hands, he screamed in pain as his shoulder stretched almost until it broke, his entire body swinging like a fish on a hook.

Eventually, he found his feet on the ladder and began climbing. Reaching the top of the tower, he crouched low and tried to catch his breath. Sweat was pouring down his back. His heart felt ready to explode. He reached to feel the side of his head. Somewhere in the chaos, he'd managed to lose his cap and the gauze pad was peeling off his wound. He peeked out through the rusted bars of the factory. Below him, a small crowd had gathered around the vehicle. Smoke was pouring from its hood. Without warning, it reared and bellowed, shaking off the pipe on its roof and crashing through another fence, nearly flattening several people in its path. He watched the vehicle speed off in the distance and out of the park.

His hands soiled with rust, Camden gingerly descended the ladder to the ground. He looked up to see Jade pushing her way through the crowd. She stumbled across the flattened fence and embraced his trembling body.

"Are you okay?" she asked

"Neeever better. You?"

She sighed. "Fine. Your leg, it's bleeding!"

He waved his hand in the air. "It's fine. Don't woorry. Just tell me one thing."

"What is it?"

"Tell me that was a faaalse memory. That was too crazy to be real."

Jade flopped down on the grass, running her hands tightly through her hair. "I wish it was a false memory, Camden."

He joined her on the ground. "Me too. Then I would've only iiimagined that your boss tried to kiiill us."

"If Walter wanted us dead, we'd be dead. Believe me. That was a warning."

"Huh. Some waarning. An anonymous threatening phoone call would've sufficed."

"Come on," said Jade. She heaved herself to her feet. "Let's go before the police get here."

Camden's ripped and bloody jeans, the shaved patch on the side of his head, and Jade's wounded forehead had drawn suspicious looks from the cab driver on the way home. Camden's response of "You should see the other guys," simply drew a wide-eyed nod from the cabbie.

Back at Camden's apartment, Jade tended to the cuts on her forehead and readied herself for bed. Camden likewise had wrapped a gauze bandage around each leg. Tonight, for a change, he was grateful he didn't need to sleep. There was no doubt that Walter could try again and Camden wanted to keep watch out the window.

"I feel safer here with you," said Jade quietly, coming out of the bathroom. She'd wrapped herself up in his robe, which was far too big for her. It looked comical; frankly, like she was wearing a bearskin, and Camden couldn't help but chuckle.

"It's a good thing I never got riiid of my bed."

"Look at us. Our own apartment, our own bed. It's just like we're married."

"We weere married. Until I woke up this moorning."

Jade drifted over to Camden and rested her hand on his chest. "Just so you know, dear, I would've said yes."

Camden was bending down to kiss her as the front door burst open. Jeremy entered in a flurry of nervous excitement, stopping dead as he saw Jade in her oversized robe.

"Uh, I can come back," he said, not bothering to look away.

"Jeremy! You staaartled us."

He closed the door behind him.

"How did everything go?" asked Jade.

"We've got eyes and ears. Everything's set up and ready to rock."

"Thank you, Jeremy."

"No, thank *you*! It was my pleasure." Jeremy gently bit his lower lip. "Once this is all over, I'm taking Chetana out to dinner," he said, making a little bow.

"Smooth operator," said Camden, patting his chest with his fist as Jade gave an astonished laugh. Jeremy looked extremely pleased with himself, standing in the center of the living room with his hands on his hips. Camden was pleased for him. He wanted something good to come out of this whole debacle.

Camden followed through on his kiss. "Get some sssleep, babe."

Jade smiled, eyelids drooping.

Ten minutes later, with Jade and Jeremy sound asleep, Camden collapsed on the couch. There was just one loose end from the day that was nagging at him, refusing to be ignored. He pulled out his phone and selected the number. Soon, the familiar raspy voice answered on the other end.

"Camden! Where are you?"

"Are you surprised to hear from me, professor?

"Yes – I mean, after what happened earlier."

"Well, I'm sorry to break the neews to you, but we're still alive."

"What? What are you talking about?"

Camden couldn't help but laugh.

"Listen, Camden, I can explain!"

"To think I trusted you."

"Camden-! Look, please, let's just meet up and talk. I'm sure we can work this out. I can help you!"

"*Ha.*" Camden sat up straight on the couch. "Listen to me very carefully. I'm sure your goons know where we are, but if you ever try to hurt Jade again... You know I'm up all night." He looked over at Jeremy's golf clubs in the corner, grasping at straws. "And I'm aaarmed. Anyone you seend after me, they're going where I'm going."

Click.

CHAPTER THIRTY-TWO

"Whaat tiiime is it?"

A gentle morning breeze rustled the leaves above the trio. Staking out the Drax headquarters from a table in Westlake Plaza, Jade watched the entrance to the building, Jeremy's eyes remained fixed on his computer screen, earphones in, and Camden's eyes were on Jeremy. Walter's meeting with Mr. Yamamoto was beginning soon, and Camden's head felt heavy, even after his fifteen-minute nap a few hours earlier. He'd taken painkillers and was forcing himself to focus on the matter at hand.

Jeremy pulled a white bud from his left ear. "You've been asking me that every five minutes for the last half an hour. Use your mental math."

"Sooorry."

"Eight thirty-eight. We're live in twenty."

Jeremy, displaying a level of stealth and cunning Camden would never in a million years have expected him to possess, had hidden one camera in Walter's bookcase, nestled among Walter's extensive collection of neurological texts, one in the middle of his 19th-century French wall clock, and the third, in a moment of irony not lost on Camden, along the picture rail, directly above the framed certificate of Consurge's approval by the FDA. All three views were showing on the laptop. Walter was pacing back and forth across his Persian rug.

Abruptly, Jeremy nudged Camden in his side. "Hey, isn't that Professor Williams?"

At first, Camden didn't recognize the professor without his brown tweed suit on. He wore grey chinos with a blue sports jacket and was walking briskly down the sidewalk.

"That's your professor?" said Jade.

"Yeah, why?" asked Camden.

"I know the face. He comes into the office from time to time. Meets with Walter."

They watched Williams walk through the front door of the Seattle Investments Tower, and within minutes, he appeared on their computer screen, entering Walter's office. It didn't appear to be a friendly visit – Williams was pointing angrily at Walter, who was shouting back. The three of them listened closely.

"*I didn't call you so you'd try and kill the kid and his girlfriend!*" shouted Williams. He sounded out of breath, his voice much higher-pitched than usual.

"*I don't know what you're talking about.*"

Williams walked closer to him and calmed his tone. Jeremy swiftly turned up the volume of the microphones.

"*Walter, you need to pull the plug on Consurge.*"

"*Do you have any idea what that would mean?*" came Walter's reply, a furious whisper. "*The financial implications – and for you, don't forget! Your name's in this as well!*"

"*I was a consultant. I offered you my advice!*"

"*And you looked the other way when I told you to. You don't think the Department of Justice is going to be interested in that? Because, believe me, they'll find out. They can decide what to do with you.*"

A brief armistice ensued, the two men glaring at each other in the center of the room. It was remarkable, thought Camden, to see them together. The same height, the same build, the same age, but one so smug, so in love with his own power, and the other suddenly looking so desperate and frail.

Williams pointed at Walter. "*You told me that what I found was a dead end. That there was no risk. You produced evidence, Walter. You gave me papers...*"

The professor stopped. Walter watched him cautiously as Williams' hands moved to his head. "*No, no...*"

"*I don't know what you're talking about, Carl,*" said Walter roughly, marching toward his desk.

"*Tell me they were real papers, Walter. Please. Tell me you did the research.*"

"*I can't tell you anything if there isn't anything to tell.*" Walter pressed the button on his desk. "*Chetana, I need someone to escort the professor out of my office, please. My meeting's about to begin.*"

"*You can kick me out, Walter, but that won't change anything,*" said Williams, his voice rising once more. "*You lied to me! You promised me I was wrong!*"

"*Get out, Carl,*" said Walter, not looking at him. "*You've gone mad. Jealousy's ruined you. I knew it was only a matter of time. You can't handle me this much further ahead than you and you're desperate to bring me down, with whatever ridiculous method you and your students come up with.*"

One of Walter's Kong-sized security guards entered the office. Williams held up his arms.

"*I'm going, I'm going.*" As he walked to the door, he fired a final shot: "*I don't care how I do it, Walter, but you won't come out of this smiling, believe me. Karma will catch up with you, and when it does, it's going to kick you square in the teeth.*"

"*Bye now,*" said Walter, waving.

Camden and Jade turned to each other, flabbergasted.

"Camden-" began Jade.

Without a word, Camden ran across the street. As soon as Williams emerged from the building, Camden took him by the arm. The older man looked around, and upon seeing Camden, his face gave way to a look of terror.

"Camden, what are you-"

"I need yoou to come with me *riiight now*, professor," said Camden quickly, trying to lead him away from the entrance. He was well aware that the last time they'd spoken he'd effectively threatened the professor's life, and didn't want the man to flee. "You waant to make this right? Come with me."

Without another word, Camden led a now yielding Williams back across the street and to the small table in the park where Jade and Jeremy waited. They both watched tensely, clearly unsure as to Camden's next move. Camden sat down, out of breath, and motioned to Jeremy to explain.

"Yeah, well, how can I put it..."

"Jeeremy!"

"Yeah, we bugged Walter's office yesterday. We just heard everything that went on up there."

Williams collapsed on a chair, clutching his chest. He turned to Camden, his breathing rushed and his voice quavering. "So what is this? Blackmail? What do you want from me?"

Camden hadn't yet recovered his breath. Jade spoke instead, pointing to the computer screen: "In eight minutes, representatives from a Japanese pharmaceutical giant are going to walk through that door and meet with Walter. We don't know why, but we know that he arranged it after we met with him yesterday. It's not a coincidence – it can't be."

"Wee thought you were iiin on it," said Camden, "because of the waay you reacted when I saaw you yesterday."

"I, I..." Williams groped for the right words. "I had my suspicions, but from months, years ago. I panicked when you saw me – I'm so sorry, I wish we'd been able to talk at the time, but..."

Jade leaned in, elbows on the table, hands clasped together. "What do you know, professor? I've worked on Consurge for two years. What did you find that we didn't?"

"Just a little something, on subconscious thought," said Williams, dabbing at a bead of sweat with his handkerchief. "An inkling I had; about the mind's capacity to compartmentalize while conscious that which it usually processed while unconscious... I mean, you can only blow up a balloon with so much air before it bursts, can't you?" The professor gave an empty chuckle. "I emailed my findings to Walter, and a month later he sent me back two papers, supposedly by his team, which showed I'd been down a blind alley."

"They weren't from us," said Jade grimly.

"You all seemed to be doing such magnificent work," continued the professor, "that I trusted what Walter had given me and thought no more of it. Everything seemed fine until..." He turned to Camden. "Until you came to my office yesterday."

Camden honestly thought he'd never seen anyone look as miserable as the professor did at that moment. In spite of everything, he felt a wave of sympathy for the man.

"I'm so sorry, Camden," said the professor. "You don't deserve this."

"Guys!" said Jeremy. "Grab some earphones, now."

At precisely 9 a.m., two Japanese men entered Walter's office with purpose. An older, distinguished-looking man, presumably Yamamoto, with white hair and a dark suit was followed by a considerably younger looking man who trailed a few paces behind, his head and shoulders slightly stooped.

Walter bowed low to his visitors, and in an ingratiating tone, spoke a few sentences of Japanese. The four eavesdroppers turned to each other in alarm. "Anybody speak Japanese?" asked Jade in a horrified whisper.

Mr. Yamamoto bowed in return. *"The pleasure is all mine. If you don't mind, I like to practice my English when in America."*

The four sighed as one. On the screen, Yamamoto's aide was presenting a gift to Walter: a ceremonial mask, deep red, its eyes and mouth wide. Walter, in return, presented a small blue box, wrapped with a violet ribbon. Yamamoto accepted it with another bow.

"How was your flight?" asked Walter.

"Very good, thank you. I always love coming to America." He burst out laughing dramatically. *"It's a big fat country with lots of space."*

Walter chuckled. *"I think I'll quote you on that, sir."*

Suddenly, Mr. Yamamoto donned his poker face. *"Now. Down to business."*

"Of course. Please, sit down. I've had my lawyer draw up the paperwork. There's a copy in Japanese as well."

The four of them watched Walter open his desk drawer and pull out an official-looking document, spinning it to face Yamamoto.

"Please, take your time. Read it over."

The aide began reading each line out loud in Japanese using a low, measured tone. Mr. Yamamoto listened with his eyes closed, paying close attention to each word, nodding affirmatively at appropriate intervals until the aide was finished.

"Fine," he said. *"I am satisfied."*

Walter smiled. *"In that case, sign on the dotted line and Drax Pharmaceuticals is all yours."*

"He's gonna taake the money and run!" exclaimed Camden.

"Can he *do* that?" asked Jeremy.

Professor Williams looked defeated. "I'm afraid so. Walter's the sole proprietor of Drax. It's not a publicly traded company – it's just him. He calls the shots. He doesn't need anyone's consent to sell..."

Mr. Yamamoto smiled and signed his name. *"I have but one question."*

"Anything," invited Walter.

"I have been offering to buy your company for two years. Why now? Why the hurry to sell? You finally have your greatest success. Your business has never been stronger. Why are you not seeking to compete with me?"

They saw Walter pause, and give a broad smile. *"Well, to be perfectly honest with you, I did have big plans for the company. To take it public – float it, appoint a board of directors. But... a few days ago, my daughter called me and told me that my grandson had taken his first steps. I missed it because, of course, I was here. And I thought to myself, What else am I missing? I decided it was time to retire."*

Mr. Yamamoto nodded in approval. *"Family first. I respect that."*

Walter pulled out an elegant bottle from his desk drawer. *"And now it's time to celebrate."*

Mr. Yamamoto's eyes lit up. *"Junmai Daiginjō-shu! My favorite saké!"* He clasped his hands together in excitement.

Walter handed Yamamoto and his aide a glass each. *"Here's to the new owner of Drax Pharmaceuticals!"*

Their bodies warmed, Walter led the two men out of the office on a tour of Mr. Yamamoto's new company.

There was a moment of silence around the park table.

"So," said Jade, leaning back. "He's dumping the whole catastrophe on someone else's plate and walking away. I'll bet everything I have that by this time tomorrow he'll have disappeared. Somewhere far away; somewhere without an extradition treaty."

Camden felt a deep well of nausea.

"What do we do?" asked Jeremy. "We've got this recorded, but I don't see it doing anything except proving he's going to sell his company. That's not gonna put anyone off Consurge, not when they all think it's the best thing since electricity."

The emptiness in Williams' eyes had now turned to conviction. All fear had disappeared from his face. "We need him to admit – on camera – that he knows about the side effects of Consurge. We need him to admit he's going to let millions of people die. Then we need to blast it on every news channel in the world. Unless we do that, Walter will skip the country tonight and he'll never be held responsible. It's our only chance of getting Consurge recalled immediately."

"I'll do it," said Jade. "I can goad him into saying anything."

Camden stood up. "No. Waaalter could kill. I'm dead alreaady. I'm the best choice." He smirked. "Blaze of glory and all that..."

Jade looked frightened, then resigned, then proud. She nodded and pulled a can of pepper spray out of her purse. "At least take this. You never know."

"Thanks." He slid the can into his cargo pants pocket. He'd never used pepper spray before, but if now wasn't a time for new experiences, when was?

"How are you gonna do it?" asked Jeremy. The three of them all stared at him.

"Well," said Camden, taking a deep breath, "iiin the immortal words of Indiaaana Jones: *'Don't know, think of something.'*"

CHAPTER THIRTY-THREE

"How did you get in here?"

By 10:30 a.m., the new owner of Drax and his aide had left to feast at a nearby sushi bar, leaving Walter to wallow in his success. The former owner, who was busy packing a suitcase, nearly jumped as Camden threw open his office doors.

"Chetana knows aall about Consurge, Waalter."

The businessman gave a smug shake of his head and sighed dramatically. "That's two people I get to fire in as many days. It's so hard to find good help."

"The gaame is up, Waalter." Camden knew he had to goad the man, but didn't know how exactly. Blocking the door and threatening him seemed the best way to raise his hackles.

Walter laughed, then abruptly turned serious. "You cocky moron. You think you can come in here and threaten me? You can barely get the words out!"

"Thanks to *yoou*."

Walter continued packing, pulling several dress shirts out of an antique wardrobe, folding them, and laying them in another case. "You can't prove anything."

Camden noticed a stray piece of paper sitting on top of the printer. He marched over and picked it up. Walter looked up and stopped packing.

"Camden, do you know what an interloper is?"

"Ahh, a one-way ticket to Cape Verde. I hear it's niice there this time of year."

"You'll never know, will you."

"Again, thanks to you."

"Get out of my office."

Camden was attempting to play it confident and assertive, but he could feel the sweat gathering on his forehead. The lives of millions of people were in his hands. This ticket proved it: if he couldn't get Walter to admit his guilt, here and now, he wouldn't face justice until it was long past due. He tapped his pocket, reassuring himself that the pepper spray was still here.

"Weee ran into a friend of yours last niiight, Walter."

Walter looked up briefly and smirked. "Is that right?"

"Your friend is a teerrible driver. Would you believe he took a wroong turn and ended up in the paark?"

"You don't say? I'll tell him to be more careful next time."

"There won't be a next time, Waalter."

Walter chuckled as he opened his desk drawer. "How cliché. Do you know what? You're absolutely right."

Walter slowly drew his hand from the desk drawer to reveal an antique-looking firearm. He cradled it gently with both hands, raising it up to admire the craftsmanship. "This beauty," he said, "is an eighteenth-century English dueling pistol. It's one of my favorite pieces in my entire collection."

So much for the pepper spray...

"Did you know, Camden, that in bygone days, when a man's honor was challenged, a gentleman would demand satisfaction in a duel? Many people assume that these duels always ended in someone's death. However, most people don't realize that they often fired at their opponent's leg or even deliberately missed, desiring only to satisfy the demands of honor."

Walter cocked the weapon, pointed it at Camden, and smiled.

"That's not going to happen today."

"Risky, Walter," Camden said in a warning tone. "You only get one shot with those, and they're prone to backfiring."

Walter considered, his face an exaggerated expression of thoughtfulness. "You know what? That's a very good point." He placed the pistol on the desk and reached back into the drawer. "These, though. These are much more reliable."

Camden recognized the black polymer of the Glock pistol, and his heart sank. Walter, hand still steady, pointed it neatly at Camden's chest, and with his free hand dialed a number on his cell phone.

"Bruno – tell Zane to escort Chetana out of the building. There's been a mutiny. Then come to my office." He glared at Camden. "We need to take out the trash."

"Do watch your head, Camden. This place wasn't designed for tall people."

The burly security guard prodded Camden through a maze of generators, pumps, tanks, and ducts. The maintenance room on the building's top floor lay beneath its expansive arched glass roof. Walter, only a few paces behind, his gun still cocked, shouted again over the noise of the machinery.

"Bruno! It's a bit stuffy in here. Would you open the door for our guest?"

A gust of wind swirled around the equipment as Bruno wrenched the outside door open. Just beyond, Camden spied a narrow ledge with a low railing.

Walter's smile was as cold as the air whipping around them. "I can see the police report now: *'Man so consumed with grief over his girlfriend's death that he commits suicide at her former workplace'*. How tragic..."

"You leave Jade alone!"

"I really don't think you're in a position to bargain, my late friend."

Walter moved towards Camden, gun still outstretched, forcing him to the door. A wave of dizziness washed over him as he approached the edge. He braced himself against the doorframe. The narrow ledge ran in both directions along the base of the huge glass arch. Through the wind swirling around his head, Camden could just make out Walter's voice behind him.

"Camden, it's time to do what scientists all want to do: take a giant leap into the unknown! I'd gladly shoot you in the back, but it looks so much better for me if it's a suicide. And plus, you get a few more moments to pray! So when you think about it, it's a win-win."

Camden dared a look over his shoulder. Walter had a wild look in his eyes; his tie was askew, and his hand was wavering. One moment the gun was pointed at Camden, the next slightly above, the next slightly to the side.

"Camden, we both know you're dead already. I just need to speed up the process so you don't do anything *stupid* before I leave town."

Walter motioned to the security guard.

"Try not to crush anyone on the sidewalk, Camden."

Camden cocked his head to see Bruno, a behemoth of a man, lumbering toward him.

This is it, the end of the road. At least I'll have a quick death.

He let out a sigh of defeat and dropped his arms at his side. As he did, he felt something poking through his pants pocket.

With the bodyguard nearly at his back, Camden plunged his hand into his pocket and pulled out the pepper spray. His arm traveled in a wide arc, spurting the hideous substance in all directions. Bruno landed on the floor with a scream, spray plastering his eyes, and Walter stumbled backward, choking and coughing.

Camden, adrenaline now pumping through his veins, took to his heels. He turned left and sprinted along the narrow ledge outside. He could hear Walter yelling at the guard to get up and pursue him, but he knew he'd bought himself a few seconds. He tried not to look down as he ran, realizing that one wrong step would send him hundreds of feet to the street below. As he reached the end of the ledge, his pace slackened. Westlake Plaza spread out below him, with three tiny dots sitting around a table. He screamed at the top of his lungs. "Jaaaade!"

The wind dragged the sound away into the void.

Before he could think, Camden heard footsteps behind, growing louder with every step. The beast of a man was staggering along the ledge, feeling his way along the wall, his eyes bright red.

There was only one way to go.

A metal ladder rose from where Camden stood, arching along the edge of the building to the top of the skyscraper. He grabbed a rung. A harsh gust of wind threatened to tear him away as he placed a foot on the first rung of the ladder. He swallowed.

No problem. It's just like climbing a tree. A really, really big tree.

Halfway up the ladder, he looked down. The bodyguard, clearly more devoted to his job than his life, was bounding up the ladder, two rungs at once. Moments later, Bruno was grabbing at his heels. Camden kicked down as hard as he could, his foot landing squarely on Bruno's face. The bodyguard simply grinned, wiped away the blood, and carried on. Camden desperately heaved himself forwards, his strength rapidly running out.

As the ladder leveled off near the top of the arch, Camden attempted to jump onto the glass roof, but Bruno snatched his leg. An epic face plant smeared Camden's saliva on the glass. He managed to scramble to his feet as the guard stepped off the ladder in pursuit, but before he'd taken three paces, he was again face down with the bear-like figure on top of him.

There's only one thing to do. Play dirty.

Camden's teeth clamped down on the bodyguard's hand. The man screamed – had he not been fighting for his life, Camden would have laughed. He swung his hand up, grabbing the side of Bruno's face, and dug his fingers into the man's swollen eyes. The guard gave a deafening roar and fell backward, loosening the weight upon Camden. Completing his trifecta, Camden landed a solid kick to the man's groin, leaving the once intimidating bully to utter a pitiful wheeze.

However, despite Camden feeling like Wesley defeating Fezzik in the Princess Bride, during the scuffle he'd failed to notice they were slowly sliding down the other side of the glass arch.

Not good, not good!

Bruno noticed it too and attempted to raise himself. But it was too late. Despite desperately scrambling to stop their slide, the glass offered no grip and the pair were soon in free fall.

Their plummet, however, was short-lived.

The first thing to break Camden's fall was the narrow ledge on the other side of the roof, the corresponding walkway to the one he'd been on just minutes before. Second, and more importantly, was Bruno, who landed on the ledge first. The momentum of their fall, however, carried both men over the ledge, dropping them twenty feet onto the top of another glass roof, fracturing both the glass and several bones.

Ugh...

Camden wasn't sure how long he was out for, but through the haze of his mind, a loud bang pierced his subconscious. The glass panel next to him exploded, raining down shards on the office workers below who had gathered to see the commotion on their roof. Camden's right arm dropped and swung in the open air. His vision finally cleared to see Walter Johnson on the ladder above, one hand holding the rung and the other his Glock.

"Give it up, Camden!" Walter screamed. "There's no way out of this!"

Camden staggered to his feet, the shooting pain in his leg telling him it was broken. He stumbled toward the wall, trying to take shelter from the madman above him. Unfortunately, Walter wasn't his only problem. Bruno grumbled as he regained consciousness.

Good grief. This guy's made of iron.

Camden was trapped. If he moved away from the wall, he'd get shot. The guard lumbered toward him, filled with a groggy rage. Camden made a feeble attempt to make contact with Bruno's broken nose; the man simply grabbed his hand, punched Camden in the stomach leaving him winded, and hoisted him onto his shoulders.

Camden, barely regaining his breath, watched the edge of the building approach. He was seconds away from taking the quick way down to Jade.

Now what?

Bruno had made one mistake: he'd left Camden with a free arm. Camden discreetly reached into his pocket and pulled out the can of pepper spray. He had no clue if there was anything left, but it was a gamble he'd have to take. Slowly, he raised his arm up to the back of Bruno's head. Walter, who had spotted what was in Camden's hand, shouted out to warn the guard, but it was too late. With one swift motion, Camden thrust his hand in front of Bruno's face and let the pepper spray fly into his bleeding eyes.

The guard immediately sank to his knees, crying out in agony, cradling his face with his hands. The swift motion sent Camden rolling forward towards the edge of the building. Only the low railing stopped him from sailing over the edge. Struggling to his feet, he turned and looked down to the plaza once more, just making out the figures still clustered around the park table. Jeremy. Chetana. The professor.

Jade.

A sudden, white-hot pain sprang from his thigh. There was a moment of silent, still realization, then his leg buckled beneath him. He fell against the railing, grasping the metal with his hands, half his body hanging over the edge.

A second shot hit the bar next to Camden's face. He cried out and turned to see that Walter had climbed to the bottom of the ladder and was standing on the walkway only twenty feet above him, both hands wrapped around his gun. Walter closed his left eye and took aim.

A third bullet, this time in his stomach. The sensation was that of being kicked by a horse, struck by a battering-ram, a huge weight thumping into his abdomen and driving the air from his lungs. He sensed himself tilting, leaning further over the edge of the building. He held on desperately, willing the fraction of strength left in his arms to pull him back to safety...

The fourth shot went through his shoulder, which exploded.

Camden fell backward, through searing agony and a cloud of blood and flesh. With his left arm useless, his right grasped helplessly at nothing as he twisted in the air. He felt his feet knock against the barrier, then nothing but his clothes flapping in the wind.

Funny. I always thought I would scream. I wonder what it will feel like to hit the ground.

There was only a faint rushing in his ears, an almost peaceful sound. The ground sped closer, the colors suddenly vibrant: yellow cars, green trees, people wearing clothes of blue, red, pink, white.

Time to close his eyes...

I'm sorry, Jade. I tried my best.

"Are you even listening?!"

Huh? He opened his eyes.

"Did you hear me? I said, *get out!* Get out or I'll have you thrown out!"

Camden stared blankly at the barrel of the pistol. He was in Walter's office. Walter stood in front of him, still holding his antique English sidearm, face screwed up in angry exasperation.

"Are you deaf?"

He finally managed to open his mouth. "I uunderstand."

Camden turned to leave, his mind sluggish. In the lobby, he could see Chetana packing her possessions into a box while the huge figure of Bruno glared at her. Camden and Chetana exchanged glances as he headed to the elevator. She looked desperate for good news, but he could only shake his head, defeated, and walk on.

Our one chance. In two hours Walter will be on a plane. I'm going to die, and how many others are going to follow, all because I couldn't do what needed to be done. I'm a failure and I deserve what's coming to me.

His spirit broken, barely able to put one foot in front of another, Camden crossed the street to Jade, Jeremy, and Professor Williams.

They know I've failed. They watched it all. I failed thirteen million people. Now what?

He couldn't even raise his head to look at them. What sort of explanation could he make? How could he face the disappointment in their eyes?

Without warning, Jade wrapped her arms around Camden and landed a firm, determined kiss on his lips. She pulled away, broad smile dominating her face. Jeremy grabbed him from behind and squeezed the air from his lungs in a suffocating hug, and Professor

Williams, all misery vanished, was clapping him excitedly on the shoulder.

"You did it! I knew you could!" cried Jade.

Brilliant. Another hallucination.

"Whaat are you talking abouut? I faailed. I had another episode. Aaanother faalse memory..."

They chuckled at Camden, apparently bemused. "You did?" asked Jeremy.

"Yeah. Walter pulled a guuun on me. Tried to throw me off the roof– make it look like... sssuicide. I fought Bruno. Waalter shot me. I fell off the building... Just before I hit the ground I was back in Waaalter's office."

Jade grinned. She seemed inordinately, explosively happy. "Camden, nobody hits the ground in a dream!"

"I thouught that waas a myth."

She laughed a beautiful laugh. "It is. But maybe there's some truth to it."

Camden suddenly stumbled, and Jeremy grabbed him. He led Camden to a chair, sitting him down. Jade sat next to him, tenderly stroking his hair and gazing at him with adoration.

She hugged him again. "Love, we watched the whole thing. Walter did pull a gun on you. But after that, you got him to confess everything. It was masterful."

"*Serious?*"

Jeremy gave him a gentle thump on the shoulder. "You did it, bro. Well done."

"I can't belieeve it. What diiid he say?"

"You can watch it later," said Jade. "Right now we've got to get this video to the police!"

"I'll stay here," said Williams. "I won't let Walter out of my sight. There's no way that plane is taking off with him on it."

"Brilliant," said Jade. "The pieces are falling into place. We have to move fast."

She already had her phone out, hailing a cab. Jeremy was hastily shoving his computer equipment into his backpack. Camden wasn't sure what to feel: the overwhelming sense of failure had been so pervasive that he was having trouble throwing it off.

"Come on, everyone," said Jade sharply. "Let's go!"

CHAPTER THIRTY-FOUR

"Shh! It's starting!"

Camden, Jade, Jeremy, and Chetana arrived at the girls' apartment just in time for the six o'clock news. The group sank into the couch, exhausted – none more so than Camden. After leaving Drax, their first stop had been the police department, then the FDA offices, and finally interviews from news reporters. There had hardly been time to breathe. Camden couldn't quite remember everything about the day, but Jade had told him he'd done marvelously, and that was good enough for him.

"Tonight on CNN, we have a special report. Consurge: Exposed! We'll take you through the today's shocking events that led the FDA to issue an urgent warning about the so-called 'miracle drug', one of the nation's fastest-ever-selling medications, and the police to arrest Dr. Walter Johnson, owner of Drax Pharmaceuticals. If you're one of the thirteen million people currently taking the anti-sleep drug Consurge, you can't afford to miss this program. Your life literally depends on it."

"The news is so dramatic now," said Jeremy loudly.

"Quiet," hissed Chetana.

"This footage, taken earlier today, shows Dr. Johnson arrested by police at Sea-Tac Airport, attempting to flee the country on a one-way ticket to Cape Verde."

Despite the sound of plane engines in the distance, and the fact that he was surrounded by a small army of security personnel, they could hear Walter shouting to the police officers, *"You can't do this! I have rights!"*

Jade shook her head. "Defiant to the end."

"A former employee of Drax, Dr. Jade Reilly, and University of Seattle medical student, Camden Walker, have courageously exposed the deadly long-term consequences of taking the popular drug. In this incriminating video footage, taken secretly in his office, Dr. Johnson shrugs off the potential deaths of millions of people. When Mr. Walker confronts Dr. Johnson, the Drax owner pulls a gun on him."

"Here it is, Camden!" said Jade.

"There won't be a next time, Waalter."

"How cliché. Do you know what? You're absolutely right."

"It's oover, Walter. We're filing a complaaint with the FDA thiiis afternoon."

"Be my guest. By this time tomorrow, I'll be sipping grogue on the beach. You think you're the one who'll stop me?"

"Caan you actually liive with yourself if you skip the couuntry? Yooou know thaat Consurge triggers sporadic fatal insomnia. Yooou know that millions of people will die by the time the FDA pulls the pluug on Consurge."

"We're all going to die sometime, boy."

"You have no conscience."

"Don't you get it? I'm in a no-win situation. My back's against the wall, kid. If I sound the alarm, the company will go under and take me with it. If I don't sound the alarm, I'll go to prison when people start keeling over – and the company will still go under."

"So yoou're gonna taaake the money and run."

"Survival of the fittest."

"Don't you caare that people will die?"

"Of course I care. Does it bother me? Yes. I'm not completely heartless, you know. But you have a very limited perspective, Camden. Where's the scientist in you? Where's the person who sees the long game? This is just a bump along the evolutionary highway. Yes, it's sad. But it's the price of progress. Future generations will build on what we've done. They'll succeed because we laid the groundwork for them."

"A twiisted mind if there ever waas one."

"Genius is rarely understood, boy, at least in its own time. You'll have to ask someone in five hundred years what they think of me. Now get out of my office... Hey! Are you even listening?! Did you hear me? I said, get out! Get out or I'll have you thrown out! Are you deaf?"

"I uunderstand."

Camden reached to touch his lips, as though unsure that they even belonged to him. Had those words really emerged from his mouth?

"Wow, I saaid that?"

"You were brilliant, babe," said Jade, a gorgeous smile on her face.

He giggled. He couldn't help himself. "Didn't know I haad it in me."

"I had faith in you," she said.

Camden tilted his head. "There's just one thiiing I don't uuunderstand."

"What is it?" asked Jade.

"I've neeveer woken up in the miiiddle of a false meemoory befoore. Yoou said my braaain was replacing actual meemories with dreams *during* the Draax Power Naaps."

Jade sighed heavily. "I hate to say it, but maybe your condition is deteriorating more rapidly."

The reporter continued. *"Why did this brave young man confront the owner of a large corporation? Because after approximately two months of use, Consurge apparently triggers a form of sporadic fatal insomnia, an irreversible rare disease. Once this happens, death is inevitable several months later. Therefore, the FDA has issued a warning to all Consurge users to immediately discontinue use of the drug pending further study. Joining us now is Professor Carl Williams, from the University of Seattle Medical School, who can explain more. Professor Williams, will everyone currently on Consurge get off the drug before this disease is triggered?"*

Williams adjusted his glasses. *"It's extremely important that those who went on Consurge during the first week it was available discontinue use of the drug within the next few days. If you know anyone in that situation, alert them. If you're a doctor that prescribed Consurge during the first week it was available, phone your patients. Do whatever it takes. I've been assured that more information will be forthcoming on the FDA website..."*

Jade touched Camden's shaking hand. "It's over, love."

It's over.

The words hit him with the force of a train. Finally, he could step off the treadmill he'd been forced to run on for weeks.

"Are you okay, babe?" asked Jade, concern creasing her brow.

He smiled at her. "I'm juuust tiired."

"Tired?" asked Chetana. "Do you want to sleep?"

He giggled again, louder this time.

"Can we do anything for you?" asked Jeremy.

"I'm thiiirsty."

Camden reached out his shaking hand to a water glass on the side table. The glass swiftly shattered into a hundred pieces, scattered across the floor. Camden apologized and Chetana brought him another glass while Jeremy tidied up the mess. Camden carefully cradled the glass with both hands, raised it to his lips, filled his mouth with water, and tried unsuccessfully to swallow. He gagged as the water dribbled down his chest.

"Babe, babe, it's okay," said Jade, gently taking the glass. "Just take it slow. There's no rush."

For some reason, this again caused him to giggle. This time, however, he couldn't stop. His three friends stared anxiously as he sat there chuckling. In the end, he mumbled something that even Jade couldn't understand.

She felt his forehead. "You're burning up." Jade turned to the others. "We've got to get him to hospital."

CHAPTER THIRTY-FIVE

"As the Consurge scandal continues, protesters have gathered around Drax Pharmaceuticals, demanding the immediate closure of the multi-million dollar corporation."

Camden stared blankly at the television from his hospital bed. The news about Consurge appeared on almost every channel, and he felt a calm pride that his efforts had been rewarded with such success. Nobody in the country with any sense was touching Consurge now, and that wasn't likely to change.

A cold shiver suddenly rippled through his body. He pulled the covers tighter. Five minutes ago he felt like he'd spent too long in a sauna. No doubt he'd feel like that again in another five minutes. As much as he shifted his body, no comfortable position was to be found. His muscles felt like the time when he'd spent two hours at the gym after not exercising for three months.

But as strongly as he desired relief from his physical discomfort, it paled in comparison to his desire to sleep. It's no wonder, he thought, that sleep deprivation is used as torture. He'd read about this sort of thing before; interrogators would keep prisoners up for days on end, then just as they were allowed to fall asleep, they were suddenly awakened and questioned.

Camden had been thirsty before. So thirsty that when he did eventually find water, he could only take small sips. He'd been hungry before. So hungry that it felt like his stomach was about to implode. But he'd never been this tired before. Not even the time he was up for 52 hours straight in his first year of medical school working on his immunology paper. At least then sleep was an option.

Fortunately, he wasn't alone. Jade hadn't left his bedside since the previous evening when she and Jeremy had brought him in, on the verge of collapse. His mom had rushed in that night as well. She'd been the hardest to see: she'd thrown herself on him and wept inconsolably for what had seemed hours. It had been a struggle to simply lift his arms to hug her.

Jeremy had been there since the early hours of the morning and Chetana had joined them not long after. She'd been to Drax headquarters only to be told by a lawyer to leave and not say anything to anyone, in common with all her other former colleagues.

Other friends and well-wishers had stepped in during the day. The triumph over Walter, however, hadn't prevented a somber and downhearted mood. Even Sam and Johnny, when they had stepped in for an hour around the middle of the day, hadn't been able to crack a smile.

Camden shifted in his bed and mumbled something to Dr. Herman, who had also spent much of the day in the room.

"What did you say, dear?" asked his mom.

Camden repeated, as loudly as he could, but it still came out as a forced whisper. "Theeere's sooome leetterrrs... My baaag..."

Herman bent down and picked up a black backpack from under Camden's bed. "May I open it?" asked the doctor. Camden managed a frail wave to signify his assent. Herman unzipped the back, pulling out a thick sheaf of envelopes. Camden's mom took them and spread them out on Camden's blanket.

"They've all got names," said Jade. A few tears were beginning to fall down her face, and this set off Camden's mom, who turned and buried her face in a tissue once again.

He'd written in his school notepad, with the little time he had left the previous evening, to as many people as he could think of: Sam, Johnny, Krista, Chetana. He'd written to his former colleagues at WestCo and to everyone who'd made him feel welcome at the hospital. He'd written to both his family and Jade's – he'd never met Uncle and Aunt O'Donovan, but he wanted them to know how much he would have loved to. He'd written to Professor Williams, praising the old man for coming good at the most crucial hour.

He'd written to Jeremy what he couldn't say in person: "I'm sorry. I should've listened to your rants." Jeremy had already opened the note and chuckled as he read it. "Maybe so," he said.

"But, somehow ignoring me saved the lives of millions of people. Work that one out."

He'd written to his mom, thanking her for everything she'd done for him, and how he could have never asked to be raised by anyone better.

He'd written to Jade. That one had been the hardest.

They were short, simple messages, some barely legible, but Camden felt he'd done his best. If he was going to leave, he wanted to be able to say goodbye.

"*Uhhhh...*" He tried to speak, but couldn't formulate the words. Jade, who had been gently sorting the envelopes, looked up in alarm.

"Doctor-!"

Herman calmly raised the bed so that Camden could sit further upright. His breathing cleared, but he still couldn't speak. He motioned weakly for a pen and notepad, which Herman placed on his lap. Camden's shaky hands managed a scribbled sentence, which he passed to Herman: '*I didn't escape from this room for long.*'

The doctor gave a sad laugh and softly patted his shoulder. "Good thing you did. It seems to have worked out for humankind."

Camden scrawled another note followed by a smiley face and turned it to Jade: '*My condition is rapidly disimproving.*'

She let out a small laugh through her tears. "So you believe it's a real word now?"

He shook his head no and grinned.

She wrapped her arms around his shoulders. He could feel her shaking, but no longer had the strength to comfort her. Jade, lip trembling, gathered his hand in hers and tenderly kissed it.

Suddenly, Jeremy grabbed the television remote and turned up the volume. "Check this out!"

A news reporter was surrounded by hundreds of people in the street.

"*...and tell me your name, sir.*"

"*Chad.*"

"*What would you like to say to Camden?*"

"It sounds cheesy, man, but you literally saved my life. Thanks for your courage."

"And what's your name, ma'am?"

"My name's Emily. And, it's already been said, but I'd like to thank Camden for standing up to Big Pharma. You're a real hero. We're eternally grateful. You won't be forgotten!"

And so they went, one after another. Outpourings of appreciation and gratitude, so many that Camden lost count.

Jeremy turned to Jade. "Where *are* all those people?"

No sooner had the words left his mouth when Betty the receptionist came hurrying into the room. "They're all trying to come in! They want to see Camden, but the security guards won't let them in. What do I do?"

"That answers that question," said Jeremy.

Nurse Sullivan quickly intervened. "We can't let anyone else in the room in his condition."

Dr. Herman sighed. "There's nothing more we can do for him now. Visitors can't make him any worse... Let them in."

A great crowd soon flooded into the room, surrounding Camden. Among them were Krista and Professor Williams. There were so many people that they overflowed and spilled out into the corridor. They passed by his bed, shaking his hands and patting his legs, their deep sorrow balanced with deep appreciation. There was nothing the crowd could do, and nothing they could say, but to Camden, it was a deafening thank you.

Jade smiled through her tears and squeezed Camden's hand. "You wanted to help people, love. You wanted to save lives and leave a legacy. Look around you."

He smiled and closed his eyes.

In the pitch black, a solitary light flickered in the distance. Soon another. Then another, exploding like popcorn, resembling countless fireflies as far as he could see along the horizon.

"Thirteen million people showed up tonight," said a voice from behind. Camden slowly turned. Eddie Vedder, the lead singer of Pearl Jam stood there, the whole of the band behind him. Vedder parted his sweaty hair with both hands and smiled. "I thought they were here to see us," he continued. "I should've known."

The band eased into one of Camden's favorite Pearl Jam songs, "Just Breathe", a ballad contemplating the nature of friendship, appreciation, love, and death. The frontman of Pearl Jam raised Camden's arm high into the air and leaned into the microphone. "Camden Walker!" he shouted.

The crowd exploded in rapturous applause.

Camden felt exhausted, yet strangely satisfied. There was a comforting weight in his chest, a feeling of fulfillment, of joy. Instead of regret, a sense of completeness; instead of injustice and loss, a feeling of peace and acceptance.

At that moment, he had but one thought.

It's time to get some sleep.

ACKNOWLEDGMENTS

This is my first novel; a labor of love spanning three years of evenings and weekends. Apart from winning the Young Author Award in sixth grade, most of the writing in my adult life has consisted of ecological reports and text on architectural drawings. In addition, my medical experience generally consists of turning my head to cough at the doctor's office. As such, this book would have never seen the light of day without the tremendous support of all those who helped bring the idea to life:

My dear wife for listening to my crazy notions, for her meticulous proofreading, and for her love and support during three years of self-imposed exile in the office. Owen for his guidance in the ways of the corporate world. Jennifer for being my pharmaceutical sounding board. My mother-in-law for her pragmatic feedback. Ryan for his fantastic artwork and his patience. Mom, Dad, and Grandma for their proofreading and encouragement from across the sea. And most of all, Eugene and Tamara Mackie from aprioriservices.com for their invaluable editing skills which helped turn the dream into a reality.

Much love and respect to you all.

TO THE READER

Thank you for buying this book! I'd love to hear from you. What did you like about the novel? What did you dislike? What would you have changed? What would you like to see in future books? You can message me at derekjpack.com. Please also leave a review on the website you purchased this book from and follow me on Facebook and Instagram.

    With gratitude,

    Derek J. Pack

Printed in Great Britain
by Amazon

58013441R00156